MORDECAI OF MONTEREY

A Novel

Keith Abbott

CITY MINER ⚒ BOOKS
BERKELEY

Other books by Keith Abbott:
Harum Scarum
Gush
Rhino Ritz

Copyright 1985 © Keith Abbott
All rights reserved including the right of reproduction in
whole or in part in any form.
Published by City Miner Books
P.O. Box 176, Berkeley, CA 94701

Mordecai of Monterey is a work of fiction. Any resemblance to
real persons living or dead is purely coincidental.
Printed in the United States of America.
Library of Congress Catalogue Card Number: 84-72513
ISBN: 0-933944-10-1 (cloth)
        0-933944-11-X (paper)

Cover painting by Tom Clark
Cover design by Nancy von Stoutenburg
Interior drawings by Anne Hawkins
Typeset in Baskerville by Heyday Books
Printed by McNaughton & Gunn

First Edition
10   9   8   7   6   5   4   3   2   1   0

"This leads us
into the problem created
by our feelings of
exuberance
joy ecstasy satori,
whatever.
These are basically
antisocial feelings."

—Philip Whalen

Book One
Monterey
Spring
1973

Through the open door of the Beer Springs bar, everyone could see that it wasn't hot enough to be in the shade. But there was a possibility that it *might* get hot later on, and so, to simplify life, three of the Beer Springs regulars had come in for a short beer a little after 10 that morning.

There wasn't much to talk about that early. Tom Soper had the *Chronicle* propped up against his carpenter's tool belt on the bar. He was reading the latest Watergate news. Jasper and Duane the Welder stared at their short beers. Ethel was behind the bar. She was humming *Red Sails In The Sunset* to herself. She had her pad of paper out, figuring the bar tabs. No one paid her much mind, or Mordecai, when he came wandering in.

But there *was* something that all four noticed about Mordecai right away. What they saw was Mordecai's roll of dollar bills. Mordecai paid for his beer with one of them. Now this was of interest because Mordecai had not been paying for his drinks the night before. Mordecai had been drinking on everyone else's money until 10:30, when his drinking buddies had retired for the night. So everyone knew that somewhere between 10:30 p.m. and 10:00 a.m., Mordecai had scored some cash.

Mordecai took a sip of his beer, brushed back his blond hair, and adjusted his Army jacket. "You know what I found out last night?" Mordecai said to Ethel.

"No, what?"

"I've been having a funny feeling lately. And I was down at Chino's last night . . . ."

"Yeah, someone said they saw you down *there*," Ethel interrupted him.

Tom and Duane and Jasper tuned in. Chino's was the fancy cocktail bar down Lighthouse Avenue in New Monterey. Usually no one from Beer Springs ever went there, except on Thursdays when they had free tiny hot dogs on the grill.

"I met this guy. He turned out to be a shrink over at the Naval Institute. He and I got to talking and that's when I found out that I had a disease."

"What kind of a disease?" Ethel asked.

"Well, I've been having this funny feeling, see, and so I told this shrink about it, because it wasn't physical so much as mental."

Ethel put up her pad of paper and looked down the bar at everyone's drinks. "Yeah?"

"Yeah," Mordecai said. "See, lately I've been having the feeling that I'm following someone and that someone's about to give me something. Or help me a whole lot. It's been driving me crazy."

"The guy you're following is going to give you something?"

"No. Sometimes I feel that I *have* to follow someone. And because I *did* follow someone, someone else's going to give me something. I don't even have to know who I'm following. In fact, sometimes I never even see the person."

"No kidding," Ethel said.

"No kidding," Mordecai said. "The shrink says that I have a real rare form of mental disease."

"What's it called?" Jasper broke in. He was old and retired, so he collected other people's diseases to pass the time. He had a wallet full of newspaper accounts of epidemics and unexplained outbreaks.

"Melanoia. It's the opposite of paranoia. And it works." Mordecai took out five one dollar bills from his pocket. He spread them in front of the fifty cent change from his first short beer. "This is what I got last night."

"How do you know when your disease is working?" Ethel asked.

"I hear a *ping*. It's this sound in my head. Then I look around and usually I'm walking along and following someone."

Duane shifted around so he was looking down the bar at Mordecai. "You *really* following someone? That could lead to trouble."

"Most of the time I'm not following anyone at all, I just feel like I am. That's why this is a mental disease."

Duane nodded. "Uh-huh," he said.

"I hear this *ping*," Mordecai continued. "And then I think I'm following someone. I get real happy and usually something good happens. Now the shrink wants to study me. He says that this is one of the rarest forms of mental disease known to man."

"Mordecai, you can't have a mental disease," Ethel said. She took his empty beer glass. "You're too poor. You can only be nuts."

"Hey, you're talking to someone special. The doctor said there were only six recorded cases of melanoia on record. That's why he gave me six dollars when we left Chino's. He was excited. He said that he could become famous and I could, too. He wants to test me. He said that he'd pay me to come out to the Institute today."

"How much?" Tom Soper said. Tom liked to talk wages, being a union carpenter.

"Twenty dollars an hour."

"For what? To talk to a shrink? That's a switch," Tom said.

"That's not a switch, that's a crock, if you ask me," Duane said.

"Well, you believe in paranoia, don't you?" Tom said. "Everyone says that's real. Why can't the opposite be real, too?"

"Yeah, maybe you're right," Duane said. "You know, I wondered why those shrinks always got some kinda *negative* way of looking at things. I thought they was in some kind of conspiracy."

"They're in a conspiracy, all right—to get your money!" Tom said. "But you're getting them to pay *you* twenty bucks an hour, Mordecai?"

"Right, but first I have to take some blood tests and stuff to find out if my melanoia is something genetic."

Ethel put a beer in front of him and swept away his fifty cents change. "You better be here tonight, Mordecai," she said. "*I'm not going to be the one to try and explain this to everybody. What can you do with melanoia, anyway?*"

"I don't know. I guess I get to find out how strong it is. Maybe it will work all the time."

"Twenty dollars a week," Jasper said. He gave a low whistle of appreciation. "You could live on that."

Duane and Tom both regarded Jasper. "Jasper must have been talking to our boss, Duane," Tom sneered. "Live on twenty dollars a week."

"Mordecai, now you know," Ethel warned him, "everybody's going to be hitting on you."

"For what? Whatta they going to do? Steal my mental disease? I'd give it to people if it would help them." Mordecai tasted his beer. "Of course sometimes it's tough to help people." He looked down the bar at Duane, Tom and Jasper. "Real tough."

— 2 —

At Beer Springs that night Mordecai did not buy one drink. When his friends heard about his melanoia, they bought all his drinks. Sal the Portagee even took him out to dinner. Mordecai was part of the longest running joke at Beer Springs, Sal the Portagee's "Army". Sal worked at Fort Ord Army base in supply. He stole Army jackets and always kept one in his car to give to hitchhikers. He had been doing this for almost twenty years. "You ever see a guy by the side of the road with one of them on? *They're in my Army!*" Then Sal would usually launch into his life story about how his father was a sardine fisherman and how the sardines left and his dad lost his boat and went on welfare and died a broken man. "I learnt then that the only way to fight the government is to have your own Army! So I infiltrated theirs and started my own!"

Mordecai always wore his Army jacket in honor of Sal's one act of rebellion in nearly twenty years of military service.

When Sal got Mordecai alone at Kalisa's restaurant on Cannery Row, he came right to the point.

"HEY!" he yelled. "You're the only guy I know who could have a mental disease turn into a full-time job!" Sal laughed at his own joke. "Looks like your vacation is over. You got a job now!"

Mordecai had to admit that was how it looked.

"So, whatta ya gonna *do* with melanoia? Huh?" He slapped Mordecai on the back. "You gonna have good luck all the time. That could prove to be fatal. Terminal good luck, huh?"

Mordecai said that he didn't know what he was going to do with his melanoia. "Maybe I'll find someone who needs good luck."

"Sure! That's what I'm saying!" Sal yelled. "What the hell do you *need* it for? You don't want nothing much. You live with whoever gives you a room. You been here in Monterey, what? Five years? You been living for five years on *air!* You hardly ever pay rent. Someone always gives you a place and food. Everyone loves you. All us 9 to 5 working stiffs like Duane and Tom Soper and myself think you got it *made.* We all *say* that's what we wanna do but you're the only one doing it. We're all addicted to that fucking paycheck. The Beer Springs Chorus is gonna say *what's Mordecai need good luck for? He's already got it made.* People gonna get jealous. You got yourself a pot of trouble if you don't play your cards right."

"I've been thinking about that," Mordecai said. Sal had called it *terminal good luck.* Mordecai did not like the sound of that phrase.

When they got back to Beer Springs, Mordecai explained about his disease over and over until his melanoia sounded like the joke that the Beer Springs Chorus seemed to think it was. People began to go *"Ping!"* behind Mordecai's back. Mordecai noticed that Duane the Welder was getting drunk and surly. He started poking Mordecai in the arm and going *"Ping!"* As Duane got drunker, the jabs got harder.

Then Rita came up to Mordecai and suggested that he come over to her house that night and look up his disease in her medical dictionaries. Rita was a short, red-haired woman with a big smile and a gap in her front teeth. Rita had been trying to get Mordecai over to her house for some time. Mordecai had the idea that she had more than a definition to give him. "I got *all kinds* of psychology books too," Rita said. She gave Mordecai her best gap-toothed grin. "We could look up your disease together, Mordecai."

Luckily for Mordecai, Katherine came by with her lover, the biker German Jock. Mordecai slipped out of Beer Springs with them, using German Jock as cover. He was good cover. German Jock had his machine gun pistol stuck in his belt and was acting irritable. On the ride home in German Jock's 1959 Cadillac convertible, Katherine mentioned that they were both speeding on Dexedrine.

When they got to Katherine's house, Mordecai left them to motormouth each other into the a.m. while listening to *Sympathy for the Devil*. He walked through to the back of the house. Mordecai lived on Katherine's back porch. He listened to the night for a few minutes. He heard crickets and sea lions and the slosh of the Monterey bay—no *pings*—so he went to bed.

— 3 —

The next morning the man with melanoia woke up early with a hangover. Mordecai stared at the ceiling and tried to figure out what kind of hangover it was. It seemed to be a stable, fairly heavy hangover with slight chance of lightning head pains. Not bad enough to really make him suffer but enough to stay in bed and risk no sudden vertical or horizontal moves. Mordecai stared at the backyard and thought about his past and what Sal the Portagee had said.

Mordecai lived in Monterey simply because that was where the Army had cut him loose in 1968. He had stayed in Monterey from 1966 into 1967 while he studied Chinese at the Defense Language Institute. He had liked Monterey then. So, instead of going back home to the Northwest in 1968, Mordecai decided that he would live there for a few months. Being trained as a Chinese interpreter had been hard work but not as hard as getting a discharge from the Army. Mordecai decided that he needed a vacation.

After two years of resting on two tours of unemployment benefits and federal extensions, Mordecai concluded that he would probably like to spend the rest of his life vacationing in

Monterey. The occupation suited him, and it suited Monterey, the vacation capital of California.

Mordecai knew that most people never find their true vocation. And during this time he discovered that lots of people needed him to be exactly as he was.

Mordecai decided to get up out of bed. He did it carefully, so as not to disturb the heavy cloud bank of hangover in his forehead. Below the bed was Mordecai's only possession, his blue footlocker. In it he kept a rat's nest of sacred items: his Chinese-English dictionary, his copies of certain Chinese philosophy books and poetry, some United States Weather Bureau books on stars and cloud formations, a collection of drawings from his young nieces, his calligraphy pens and brushes plus other items. He opened the footlocker and took out a thin Japanese tablet of fine linen paper. He turned to the last page and regarded a new translation he had made from The Book of Songs. He corrected one word and then wrote it out in sloppy calligraphy. He stuck it on a nail by the back door and read it again before walking into the kitchen to make coffee.

In the Nine marshes a crane cries
In the wild its voice carries
In the lake by the bottom spring the fish lies
In the garden by the trees leaves fly and fall
In the hills by my side the rocks stay
In time let someone else
Turn them into millstones

Mordecai moved German Jock's machine gun pistol off a stool next to the gas range and sat down to watch the water boil, reflecting on his pleasant life at Katherine's house. She let him sleep on the back porch in exchange for free babysitting. He liked children. He got along fine with Katherine's two boys.

Mordecai made coffee. He wondered whether or not melanoia was going to change his life. Mordecai was not afraid of change, but *terminal good luck* sounded ominous. The coffee lifted the hangover cloud and Mordecai thought about his responsibilities —did he now have a responsibility to *do right* by his disease? Was it some kind of magic? He thought that if it *was* magic, then he had the responsibility to do the right things with it.

As Mordecai finished his coffee, he heard a tiny sound inside himself. *Ping.* He listened again. *Ping.* The sound was close to the ring of a wind chime. Mordecai listened to it and tried to describe the sound. The *ping* sounded like the *inside* of the ring of a wind chime.

Mordecai walked out the back door and began to stroll up Hawthorne Street toward Pacific Grove. In his mind he was seeing the back of the person he was following.

— 4 —

An hour later Mordecai was standing at the foot of Rita's stairs. He did not want to be standing there. Mordecai was having his first crisis with his mental disease. He could not believe that his melanoia had led him to Rita.

Ping.

Mordecai walked to the corner of the house. *Maybe,* he thought, *my good luck is waiting somewhere behind the house.* He continued into the backyard. There was no back apartment, nothing but an overgrown lawn.

Ping.

Mordecai sighed and turned around and walked back to the front stairs.

Ping.

Mordecai went up the stairs and stood at Rita's front door. He knocked on the door and the *pings* inside him motored into a smooth fast purr. Rita opened the door. "Mordecai!" she said. She was wearing a bathrobe with nothing on underneath. Mordecai saw that right away. He also saw Loser Rred sitting at the kitchen table. *Thank god,* Mordecai thought. Last night Rita had not gone home from Beer Springs alone.

Mordecai walked into the kitchen. As he passed through the living room he saw Rred's Swiss hiking boots on the floor beside the coffee table, where two half-finished Coors were standing. Halfway between the couch and the bedroom door were Rred's socks.

"Mordecai," Rita said, taking his arm and pressing it to her side, "I was just thinking about you."

"Hi Mordecai," Rred said, "and we were talking about you too. You'll never guess what happened?"

Mordecai looked at the socks on the floor and then at Rita's sleepy pleased expression. "No, what?"

"You know Jesus John, he's going to New York."

"Oh Mordecai," Rita said, squeezing his arm and pulling it into her side harder, right under her breasts, "I'm so *excited!*"

"About Jesus John going to New York?" Mordecai said, pulling away from her and sitting down.

"No," Rita said. "About him giving you his truck."

"Jesus John gave me his truck?" Mordecai remembered the dilapidated '48 Dodge. "Couldn't he have just left town and let it rust?"

"No, that's not the whole story," Rred said. "See—last night, after Jesus John left Beer Springs—he wrote a play. It's about a guy who's in jail and there are two other thieves in the cell with him. Then the guy turns out to be Jesus."

"That sounds like Jesus John's life story," Mordecai said. He accepted a coffee from Rita. "Was it the *Salinas* jail?"

"Yeah, well, I think Jesus John forgot about his own cover story there for a while. He's sort of a professional amnesiac," Rred said. "He got kinda excited listening to you talk about your disease, so he went home and wrote the play, see. But uh, the only story he could remember was his own, only he didn't remember that it was his own story, so he wrote that, thinking it was a whole new story." Rred laughed. "Anyway, he dropped the keys by and the pink slip for the truck on his way to catch the Greyhound to New York to give his play to Broadway producers." Rred leaned back and smiled at Mordecai. "So we're partners."

"In what?"

"A hauling business," Rita said. "You can use my phone for the hauling ad. I'll be you guys' secretary."

Mordecai considered this arrangement. He had the feeling that Rred had sandwiched himself in this deal somehow. Rred kept talking; he claimed that Jesus John thought Mordecai would die from the melanoia soon, so he gave him the truck to help defray his medical expenses. Rred being a mechanic, Jesus John made him half-partner so he could help keep the truck running. To Mordecai's knowledge Jesus John didn't usually think things out so completely.

"Does that truck run?" Mordecai asked.

"Sort of," Rred went into the living room and put on his socks. "Jesus John ran it down pretty hard after he bought it from Buck. I know that's hard to do after Buck gets done with a truck, but Jesus John did it," Rred continued. "I gotta put some points in it, new brake linings, and then I'll head down to the *Monterey Herald* and put in our first hauling ad in the classifieds."

"I'll take any messages," Rita said. "You can come by every day and pick them up." Rita stuck her toe up Mordecai's pants leg and gave a jerk.

"Only thing is," Rred said, putting on his Swiss hiking boots, "what are we going to call ourselves?"

"How about International Trash?"

"That's a good name, Mordecai. There's a lot of foreigners on the peninsula," Rred said. "Yeah, and International makes us sound *cosmic*, too."

Rita put her hand on Mordecai's shoulder as Rred started for the front door. Mordecai looked up at Rita. "Isn't it funny, Mordecai, how your disease really works? I wonder what you'll get next?"

"Yeah, first six dollars, then a truck and a new business." Rred opened the front door.

Mordecai squirmed out from under Rita's hand so he could leave with Rred. Rita slipped her arm through his. "Mordecai, will you come in here with me and help me get my psych dictionary down? I want to look up your disease."

"Bye," Rred said, walking out the door. Mordecai looked at the bedroom door. Rita began to tow him towards it. "That dictionary is on the top shelf and I don't trust that chair," she said. "You can hold it for me."

Mordecai hoped that Rred had tired her out a little, but it wasn't much of a hope. It occured to him that he and Rred might be sharing more than just a truck.

— 5 —

That night the Beer Springs Chorus gave advice to Mordecai about his new business. "Let me buy him this round, he'll need to be drunk all the time with Loser Rred and Rita. Wow-eee!" German Jock laughed. "I think with those two you got a chance to be both financially *and* morally bankrupt. Ha! After *that* you can join our motorcycle club, Mordecai!"

"Mordecai, be sure you have Rred check the emergency brake on that old Dodge. I heard a little something about that before Buck sold it to Jesus John." Ethel put the Coors in front of Mordecai.

"Boy, are you going to need good luck with those two," Tom Soper said to Mordecai. "You remember that pot rap Rred got busted for? He put his stash up on the dashboard of his car. You know what he said: *"if President Nixon can declare war on Cambodia without the Congress, I can declare dope legal."*

"Yeah, and the newspaper ran his name as Rred, two R's. He liked it so much he had a belt buckle made with Rred on it, *Hooo-eeee!*" Sal hooted. "He's the only guy I know who named himself after a typo!"

"Yeah, he used to take out the clipping of his pot bust and say, *that's unique. Rred with two R's,"* Duane said.

"But what I want to see," Tom broke in, "is both of you working. That's almost ten years of unemployment on the line."

"We oughta put a statue on the spot of their first job, of two guys yawning and waking up," Sal yelled. "On the bottom it'll say, *Here ten years of vacation came to an end."*

"Rred will still be on his mental vacation, if you ask me. He ain't never coming off that." German Jock said.

"Lay off Mordecai," Ethel said. Then, to Mordecai, "Has anyone called about your hauling ad yet?"

Mordecai shook his head. "I don't know, I haven't been back to Rita's."

"Let me take you out to a steak dinner before you go." Duane poked Mordecai in the arm. "You'll need the extra strength. Rita can really take it out of a man. Show them the bruise on your arm, Mordecai. Little love bite, size of a silver dollar."

"I got that bruise from *you* poking *me* last night. And besides,

I'm sending Rred over to get our job calls."

"Why's Rred got to do that?"

"He's the President of International Trash," Mordecai said. "I'm only the Vice-President. I'm the one in charge of good luck."

— 6 —

That night, as Mordecai treked back to Katherine's house on Hawthorne Street, he had a thought about his melanoia. What prompted this thought was that his Army jacket kept slipping off his left shoulder. (He had a six-pack in his left hand and that side of him drooped a bit.) Mordecai realized then that his getting melanoia was just like a hitchhiker getting one of Sal the Porta-gee's Army jackets. Melanoia was an idea but it was real too. Just as Sal made a gift of his Army jackets, some fate had given Mordecai the gift of melanoia.

Mordecai was pleased with his notion. It meant that while he had his disease, he was part of something much larger than himself, just as by wearing the Army jacket he was part of Sal's Army. *And when I'm out of it,* Mordecai thought, *I'm still me. Or maybe I'll be someone else.*

The next morning he spent some time rifling through his Chinese philosophy books, looking for the right discussion about such a notion. The question he asked himself was: *If I've got melanoia, what will losing it do to me?*

The closest he could find was the story about Master Yu and Master Ssu. Loosely translated the story went like this. Master Yu was sick, his body all crooked from his disease. When asked by Master Ssu if he was resentful, he said, "Oh no, maybe next my left arm will become a rooster. Or my right arm will be a crossbow dart and I'll shoot an owl for dinner. Or maybe the cheeks of my butt will turn into wheels and I'll go for a ride with my spirit for a horse. Hey, this is my big chance to get in the swim of things, to free myself from all this junk."

But before Mordecai could continue with his reading, Loser Rred stopped by Katherine's house. Rred told Mordecai that International Trash had just got its first job.

— 7 —

"Just get out there and haul that old trash away. I'm sick of it. I can't do a thing about it, what with my hip. It's been there for years. Fifteen dollars? Good, haul it away. Just haul that old trash away. I don't even know what's in it. Most of it is my eldest boy Paul's trash. But he's never coming back. Not unless the parole board gets generous. Just go ahead and haul it away. Knock on the back door when you're done, and I'll pay you boys."

Her aria completed, Mrs. Blier turned. With her faded peach-colored house dress wobbling about her ankles she made for the front room and her TV set. Rred and Mordecai walked across the backyard to her garage. Mordecai opened the lock on the door with the key that Mrs. Blier had handed him. Parked to one side of the garage in the alley was Jesus John's red and black 1948 Dodge truck.

Rred was no help. The night before Rred had driven the Dodge on a test run over to Salinas to visit a Chicano sweetheart. Her brother had been there. He had tried to tear off Rred's left arm. He wanted it for a club to beat in Rred's head. Rred didn't say much more than that. He didn't have to elaborate once Mordecai saw how his left arm was hanging.

Mrs. Blier's garage roof was covered with a thick green mat of blackberry vines and the weight was bending it down to one side. Mordecai swung open the garage doors.

The garage smelled of mold and dust and rotten wood. There were boxes of clothes and a broken tricycle, an old basketball hoop, a bundle of garden stakes, a mattress which had grown white and puffy with mold, black stuff, paint cans, two busted ski poles, a burnt-out steel barrel, a refrigerator door with NO GOOD crayoned across it, a headlight from a 1930s car, a battery, rusty green tin flower pots, a slimy footlocker, eight pairs of rotten shoes, a couple of rusty garden tools, and a lot of nameless junk.

Given his condition, Rred supervised the Blier garage cleaning while Mordecai threw the junk into the Dodge's back end. Rred did hold one end of the rope with his good hand as Mordecai tied the load down. Then Mordecai went into the house and got fifteen dollars cash from Mrs. Blier. She heaved herself out of her armchair and followed Mordecai onto the back porch to warble the coda to the trash opera. *"My, my, my! I appreciate that, boys! My Lord! I can see right through the back window of the garage to the alley for the first time in years! Don't bother closing the doors, I like it that way!"*

The Monterey public dump was out past Seaside, on the north side of Fort Ord Army base. It was a long, slow drive. When they got to the dump, Rred let Mordecai unload the truck, too. Mordecai had experienced a mild melanoia attack as they drove up to the dump, the *pings* purring just under the low roar of the Dodge. He had thought it was because everything at the public dump was free. But as Mordecai was spilling out the contents of the slimy footlocker, it hit him.

PING.

Mordecai looked down at a mound of old clothes and spied the corner of a small burlap sack poking out from under a wool shirt. Mordecai lifted out the sack and something small, square and hard was inside. Opening the shirt, Mordecai found a wooden box. He pried the top off with his pocket knife.

Rred climbed out of the cab to see why there was a slowdown. He found Mordecai staring into the box. "What's that?" Rred looked in. "No shit!" he said, looking down at the gold and silver coins. "I wonder if they're real."

"Jesus," Mordecai said. "Hell yes, they're real!" He jumped down into the garbage pit and hoisted up a cardbox box that he had thrown away. Loser Rred began to paw through the boxes. The sight of the gold limbered up Rred's arm considerably. He knelt down behind the Dodge and began to feel each piece of clothing, running his hands along the seams.

— 8 —

With the seven hundred and twenty four dollars from the sale of the coins and the fifteen dollars from the job, Mordecai and Loser Rred stopped first at Beer Springs. Mordecai and Rred barreled through the swinging doors arm and arm, doing high kicks all the way to the bar. There they told the Beer Springs Chorus the story of how International Trash had struck it rich on their very first job. Mordecai paid off his bar tab of thirty-nine dollars and they bought everyone a round of beer.

"To Mordecai and his Melanoia!" Rred toasted.

Then they left in the Dodge for a big dinner at the Nepenthe restaurant in Big Sur. When they arrived, they had a few drinks inside the Nepenthe bar first. Those drinks became more than just a few. Rred decided that Nepenthe was not the right place for dinner. He didn't feel comfortable with the other highclass people there. Rred suggested that they spend their money instead at Kalisa's on Cannery Row. Loser Rred remembered when Kalisa had hired him as a bus boy when he first came to Monterey. Rred wept, remembering how kind Kalisa had been to him. Now he wanted to repay her. It had been his fault that she had to fire him. Rred recounted the story of how he had stepped out in the alley on his break and smoked some dynamite Thai weed. When he came back in, the restaurant seemed too solemn. To liven things up, he had strolled among the diners with raw squids dangling from his fingertips, a humorous gesture which failed to amuse his audience. Remembering this, Rred got moody. "It was all my fault," he said, turning to the rest of the bar. "I'll admit it." The other people seemed interested in hearing what else Rred might confess. The squid story was a big hit with them. "What are *you* looking at?" Rred said to the guy nearest to him.

Mordecai took Rred by the arm and led him out of the bar. He could see that it was time for them to go somewhere else.

On the way back to Monterey, Rred decided that he had to take a piss. That was fine with Mordecai. Rred stopped the truck in front of a field of iceplant overlooking the Pacific Ocean. "Look at that moon," Rred said, "so white and pure. You ever think of that?"

Mordecai said he had, often. Rred didn't believe him. "You don't think about shit like that, you don't *have* to," Rred told him. "You got that disease. All you got to do is kick back and wait for all that good luck to come in the door."

Mordecai decided it was time for him to take a piss, too. He got out of the truck and walked down into the iceplant. He strolled closer to the edge of the cliff and looked out over the ocean. Behind him he heard the truck door slam shut. He turned and saw Rred coming after him. Mordecai took a piss. Rred stood off to one side and relieved himself too. The sea breeze was blowing in their faces. The sound of the surf boomed up over the cliff. The moon was beaming down on them. The air was cold and moist, and smelled of salt. It seemed so peaceful.

Mordecai turned to say something to Rred about how peaceful it was. Rred was still taking a piss, and as he looked back at Mordecai, Rred's eyes widened, his mouth dropped open, and he looked very alarmed. For a moment Mordecai thought Rred was about to keel over and pass out. Then Mordecai realized that Rred was not looking at him.

Mordecai turned. Behind them the Dodge was rolling slowly past, the twin tracks of its tires leaving a dark wet green trail through the iceplant.

The Dodge bumped along as if it were an old car out for a walk. The full moon cut a path of light to the cliff. The Dodge toddled along into the path of light and followed it toward the ocean. The top of the steering wheel lit up in a shining crescent as it joggled back and forth. There was a little hesitation, a minor bump, as the front wheels hit the edge of the cliff. The moon was shining through the back window and then the moonlight swept down the bed of the pickup as the truck tilted up and slipped over the edge.

— 9 —

The next morning Mordecai told the Beer Springs Chorus of his new plans for International Trash's assets. After Mordecai had bailed Loser Rred out of jail the night before where he had been held on the charge of littering a state beach, they had agreed to dissolve their partnership, since there was no longer a truck. Mordecai then decided to offer their remaining assets to Buck.

"Not Buck," Duane said. "Why you going to give your good luck to Buck?"

"What's wrong with Buck? I've got a hauling ad in the paper and an answering service but no truck and no partner anymore. Buck has a truck and he's not working."

"Yeah, and there's a reason he's hiding out down there at Jasmine's house in Big Sur. You don't know about Buck," Tom Soper said.

Old Jasper bellied up to the bar behind Tom. "He's a pistol, Buck is," Jasper said.

"So tell me about him," Mordecai said. "I've only met him a couple of times at his Alice street house when I borrowed books from his library. He's got a great paperback library."

"He's got women, too," Jasper said. He looked at his empty glass. Mordecai signaled for Ethel to fill it. Jasper licked his lips as Ethel drew another draft. "He can't stay away from them. And they can't stay away from him."

"Oh bullshit," Ethel said. "Buck's got a line of Irish blarney with that Southern accent of his. And women would rather hear *that* than rehashes of pro football games. Buck can be one of the most generous people you will ever meet, but you got to watch out for his optimism. When he gets a head of steam up on a plan, stand back."

"Sounds like a perfect candidate for a good dose of melanoia," Mordecai said. "I'd like to see what he does with it."

"AHHHH," Sal yelled, "you need someone who's got the brains to see that this disease of your is a *fantastic* breakthrough for the human spirit, huh? Am I right or what?" Sal poked Tom Soper in the chest. "You knotheads don't know a brain when you see one—like me, for instance."

"What do you think, Jock?" Mordecai said, turning to German Jock. He was playing the pinball machine.

"Buck is a perfect partner for you, Mordecai," German Jock said. "He'll always need your good luck. Buck's the kinda guy who can fuck up a two-car funeral."

—10—

German Jock dropped Mordecai off at the mouth of Garrapata Canyon in Big Sur. Mordecai was walking up the canyon to Jasmine's house when he heard the first *Ping*. As Mordecai rounded the bend of the road and looked up at the house on the bluff, a shotgun went off. *Ka-boom!* Then as if in answer, he heard another *Ping*. Mordecai took it easy, skirting around the bluff so he approached the house from the back. *Ka-boom!* When Mordecai peeked over the brush at the back of the bluff, he saw Buck's Nash Metropolitan coupe and his 1954 Chevy truck, the Grey Ghost, parked in front of Jasmine's house.

Ka-boom! Then Mordecai saw Buck.

Buck was lying on a mattress in the tall grass by the edge of the bluff. He had a smoking shotgun in his hands and a naked woman next to him. He was reloading. The two of them would have made a perfect illustration for some men's magazine. *Buck and his woman held off the bandits at the top of the bluff.*

The only things wrong with the picture were that the naked woman was handing Buck some suntan lotion instead of ammunition, he was wearing a pair of baggy swimming trunks with hula girls on them, and instead of banditos at the base of the bluff there were about twenty loaves of Wonder Bread in a garden plot. *Ka-boom!* Buck blew a loaf of Wonder Bread into a fan of red white and blue confetti.

"Hello, Buck!"

Buck saw Mordecai. "Hi, Mordecai," Buck said. He acted as if he had been expecting him. "How do you like my garden? I decided to combine hunting and gardening this morning. You want some coffee?"

Mordecai walked up to them and looked down at the dark-haired woman. She had a tiny flower tattooed on her left hip.

"That's Jasmine," Buck explained.

She took off her sunglasses and looked up at Mordecai. He nodded a hello to her and followed Buck into the house. As Buck heated the water for some coffee, Mordecai told him of International Trash's spectacular rise and fall.

"Rred claims he doesn't know how it happened. He said he put on the handbrake, but I've been thinking that perhaps Rred likes fuckups a little too much."

"Ahhhh, you're *absolutely* right, Mordecai," Buck said. "He's a tightass Protestant drone." Buck scooped a lethal dose of coffee into the Chemex top. "Boy's got no poetry in his soul. Minute he feels any joy he wants to get slugged. *Demands* it in fact. What'd they book him for?"

"Littering the beach with our truck, a five hundred dollar fine. Rred got smartass with the cop. I bailed him out by loaning him my share of the coin money. Anyhow I came over to see if you would want to take over our leftover job calls and our ad since we no longer have a truck."

"Sure, Mordecai, but we go 50-50 right down the line. We'll be partners." Buck paused. "I don't want to be critical, Mordecai, but it seems to me that it's time for you to get *out* in the world, stop cheesing your brain down at Beer Springs. That old Chinese recluse routine is no good *all* the time. Hot damn, Mordecai, I appreciate this, I really do. I need a new start, I've been hiding out from my creditors down here."

"That's the way our country was founded, by people on the lam from the law," Mordecai pointed out tactfully. Seeing Buck fight off those red, white and blue Wonder Bread loaves had sparked off a chain reaction of patriotic knickknacks in Mordecai's head: the Battle Hymn of the Republic, Valley Forge, John Paul Jones, Stephan Decatur in the prow of his boat . . . .

Buck moved over to the windows and gazed off at the Pacific Ocean. Mordecai watched as Jasmine rolled over and applied some lotion to her thigh. Buck saw him watching her. "Ah, yes," he sighed, pouring Mordecai some coffee, "a naked young body in front of a sea of carbohydrates. Got any new Chink translations?"

Mordecai recited his translation of the Nine Marshes poem. Buck contemplated Jasmine sunbathing. "Lovely, Mordecai." Buck said. He repeated the last lines. *"Let someone else turn them into millstones.* My philosophy entirely this morning. Say, you wouldn't want to take a half hour walk to the beach? Gunpowder and suntan lotion are always an aphrodisiac for an Alabama boy like myself."

With Buck's brain wowser coffee surging through his body Mordecai felt only too ready to go for a walk.

"Stay out of the poison oak and the trail's that way." Buck winked. "See you in thirty minutes." He jerked his thumb at the windows behind him and got up. He walked out toward Jasmine, musing outloud to himself in his best W.C. Fields imitation. "After a man finishes shooting up the back forty, his thoughts turn to love."

— 11 —

It was early evening when Mordecai returned. On the way to the beach his melanoia attack had continued. Mordecai showed

Buck and Jasmine an Indian pestle that he found in a creek bank, exposed by the winter floods. Jasmine was in the kitchen with Buck. She had on a maroon gown and she was mixing the dinner salad. Buck stared out the window at the ocean. From the living room the stereo was playing Marvin Gaye's *Can I Get A Witness.* There was an unopened bottle of cognac on the table in front of Buck, along with two glasses and an opened edition of Boswell's *Life of Johnson.* "I was just thinking," Buck said, "that you could be the Vice-President of GTM."

"Sure," Mordecai said, eyeing the cognac.

"We shall aspire to be heroes," Buck said, "and we shall begin with this bottle of con-yacky." He poured a drink for Mordecai and one for himself.

"But what's GTM?" Mordecai asked.

"Oh, that calls for a toast," Buck said, raising his glass. "To GTM, known to the public as *Good Times Movers,* but among us, it's *Get The Money.*"

— 12 —

Later, as the sun fell into the sea, and the cognac fell into Buck and Mordecai, Buck told the story of his recent fall from economic grace. "Stoney broke. Lost my hauling ad, lost my phone, no way for GTM's customers to contact the service, three months behind on my rent . . . Ah, it was the Nose. The Nose, the Nose, the Nose," Buck said. "It was the Nose."

"I tried to call you at your house on Alice Street," Mordecai said. "I got the Nose instead."

"Ah yes, the Nose was snuffling down my trail. Finally she cut off my connections to the economic firing line. Not only that, but she snuffed out GTM's financial angel."

"I didn't know GTM *had* a financial angel," Mordecai said. He held out his glass. "More con-yacky?"

"Certainly my son." Buck poured another drink for Mordecai. "Yes," he continued, "GTM's financial angel was the Reverend Duncan Dennis David. GTM was one of the many sound financial investments which the Reverend made with his church's funds."

"What funds?"

"You're right, it was the Reverend's good name that he lent to GTM. He had a trash hauling ad put in the Herald and put his good name on the phone bill, too." Buck tasted the cognac. "No deposit, you know, for a man of the cloth. It's comforting to know that the phone company and the newspaper still respect religion, . . . as our Vice-President Spiro Agnew has so elegantly said, no nattering nabobs of negativity they."

"I can see the Reverend was a man of the people, what happened to him?"

Buck contemplated the Pacific Ocean. It seemed to whisper further information about the Reverend Duncan Dennis David. "Yes, he was rumored to have gone to Hawaii, . . . to spread His Word."

Jasmine snorted and sat down opposite them. She put her long legs up on the empty chair and adjusted her maroon gown and inspected the satin lining. "He took a powder," she said. Then, with a perfect nasal whine, "*I am sorry, but the number you have reached is out of order at this time. There is no new listing.*"

"Why, that's almost perfect," Mordecai complimented her.

"What do you suppose the Nose wears?" Jasmine said.

"To work? Cardigan sweaters," Buck intoned, "cart-di-gan only. The Nose is surrounded by a system of tweezers and claws which she operates with her powerful nasal hairs. The telephone company spares no expense for the Nose. After all, who else can smell a bad debt coming over miles of telephone wire?' Buck paused. "The Nose doesn't have much of a social life, floating in *that jar* after work, but in these lean Republican times, a Nose doesn't have the choices that it used to have for a career. But speaking of careers, Mordecai, what's this about your new found disease?"

"Melanoia?" Mordecai described his melanoia to Buck. "Some philosophical questions have, however, been raised. Such as— what can you do with nonstop good luck? The trouble with constant good luck is that it doesn't give you any peace."

"You're right, Mordecai, I hadn't thought of that."

Both Buck and Mordecai contemplated this idea for a few more sips of cognac. Jasmine got up. "You two are slipping into *the fool zone*," she said. She left the room. "I'm going to bed."

Buck watched her walk out of the room. "Whenas in silks my Julia goes, ti-tum, the liquefaction of her clothes . . . ah, the

Eternal Verities. Farewell, my lovely. Well, Mordecai, look at the bright side. After all, this is America. There's no telling how far you can go if you have the right mental disease. Look at our sainted forefathers. Look at our Head of State, Mr. Nixon."

Buck and Mordecai meditated on this historic truth some more and then Buck poured a nightcap for them.

"Yes," Buck said dreamily, "this melanoia of yours is a whole new frontier."

— 13 —

The next morning, when Mordecai tottered into the kitchen after a night of con-yacky, he was amazed to see Buck up and bustling around. Mordecai had no such energy in him. He numbly accepted coffee and ham and eggs from Buck. When Buck said they best be rolling, Mordecai followed him out to his Chevy truck and got in. They drove down the canyon and Buck turned south on the highway. Mordecai stirred. He asked him where they were going. Buck acted surprised. "We're going to see *about the truck!*"

"The truck?"

"Yeah, my old truck. The Dodge."

Mordecai's brain staggered under the hallucination that the truck had never gone over the cliff, he was only visiting Buck, the entire episode with International Trash was just a dream.

"Where is it exactly?" Buck said.

"Where is it? It's at the Big Sur garage. They winched it off the beach. It fell, *over two hundred feet straight down*, Buck."

Twenty minutes later Buck and Mordecai were standing in front of the Dodge. "Hmmmmmm," Buck said, eyeing it, "now you're sure Rred doesn't want it anymore?"

Mordecai didn't answer. He wanted to say *no one wants that any more*, but his tongue couldn't get the words right. He watched helplessly as Buck circled the Dodge. Buck had the same look on his face that General Custer had when he saw the first Indian on the last day of his life: *oh boy.*

"Well," Buck said, squatting down and looking under the Dodge, "all we have to do is straighten the frame a little."

Straighten the frame a little? Mordecai stared at the Dodge. The cab of the Dodge was a good foot off the frame. Half of the truck's bed was jammed up on the roof of the cab, making an A shape. The front end of the truck was rippled back like an accordion.

"Hell this is in okay shape," Buck said. "How far did you say it fell?"

"Two hundred feet. That's why the engine is jammed into the front seat."

"Hmmmm, so it is," Buck said, peering into the cab. The back end of the engine was poking out from under the dashboard. "But you can't hurt these little 6-banger engines. I bet it would turn over in a minute." Buck reached in and touched the speedometer and it fell off into his hand. "I don't remember that speedometer working when I owned this truck anyway."

— 14 —

On the ride into Monterey, Mordecai began to catch the scope of Buck's hopes for their business. Not only were they resurrecting GTM from its financial grave, they were going to operate a *fleet* of two trucks, Buck's Grey Ghost and a fixed-up Dodge. Buck threw in a pep talk, too. "Mordecai, you could sit on your ass down at Beer Springs, cheesing your brain on free drinks, but don't you see that would be *chippying* on your melanoia. You got to get out in the world and *work* with that disease of yours."

When Mordecai told Buck that Rred had gone to work at the Beacon gas station as a mechanic, in order to pay Mordecai back the two hundred and fifty dollars he owed him for half of his littering fine, Buck appropriated that debt for his truck. "We'll just stop off to arrange for a thorough tune-up for the Grey Ghost," Buck said.

But, because Buck owed the owner of the Beacon gas station some money, Mordecai dropped Buck off at Beer Springs first. Then he drove the truck to the station. Rred agreed to do the repairs.

"Hey, uh Mordecai, one more thing. Rita has got some job calls for you," Rred said. "She's been pestering me to get you to drop by."

Mordecai returned to Beer Springs. He had forgotten to mention to Buck that one of his duties as President was to pick up the job calls from Rita. "Oh hell, Mordecai, you stay here and have a few beers, I'll be back in a minute," Buck said. "Leave that part of the biz to the President of GTM."

"GTM?" Ethel said, "what's GTM?"

"Good Times Movers," Buck crowed, going out the door. "I'm the President."

"What's that make you, Mordecai?" Ethel said, putting his beer in front of him.

"Well, I'm his VP and spiritual advisor," Mordecai said. "And principal investor—my melanoia is the raw capital for GTM's Western movement into capitalism."

"Uh-huh," Ethel said. "So what's GTM really mean?"

— 15 —

Buck did not return for three hours. While Mordecai was waiting, Rred came in to tell Mordecai that the Grey Ghost had a tune-up and the brakes were adjusted and new filters installed all the way around. Rred joined Mordecai in a beer and they watched the mid-day TV news about Watergate with Ethel. "Look at that goddamn crook," Rred said, pointing at President Nixon. "Turn off the sound, will you?"

Ethel turned the sound down. "Well, Rred, you should talk," Ethel said, "you were a dope dealer for eight years or more, weren't you?"

"Yeah, but I wasn't a *crooked* dope dealer," Rred said.

"You know Ethel, all the time I spent in here, I've never heard you say word one about politics," Mordecai said to her. "Why's that?"

"No percentage in it, Mordecai," Ethel said. "Only thing that happens to people when they mess with politics is they either get rich or mad. And no one's going to get rich in this bar."

"These are lean Republican times," Mordecai said.

"Well, you want to know what I think the difference is between those two?"

"What two?" Rred asked.

"The Republicans and the Democrats," Ethel said. "I look at it this way—I was born in 1920, raised New Deal Democrat. I'm fifty-three years old, so I've been around the block—this is the way it seems to me: the Democrats now, they know when they get in office, it is going to take some time before they get voted out. So they take their time working over the treasury. They set up this program and that, and some trickles out to the people, but all the while," Ethel rubbed two fingers together as if cash were between them. "But you see the Republicans, now they usually only have one term or two at the most, so they have to get it fast. That's why old donkey nose Nixon's advisors," she pointed at the TV screen, "cleared out of his administration before the ship began sinking, which it is. Only the truly greedy ones are left, and it's a pleasure to see them drowning with their boss, let me tell you."

Ethel took Mordecai's dollar and put it in the till. "But I guess the real difference between the two is that the Republicans have plundered what they call the private sector, that's us, the working people, of what money they could get and now they are busy robbing the government itself. That's the new frontier to them— not Outer Space—the government itself. They don't even bother to set up new programs, they just rob the old ones, sell what they can get their hands on, deal away anything else, and the smart ones clear out by the third year. I guess that's why I don't talk about it much." Ethel looked out over Beer Springs. "Makes me sad, to tell you the truth. I guess I was brought up differently."

— 16—

It was a little past four when Buck and Rita showed up at Beer Springs. Rita seemed quite content with the way that the GTM President handled the negotiations. From the pleased look in her eyes, Mordecai could see that she had driven a hard bargain before she turned over those job calls, but he still got a little squeeze on his upper thigh from her as he went out the door.

With International Trash's job calls in hand, Buck and Mordecai began to make the rounds of their potential customers. "Gaaaawdamn," Buck sighed. "It sure is good to get GTM Movers back on the road again. I was getting tired of living on Safeway garbage and remaindered Wonder Bread down there in Big Sur. Jasmine's a nice girl but things get too squirrelly out in the country. That's a sweet little deal she's got, though, taking care of that trout farm. I'd like to get ahold of that some day."

"That your dream, Buck?" Mordecai said.

"Wouldn't you like to own a moving business *and* be caretaker for a trout farm?"

"I hadn't considered the two together."

"Fish move real easy, don't they?" Buck said. "And so does GTM."

As Buck and Mordecai drove around the Monterey peninsula and gave bids on the moving or trash hauling jobs, Mordecai began to see that Buck was perfect for developing his melanoia to its full potential, Mordecai's disease needed to interact with the world of work. Mordecai knew that he had always had an image problem in regards to work. People would look at him and realize that Mordecai was on vacation. This prevented them from burdening him down with jobs. But with Buck it was different.

Buck was the perfect image of the American working man. He was big, he was Irish, and—what was best—he was optimistic. That was the most important part. When Buck's ego got in a waltz with his optimism—it was hey nonny nonny, and Katy bar the door.

People were never calm when they moved. They got nest upset fever. But with Buck the message was always clear: *everything was going to be fine.*

Buck talked and their customers were convinced and calmed. After their first three bids were accepted, Buck revealed the GTM formula: "Figure out what you'll do it for, double it, and add five for the beer."

Mordecai was even more pleased when he saw that the GTM Formula was subject to experimental bids. Once they had three jobs sewn up, Buck started to freelance on the bids. What created the first experimental bid was the Reverend Duncan Dennis David's phone bill. The exact figure popped up in Buck's mind for some reason: 154.87. While they were driving between bids, Buck kept muttering about that. "Of course, we'll have to do something about the phone bill, can't always be wasting time at

Rita's . . . . 154.87." Then, "I don't want to go down to the phone company and go through all that rigamarole of getting a new phone . . . 154.87, humph!" So, on the next bid, Buck tacked on a religious surtax of 155 dollars but the bid was refused. "Well," Buck said, as they drove away, "that screws the Reverend's chances for financial redemption."

But what Mordecai loved most was that not only was his melanoia going to get a chance to interact with the world of work, it was going to have a chance to effect the past and future worlds of Buck's life. On the next bid, Mordecai found out that Buck had always wanted a fireplace in his Alice Street house. This dream of Buck's was revealed as they bid on a moving job for Manny, a Portuguese fisherman.

Manny was selling a rundown old house on David Avenue. He showed them what had to be moved out of the house and then he led them to his backyard. "There'll be some trash," Manny said. "We'll throw it out in the backyard with that stuff there." He pointed at the junk in the yard.

"You mean, you're going to *throw* away that bellbuoy?" Buck said. In the corner of the weedy yard a rusty bellbuoy with a big chain hanging from the top was parked next to the fence. "How much do you want for it?" Buck said.

"What are you going to do with a bellbuoy?" Mordecai said.

"We'll get it in the house," Buck said. "Don't worry about that."

"*In your house?*" Mordecai said. "What do you want a bellbuoy in your Alice Street house for?"

"Twenty bucks," Manny said. He shrugged. "I let it go for that."

"Fifteen," Buck said.

"Seventeen," Manny said, eyeing Mordecai.

"Hold it," Mordecai said, pulling Buck to one side. "Buck, how we going to get that bellbuoy on the truck? Let alone in the house?"

"It'll fit right in there," Buck said. He spread his arms out and encircled the bellbuoy in his imagination and lifted it up and put it on the back of the Grey Ghost. Manny and Mordecai watched this. "Okay, fifteen," Manny said.

"*What the hell are you going to do with a bellbuoy in your house?*"

"I've been looking for a way to heat up the old dump. I'll get

Duane the Welder to put a smokestack on it and cut a hole in the front, and make a fireplace out of it."

"Oh hell," Manny said, "if you can use it, ten."

"Done," Buck said.

"Wait a minute," Mordecai barked. "He was going to pay *us* to take it away, remember?" Mordecai pointed at the bellbuoy. "That's bigger than your whole truck, Buck, forget about the house."

"I wanted to remodel the house anyway. Tom Soper is willing to put a bigger doorway in and while we're at it, we might as well take off the whole front of the house and put in a sun deck. We can roll the bellbuoy in there then." Buck nodded and jerked a thumb toward Manny. "Give the man his tenspot."

"Not me, not my money," Mordecai said.

"If you take the chain off the top, it'll roll *easy*." To demonstrate, Manny walked over and tried to lift the chain.

"We'll hang it from the ceiling by that chain," Buck said. "No, from the beam Tom Soper will put in, and then we'll have a hanging fireplace, radiating heat 360 degrees!"

Mordecai was speechless. In his mind he saw the bellbuoy hanging from Buck's sagging roof, glowing red hot and frying the paint off the walls.

Buck brushed past Mordecai. He bent over and tried to help Manny lift the chain. The chain seemed to have different ideas about its fate. "Hell," Buck said, "we'll get Duane to *torch* off this chain, then we'll rent a little bigger truck, park it downhill on David Street there, lay a plank up on the back end and let that bellbuoy *roll* right up onto it." Buck pointed down the steep incline of David Street at the Monterey bay. Mordecai looked at where Buck's finger was pointing. He imagined a big splash out in the blue water.

— 17 —

By the time GTM drove down 5th Street in Pacific Grove, they had seven jobs for sure and a possible bellbuoy. Buck was figuring how they could subcontract the seven jobs and make enough money to rent a 2-ton truck with a winch on it for the bellbuoy.

"Duane hasn't worked for awhile, maybe if we gave him the Manny moving job, he'd torch that chain off for free."

Buck parked the Grey Ghost in front of a modest stucco house on 5th and got out of the truck. "You coming in?" he said.

"No," Mordecai said, "You talk to them." He held up the job call slip. "This is only a garage clean-out job. Lazarchuk's the name." He gave the slip to Buck. *Let Buck do it,* he thought. Mordecai stared at the Monterey Bay. He watched a lone sailboat tacking into the harbor. Easy enough to do. *Forget about winches and bellbuoys and 2-ton trucks and subcontracting jobs, just watch the sailboat sail in.*

It was only when Mordecai noticed that the sailboat was safely in harbor that he roused himself. The afternoon sun was turning orange-red below the long wisps of clouds over the ocean. Buck had been in the house for a long time. Mordecai tried to re-member what the woman looked like who had opened the front door. He really had not been paying attention. Then he re-membered the job slip; squeezed in between the address and the name Lazarchuk was the word "Widow". Mordecai looked at the front door. During their ride around, Buck had hinted that GTM often accepted *any fringe benefits* that a job might offer. Some of them, Buck had said, even took precedence over the base pay.

Mordecai couldn't recall the Widow Lazarchuk that well, he had only seen her open the door and let Buck in, but he decided against going up and ringing the doorbell. He got out of the truck and started to walk down 5th Street toward Cannery Row. *Buck might be bidding on that job all night,* he thought.

When Mordecai got to Cannery Row, the air was turning cool with a delicious thick misty taste to it. He strolled along the boarded-up canneries and watched the women and men getting out of their cars in the parking lot beside the old Chinese grocery store. He saw a woman with a brilliant red dress on climbing out of a tan Mercedes. He felt something revolve inside himself and he started out across the parking lot. Mordecai turned to watch the woman in red walk toward the street. Her legs looked long and fine. Mordecai felt a soft *ping.* Of all the *pings* Mordecai had heard so far, this one was the softest, the edges of the sound bleeding out into his imagination just as the woman's red dress seemed to fuzz out into the Monterey mist. And there was a prickly, erotic tickle to the ping.

Feeling as if he were following someone, Mordecai walked up the railroad tracks. In his mind a figure was ahead of him. He continued along the tracks until it crossed back onto Cannery Row. He walked toward the old Coast Guard station. Parked facing the bay were several scuba diving vans. The sun was setting in the west. Mordecai heard the *pings* inside him level out into a soft teasing sexy drone. The sensation almost made him dizzy. He stopped and concentrated on them and they turned into a delicious itching sound. He walked up to an old grey Metro. The back door was open.

A dark-haired slim woman in tight black jeans and a vaguely Hawaiian blouse stepped down from the van, then she stepped back up when she saw Mordecai. She knelt on a blue foam pad. "Hi," she said.

"Hello," Mordecai said.

"You a diver?" she said.

"Depends."

"Really?" she said. "What kind of a diver?" Mordecai shrugged. "I'm Francine," she said, "Francine Fingers."

Mordecai nodded and took out a cigarette. His fingers felt so hot he thought he could light a cigarette by touching the end. "I'm Mordecai," he said. "I don't really scuba dive."

"Your hair looks bleached enough," Francine said. She reached out and touched it. "It's really thick." She looked back in the van. "You want to look at some of the latest gear and watch the sunset?"

"Sure," Mordecai said. He climbed in beside her in the van. She shut the door. It was dark except for the spectacular reddish light of the setting sun coming through the windshield. The van smelled salty and wet and sandy. There were a few pieces of scuba diving equipment in the right corner, in the left corner was a big red beanbag chair. She leaned back into it. Mordecai felt the back of his head begin to grow lighter. "Where's this equipment?"

Francine lit a match and held up a bong pipe. She handed the bong to Mordecai. He waited until she passed the match over the top. He breathed in the smoke. Then he handed it back.

"You scared?" Francine asked.

Mordecai felt the soft touch of the smoke at the nape of his neck. "No," Mordecai said. "Why should *I* be scared?"

"It's dark in here," she said. "The sun will be completely down in a few minutes." She took a hit off the bong and laid it down on the floor behind the spare tire. She picked up a long drawstring bag. Inside was a bottle of wine packed in blue ice. She took it out and drank some and handed it to Mordecai. He took a drink. It was dry chilled white wine. Delicious. He took a second drink. Then he handed it back. As she turned west her face was glowing red from the sunset.

Watching the light change on her face Mordecai finished his cigarette and ground it out on the top of the wheelwell. He moved over and sat down on the beanbag. They stayed that way for a few minutes.

"What shall we talk about?" she said.

Mordecai couldn't think of anything to say. His body felt light and floating and yet there was a tremendous pressure inside his skin. The sun was a sinking ball of yellowish red fire at the mouth of the bay.

"All right, let's not talk, let's watch the sun," she said. Then he felt her face coming close to his ear. "You're really not scared?" she whispered. "You're trembling."

"No, that's not fear."

"You're different. Most men are nervous if a woman comes on this strong to them," she said, leaning back on the beanbag. Inside it there was a sliding, rustling sound as she settled back.

"Really? How long have you been making this survey? How many men have you scared?" Mordecai laid back next to her and she brought her face close to his and looked in his eyes.

"You're really *not* scared, are you? That's amazing."

"I don't know why not, but that's right. Am I supposed to be?"

"I've seen you around."

"No you haven't. I don't miss much and I wouldn't miss you if I saw you. We're total strangers."

She laughed. The last after-image of sun dipped below the horizon leaving red streaks of clouds arcing over the bay. She pushed herself down on him. "Okay, I've never seen you before," she breathed into his mouth, "but I'm going to now." She kissed him. Then she began to take off her blouse.

"Wait a minute," Mordecai said. "What are you doing? This isn't some movie."

"Stop complaining." She held up her watch and read the glowing face. "By the way, we'll have to hurry—my husband'll be back up to the top in twenty minutes. He's diving."

Mordecai laughed. "You don't have a husband." He opened up his Army jacket, slipped his arms out and spread it under him.

"Yes, I do." She wriggled out of her jeans. She had on silver panties with a blue lightning bolt up the left side. She pulled his foot to her and began to unlace his tennis shoe. "You don't believe me, do you?"

"Why should I?" Mordecai said, working the belt of his pants loose. "This is insane."

"I know," she said, tossing his shoe into the front seat. "God, I've never done anything like this before in my life."

Mordecai gave her his other shoe to unlace. "This doesn't really happen," he said. "This is someone's fantasy."

"I know, it's *ours*."

He unzipped his pants. "I'm really shaking. Feel my hand." He held out his hand. She held it for a moment.

"Ohhh, you *are* shaking." She leaned over and pulled at his other tennis shoe. He ducked as she threw it over his head into the front seat.

"Well, Jesus," he said, pulling down his pants, "what the hell, there's only one way to get rid of this much tension."

"You said it." Francine lunged on top of him and then he rolled her back over onto the bean bag and they both disappeared under a wave of lust.

— 18 —

Buck took the cup of coffee off the kitchen counter, walked over to the table, and sat down. On the table was a jade figurine of a Deva dancer with flames shooting out behind her. She was next to a fat translucent jade Buddha. "Mrs. Lazarchuk," Buck mused aloud, "a thousand cranes wave at you in thanks."

Buck sipped his coffee and then looked up at the silk mandala painting on the wall next to the table. He didn't like it there, so he rehung the mandala on a nail sticking out of the orange crate bookcase. As a final touch, Buck fetched a large silk portrait of a Chinese lady with her parrot from the pile of scrolls draped over his water bed and hung that on the wall behind the table.

Buck sat down, picked up his coffee and viewed the effect of the two jade figurines in front of the portrait of the lady and her parrot. Satisfied, he took another sip of his coffee. Then he wandered out the door and went around in back of the house. The lady and her parrot billowed out and flapped in the wind of the door slamming shut.

About twenty minutes later, Mordecai walked in. He sniffed and went for the coffee. He poured himself a cup and then he noticed the Chinese lady and her parrot scroll. He looked down at the two jade figurines on the table. "Jesus," he said, picking them up. He put them down and reached over and inspected the wall hanging. He felt the silk backing, checked for any rips. "Holy mother of god," he said. Mordecai walked into the other room and saw the mandala on the bookcase nail, then he noticed the pile of wall hangings on the waterbed.

Just at that moment, Buck came in. "Mordecai!" He laughed, seeing Mordecai with a Chinese ancestral portrait in his hand. "How about that? huh? You got any money? I need some capital."

"Where the *hell* did you get these?"

"You ran out on me last night. Christ, I had to race down to Beer Springs, tap into Sal for some cash and scoot back." Buck did a little dance around the front room. "Oh god, Mordecai, you should have *seen* it!" Buck suddenly bent over and began to wobble from the waist up, going into his old lady imitation. "*I was going to wait until after I had my garage sale before I had any one in for the cleanup,*" he said in a cracked old lady's voice, "*but then I got to thinking, maybe I better have an estimate first, so I know how much money I need to make.*"

"Well," Buck said, straightening up, "I said that I would be interested in anything she had to sell. *Oh I love garage sales, Mrs. Lazarchuk,* that's what I said, and she took me into the garage and opened up this trunk and lord in heaven, did I ever get an eyeful!"

Buck went back into his palsied old woman routine, holding up one of the rolled up scroll paintings. "*Mr. Lazarchuk was in China before 1920 and he got all those old things.*" Buck thwacked the scroll painting in his palm a few times. "*I'm just going to get rid of them. Yes, I've got to get rid of this old junk before I move to the retirement home.*"

Buck grinned insanely at Mordecai. "So I bought these fourteen scrolls here for $45 and those jade figurines on the kitchen table for $25 and I'm going back there this afternoon to get some more. She said there were more old trunks in the attic! Look at this embroidered silk kimono," Buck reached into the bathroom and unhooked a gorgeous pale pink kimono from the hanger on the door, "I had to give her the pink slip on the Grey Ghost for collateral. This is Score City, baby! Don't you have any more money left from the International Trash score? I heard you made over seven hundred. You think Loser Rred got paid yet at Beacon? How much cash is he paying you back? Think you can get some?" Buck turned in circles, revolving out to the kitchen. "Lord, where can I get some more money? We've got to *buy* the old girl out and we'll have it made! Look on this as an investment, Mordecai! I'll cut you in on the deal, you want breakfast? Why don't you move into the shed in back? I got a bed in there. You can move out of that squirrel Katherine's house. You need a rest from German Jock and her and their twitch methedrine runs. Your melanoia is working overtime for GTM! I need cash, though. Cash." Buck began to lay some bacon in the frying pan while muttering to himself. "It's Fat City for us, right? Hmmmmmmmmm?"

"Hey, slow down a bit. Something funny happened to me, too." Mordecai sat down at the kitchen table. "See, when I left you, I went down to Cannery Row and I was having a melanoia attack . . . . "

"You bet you were!" Buck crowed, cracking the eggs into a pan. "Fat City! here we come!"

"No, it was a different kind of *ping*, and uh . . . ."

"It was the ping of hordes of little gold coins dropping, baby!"

"No, see, I met this woman named Francine Fingers down at the beach. And see we uh . . . it was the damnedest thing, Buck, she asked me into the back of this van, and it was uh . . . well," Mordecai leaned back and closed his eyes. "I never had anything like this happen to me before. It was like she was expecting me, or something, and that we already knew each other. It was more like we were brother and sister, at first, that is."

Buck sighed, rubbing the jade flames of the dancing girl with his finger. "What's that, Mordecai? You got your ashes hauled?"

"It was more than *that*," Mordecai said to Buck. Buck circled back into the bedroom and came out with a scroll painting of an old Chinese gentleman. Buck held it up alongside Mordecai's head. "This old guy sort of looks like you, don't he? Look in the mirror there."

Mordecai looked at himself in the mirror as Buck held the old Chinese gentleman behind Mordecai's head. "See, she said her husband was going to be back in twenty minutes and we uh . . . I mean, it was . . . well, hell it was a frenzy we fell into, no other way to say it. Just out and out *lust*."

"Ah yes," Buck said, fingering the silk backing to a painting, "know what you mean."

"I'm not that way, never have been, but she got me *going*. There wasn't any yes or no about it. Magic. Incest, adultery, you name it. We had it all. And the next thing I know I'm hiking up Prescott Street with my shoelaces untied." Mordecai shook his head. "I said to myself, wait a minute, and I doubled back. She claimed her husband was coming back from diving in the bay. I didn't believe her but the Metro van was just pulling out and all I could see was the driver, a big dark-haired guy." Mordecai paused, remembering. "I don't know about this melanoia if it's going to get me into scenes like *that*. It shook me up. I don't mind being friendly, but this was crazy."

"Well, you like your animal, don't you?"

"Well, uh, yes, I do, I guess."

"She likes her animal too, it sounds like," Buck said. "I mean, one of the reasons people *like* you, Mordecai, is because you're warm and friendly. This woman obviously caught that right away and decided to take it to the limit—rub up against it for good luck. Your animal, her animal."

Buck laughed, catching Mordecai's expression. "Christ, Mordecai, grow up a little. You've been locked up in that hermit life too long. This melanoia of yours may take you into a few places that you can't handle, you know, and then it's . . . ." Buck picked up the silk kimono and began dancing with it, "bossa nova time."

Mordecai looked over at the gas range. The frying pan was sending up a column of smoke. "Buck," he said, "your bacon is burning."

— 19 —

Mordecai had no doubts about the power of his disease. In two days he had founded and liquidated International Trash, recovered buried treasure and lost a fortune, gained and junked a truck, and become a Vice-President of GTM, a company with over seven future jobs. He had fallen in lust and been waylaid by a mysterious woman. Also, with half of his previously hidden hundred dollars from the International Trash score now in Buck's pocket, Mordecai was an investor in what Buck was now calling "*The China Estate*". So far there was only one problem with this last item: Buck was going crazy with greed.

The Beer Springs Chorus began to monitor Buck's scams as he purchased more and more artifacts. Buck had pledged Mordecai to silence, so no one knew where he was getting the China Estate. This caused even more interest among the regulars, which was only topped by the Nash Caper. In one day Buck sold his Nash Metropolitan to Tom Soper and then, before Tom could drop by Jasmine's place in Big Sur and pick it up, Buck sold it again to Duane. And before either of them got it, Buck drove down to Big Sur to borrow money from Jasmine and took the Nash on a test drive up the canyon to view Jasmine's herb garden and blew the head gasket. At least that's what Buck said had happened.

Buck's ability to perceive the truth began to fluctuate as wildly as the value of the Chinese Estate. As Buck's ideas about the value went up, his notions of himself also began to inflate. Mordecai remembered what Ethel had said, "*When Buck's ego gets in a waltz with his optimism, watch out!*"

Duane drove down to Big Sur with his one ton truck to tow the Nash out of the canyon but he found that Buck had cut the top off with a hacksaw and turned it into a convertible. Disgusted, he had left it in the canyon to rust. "Buck obviously thinks a man with that much fine art should ride around in a convertible," Duane grieved. "Damn! that was a fine little car! And now the thing looks like a convertible all right, *an Okie convertible!*"

Both Tom and Duane began to lean on Mordecai to get Buck back in line. "What the hell have you unleashed on us?" Tom complained. "Hell, Mordecai, you're the Vice-President, aren't you? Get some of those assets liquidated and pay us our money back."

"Hey, any deals between you and Buck are none of my business. I'm the Vice-President of a moving company, GTM. In regard to the China Estate, I'm an investor, same as you. Don't blame my melanoia."

— 20 —

Mordecai had taken Buck's offer and moved up the hill to the shed in the back of the Alice Street house. From there he got a better view of the wildfire he had started in Buck's life. When Buck began to flash around the Widow Lazarchuk's silk kimono, his chances of persuading his women friends to loan him money blossomed, along with his dinner invitations. Buck began to sag under a twin load of greed and gluttony. He seemed to be eating out every night. Jasmine actually got to keep the kimono for one night, but Buck turned restless the next morning and drove down to the Big Sur trout farm and got it back through a combination of exercise and guile.

Mordecai, being an honest man, began to worry about the Widow Lazarchuk. She was doling out a trinket here, a silk screen there. Mordecai wondered how long her trunks would hold up. Was she senile? Was she throwing away her retirement nest egg on Buck's charming Irish company? And more serious, was any of this stuff worth it? Some of the scroll paintings were torn and tattered. Buck talked about getting them appraised, but he was too busy eating, borrowing money and attending to the Widow, to go have it done.

One morning when Mordecai asked Buck about this, he was offended. "Are you nuts?" he said, holding up a brass incense burner to the sunlight. "This stuff is worth a fortune! Leave it to me . . . . and say, you couldn't see your way clear to go do Manny's moving job for me? You could hire Duane maybe. I'd loan you my truck . . . I don't have time . . . ."

Mordecai declined the offer, but he realized that none of the seven GTM jobs had been done. Furthermore, Buck was in debt to practically everyone in town. Mordecai asked Buck to take him along on one of his visits to the Widow. He wanted to see if he could tell how long this routine was going to last.

"What for?" Buck said. "Now look, Mordecai, everything is on the up and up. I got the receipts for buying this, fair price," he chortled. "Oh yes, a fair price . . . And you can't *guide* this melanoia of yours, you know," Buck lectured him, holding up a thin jade figure of dancing Deva girl to the light so it cast a pale green shadow on the table top. "Remember, *He who kisses joy as it flies, lives in eternity's sunrise.*"

"It's noon," Mordecai said, looking at the same sun. "Hadn't we better be going?"

"All right, just this once, but don't queer this deal, okay?" Buck got up from the table and they went outside and got in the Grey Ghost.

It turned out that the Widow Lazarchuk had all her marbles. Mordecai had been wondering about that. There were laws against bilking old ladies and Mordecai had been thinking that Buck might have stepped on a few of them in his haste. "I just put on the tea," she said, "and I found another old trunk in the attic, Buck. You'll have to drag it out where you can see it, but go ahead on up and look at what's there."

While they listened to Buck wrestle the trunk around in the attic, Mordecai and the Widow Lazarchuk had tea. "We'll have to start thinking about that move soon, Buck!" she shouted up at him. There was no answer, only scrapes and thumps and curses. The Widow Lazarchuk winked at Mordecai. "He's not really a moving man, is he?" she said in a whisper to Mordecai "He's a con man, isn't he?"

Mordecai almost choked on his tea. "Well, uh . . . ."

The Widow smiled and drank some more tea. "When my Mishka died, the bank people told me those kind of people might come around. I waited and waited but none of them showed up. Oh well, he's lovely company, he's . . . ." she searched her memory for the right word, "he's so *optimistic*. Yes, you can't find that kind of enthusiasm any more. People used to have it all the time but now they don't."

"Uh, if you think that about Buck, then why . . . ?" Mordecai waved at the attic.

"It's such a relief to get *rid* of it," she said. "And I know Buck takes such *pleasure* in that old junk." She beamed at Mordecai and winked again. "I knew that I had found the right person for it."

— 21 —

After Mordecai left the Widow's house, he wandered back down toward Cannery Row. As he crossed Lighthouse Avenue and began to walk down toward the Stanford Marine Biology lab, he thought he saw someone walking on the railroad tracks toward Monterey. Mordecai turned east on the tracks and followed along, even though he could no longer see who he was following. Mordecai began to have fantasies about the man. He began to say a line of Chinese poetry over and over to himself. Translated the line read: *"Men like that should stick to making money."* Mordecai could remember vaguely that the line was referring to a quarrel with a critic by the poet, but Mordecai applied it to the ghostly figure somewhere ahead of him on the railroad tracks. He wanted to see this man who was only good at making money.

It was a misty, overcast day. When Mordecai reached the wharf down in Monterey, rain was falling. He watched the sparse tourist crowd, wondering where his money man had gone, and then he turned around and walked west on the railroad tracks, back toward Cannery Row. He was a block away from where he started when he heard a soft *ping*.

— 22 —

Mordecai found himself in front of what had once been a health food store. After that a Filipino family had lived there for a few months, and then the storefront had been changed into a regular neighborhood grocery store run for Chicanos, Portuguese and Italians, featuring their foods. Mordecai could not remember how long that had gone on. Now the storefront looked desolate. The last owners had put up a wide band of pale green paper across the window, about six feet high so no one could see in. Still visible above the green paper was a scale hanging from the store ceiling, the red arrow tilted out at a forty-five degree angle, even though there was nothing in the scale's basket.

Mordecai stood outside the storefront, his *pings* were now rippling along under his consciousness like a fast-running brook. He liked the sensation and didn't particularly want it to stop. So he stood there, letting his melanoia meter run. Finally, he stepped forward and tried the storefront door. It opened.

Mordecai stepped in. The counter was still in place but only a few old empty cigarette cartons stood where the register used to be. The light was dim. One long flourescent light fixture was on in the back. Someone had fixed the store up into a studio of some kind. Instead of shelves there were three old couches, facing each other in an open-ended square. On one of the couches was a tattered black paperback of *Cannery Row*. Behind the back couch was a counter with a sink, a refrigerator, a hot plate and kitchen utensils. On the floor in the middle of the couches was a blue plastic mat.

To the right on the wall facing the three couches and the blue mat was a long three-piece mirror. At either end were two big lightstands with huge bulbs, the kind that were used for photography. A backless bookcase filled with paperback books was behind one couch. A shaft of light suddenly swept up the books as a trapdoor in the floor opened. Mordecai took a step back. Up from the basement a figure emerged, holding a large bellied vase. "Hello," Francine said, peering at him. "*¿Quien es?*"

"It's me," Mordecai said. He reached for his cigarettes. "Mordecai."

Francine held the vase up and back toward her right shoulder and regarded Mordecai. "Hello Mordecai," she said. "How'd you find this place?"

"Chance," Mordecai said. "I stumbled in here." He lit a cigarette and noticed his hands were trembling.

Francine had on a blue smock tied tight around her waist. Her legs were bare, a pair of black thin sandals on her feet. She turned and set the vase down on the floor. Her arms were smeared with clay. "So what have you been doing?" she said, backing up and looking at the vase.

Mordecai could see through the opening in the back of the

smock that she had on a pair of cutoff jeans and a loose silver blouse. Her hair was drawn back up under a black scarf. "Nothing much," Mordecai said.

"You didn't come back the next night like you said."

"I got held up," he said. He sat down on the couch. "So, this your studio?"

"No, I'm borrowing it." She smiled at him. "Would you like some soup? I'm about to eat." He nodded. She moved over to a counter behind the couch and put a pan on the hot plate. "This was a mom and pop store last time I passed by here."

"Yes," she said. She opened a can of Campbell's Beef Noodle Soup and poured it in the pan. She added a can full of water from the tap above the sink. Then she put the can in the sink and turned around.

Mordecai watched her survey him. "What have you been making?" he said, looking down at the vase.

Francine began to laugh. "Oh," she said, "oh, wouldn't you like to know?"

"Yeah I would," Mordecai said. "As a matter of fact, tell me all about it!"

"We'll need a drink for *that*," Francine said. She reached down under the counter and brought up a full bottle of Jack Daniels whiskey. "Soup first or this?"

"That," Mordecai said, pointing. "Fuck the soup."

Francine poured two glasses of whiskey. She opened the refrigerator and in the dim light her face seemed concentrated as she took out the ice tray. *She's in a role,* Mordecai thought.

She came over to him and gave him a glass of whiskey. Then, as Mordecai saluted her with his drink, she stepped back and turned on one of the photographer's lights. The glare off the mirror blinded Mordecai for a minute and then his eyes adjusted.

"Why'd you do that?"

"I don't know."

"I keep getting the feeling you know everything you do."

"Maybe I do," she said. "What's the difference?"

"To me?" Mordecai had to think that over. Francine came over to the couch and sat down beside him. She drank. "Nothing, I guess," Mordecai said. "No, I like it. It's like dance or something. Choreographed."

"I dance," she said. 'Want to see?"

Mordecai nodded. Francine took another sip of whiskey and got up, untying the smock in back and letting it hang loose around her. She stepped in front of the blazing light and tripped the switch for the other light, pinning her between the two and her own image in the mirror. She shook out her hair from the scarf, pushed her head forward so her hair covered her face, and let the smock slide down her arms until it dropped to the floor under a curtain of hair.

— 23 —

Mrs. Edith Spinoza Villareal needed one jicama to shred as garnish for her salad. She had just returned from a three month trip to her relatives in Brownsville, Texas and her sister was coming over from Salinas to chat about her trip. She got her string bag, put on her scarf against the mist, and hurried out the door, not forgetting her change purse. She walked down David Avenue toward Cannery Row, ignoring the supermarket on Lighthouse Avenue. She was thinking of many things she had to tell her sister about what had happened at the wedding and what poor Carmelita, their crazy half-sister had done, when she opened the door to the Aurelia Market and found herself in a blinding light staring at two naked people screwing like billygoats on a big blue mat in front of a huge mirror. "AY!" she said, "this is not a store!"

— 24 —

"I've got to remember to lock that damn door," Francine said, pouring some soup into a coffee cup and handing it to Mordecai. "People just barge in all the time, talking Spanish."

"You like it," Mordecai said, adjusting the blanket around his shoulders. He laughed. "I can't believe what went on there. I used to be a really shy guy."

"Yes," Francine sighed. "You didn't miss a beat."

"Now come on, do you really have a husband?"

"I did."

"You did."

"I sort of do. I don't want to talk about that.'"

"You set that up, didn't you?"

"What?"

"You get off setting up scenes, right? Danger." Mordecai shrugged. "I mean, I'm not saying it's *bad* or anything. You like to direct things, don't you? You were sort of in control, weren't you?"

"I believe," Francine said, demurely, sipping her soup, "I was approaching something out of control right then."

"I don't want to ruin everything but uh . . . ." Mordecai paused. "How can you like control so much?"

"So what do you want to know? Life story? Okay. I was married to a lawyer. I wasn't ready for that kind of life. It got so I couldn't tell where my feelings ended and somebody else's anticipations started. It was boring. It got so things felt so pre-planned, that after a few years, I felt like every time I had an orgasm or ate a peach, some statistic was adjusted in an insurance company."

"So now you feel in control?"

"No, I feel as if I have a choice now, free in a way I think I should have felt maybe five years ago, maybe in 1968. I'm catching up, let's say."

"Hey, 1968 is never coming back," Mordecai said. "That's over. I'm not sure I'd *want* it back."

"Well, let's say I'm creating five years past history for myself."

"Look, I'm really not worried, but you're divorced?"

"Everything I just told you is a fantasy, okay? Five years of fantasy."

"You said you'd seen me, where?"

Francine sighed. "A bar."

"Which bar?"

"You're ruining a perfect relationship, Mordecai. We don't need our personal histories all the time. Most of the time we need to get *rid* of them."

"I'm not asking for anything major, just where you saw me."

She drew the blanket around her closer. She drank some soup, and carefully ran her finger along her lower lip, removing some overflow and then sucked it off. "On Lighthouse."

"Beer Springs? No. Chino's!" Mordecai got excited. "Two weeks ago?"

"You were talking with some doctor type."

"That was when I found out about my disease." Mordecai told her about his melanoia.

"And you haven't been back to the shrink?"

"I've been too busy," he said.

She laughed. "You're really crazy," she said. "Don't you want to know?"

"What more do I have to know? It's working."

— 25 —

Just how far Buck had strayed from their business arrangements wasn't made clear to Mordecai until a day later down at Beer Springs. Mordecai had settled in at his favorite corner and was having a short beer and reading the *Chronicle* about the latest Watergate scandals. "Look at this Ethel, talk about melanoia— this guy hands over $220,000 and doesn't ask for any identification," he said.

"Don't be so *hard* on him," Ethel said. "This was probably the first time he had ever done something like this. Ha-ha. He didn't know he was supposed to get a firm handshake and the password in return for all that dough."

"What do you suppose the password was?"

"Loose lips sink ships," Ethel said.

Mordecai looked up as the front door swung open and he saw Rita come in. "Speaking of loose lips," Mordecai muttered. She marched over to him.

"Mordecai, the customers are wondering when the moving men are coming," Rita said. "They call up all the time. They wonder why the moving men haven't come. They are wondering if the moving men are going to come at all. They are wondering about *that advance*."

"*That advance?*"

"That advance," Rita said. "I don't know what to tell them, Mordecai, some of them are really mad. They yell at me." Rita sat

down, blocking Mordecai's exit from the bar. "You should come by right now and pick up the new job slips too," she said. "It's the least you can do."

Mordecai looked across the bar for help from Ethel but she turned her back on him. *Women*, he thought, *they stick together*. Rita took Mordecai by the arm, drinking the last of his beer for him. "Now come on," she said.

Mordecai and Rita emerged from the darkness of Beer Springs into the bright light of day. "I gotta . . . uh . . ." Mordecai looked up and down the street.

"You gotta what?" Rita said, hooking her arm in his.

Mordecai looked down the street at the Beacon Farm Milk gas station. "I gotta get some money from Rred." But Rred was out to lunch.

As Rita and Mordecai strolled back arm and arm toward Rita's house, Mordecai wondered if Rita had been up to see Buck's silk kimono yet. "Seen it?" Rita said, "I've got twenty dollars down on it."

A half a block away from Rita's house, Mordecai got a sudden urge for an ice cream cone. "Whew, I didn't think it was this hot," he said, "I could go for an ice cream cone." He looked back down Lighthouse Avenue at the Dairy Queen. "I've got a whole half-gallon at the house," Rita said, "Baskin-Robbins Rocky Road. Come on." She yanked at his arm.

Mordecai, whose capacity for accepting anyone's personality was the cornerstone of his popularity down at Beer Springs, suddenly became critical. In the bright daylight, he began to notice things about Rita, things that he hadn't seen so clearly in the shadows of Beer Springs.

That mole on her cheek. That ingratiating way she had of hanging onto his arm as they walked. Her frizzy red hair that looked a little greasy in the sunlight. Mordecai began to think of folk sayings, such as, *you can lead a horse to water but you can't make him drink.*

By the time they turned the corner to Rita's house, Rita had him in such a clutch Mordecai felt as if he had a python on his arm. And that's when he saw Buck, standing beside the Grey Ghost at the curb. "Goddamn, what took you so long, I called Beer Springs and they said you just left. You got any money?"

Mordecai took out his wallet and handed Buck a five dollar bill.

"The China Estate negotiations are finished! The China Estate is ready to go to the Avery Brundage Collection in San Francisco for appraisal. And then be exchanged for big money! Whoopee! Let's eat! Let's celebrate! We're in the money! GTM forever! Whaaaa-hooey!"

Buck lifted Rita right off Mordecai's arm and gave her a bear-hug. They all began to walk up the steps to her house when Mordecai remembered that they needed some wine. Buck gave him back his five dollar bill and Mordecai hurried off. "Get some food, too!" Buck yelled down the stairs. "Bread, wine, and cheese! Goat cheese! Brie! Sausage! Whoopee!"

When Mordecai returned two hours later, Rita was taking a nap. Buck was sitting on the couch in the front room in his jeans, barefoot, with his shirt off. He was sorting through the job calls, looking like an overworked exec.

"Goddamn, Mordecai, we're on our way. Riches, fame, and fortune, When I called the De Young Museum, were they hot to see this stuff? Hot damn!" Buck showed Mordecai a job slip. "This a new one? We might need a little trash job to firm up our cash flow."

Mordecai inspected the address and agreed. He uncorked the wine.

"Good, and while we're in the city, we have a place to stay. Don't know how long it will take the museum people to appraise our goodies . . . . We're staying with Jane James. You remember Jane, don't you? The one who married that Portuguese bullfighter and brought him to Big Sur about six months ago." Buck snorted. "Portuguese bullfighter, that's like marrying the Studebaker of bullfighters. Jane was always *trying* to be different, English accent and all, but she's as middleclass as a goddamn box of Cheerios."

Buck took a glass of wine and sipped it. He spread the job slips out on the table. "So we've got two rent-free months up in the city, if we want them."

"Two months?" Mordecai said. "Why two?"

"Jane is moving back to Missouri and wants GTM to look after her apartment in exchange for shipping her things back there. You know Miss Jane. Can't get good help and she was too busy shopping to pack up her junk. So we'll have time to spend all that

money! Sharkfin soup, Mordecai! Pork dumplings at Wooey Gooey Louies! Cezannes at the Legion! The newest used books in Berkeley! Poetry, Mordecai, light on white Victorian houses! Music! You can check out the Brundage collection of Chink art! And all that lovely money! I believe this disease of yours is catching! Whoopee!"

And with that declaration of financial independence and lust for the good life, the upper echelon of GTM took the rest of the day off and began their lunge into good fortune with a bottle of cold white wine.

"San Francisco, here we come!" Out on the front porch, Buck toasted the Monterey Bay. Then he toasted Mordecai. "It's a great day for melanoids!"

Book Two
San Francisco
Summer
1973

WHEN MORDECAI WEAVED
into Buck's kitchen at noon the next day, certain tangible pro-
cedural difficulties relating to the move to San Francisco were
much on his mind. They didn't have any food for breakfast.
They didn't have any money. The gas tank of the Grey Ghost was
empty and Mordecai's brains felt like a pile of alcoholic gravy.

Mordecai put water in a pan and lit the gas range and put the
pan over the flame. Then he looked in the refrigerator. After the
euphoria of the previous evening it seemed remarkable to him
that so able a President as Buck had neglected to provide for
breakfast.

"Buck, . . . are you there?"

"You don't have that camera around anymore, do you,
Mordecai?"

"No," Mordecai said, "I pawned it."

There was silence in the next room. Then the thump as Buck's
feet hit the floor, the slosh of the waterbed and then a groan.
Mordecai walked into the other room. Buck was standing there
naked, looking at the cleverly concealed fortune strewn all

around him. He stared at the silk kimono hanging above a chainsaw sitting in a pool of cold oil on the floor.

Mordecai saw the temptation in Buck's eyes. "Don't do it, Buck."

"Just one jade figurine," Buck said. "For breakfast."

"You can't take a piece of the China Estate down to Sol's pawnshop, not after all this. Don't chippy on our fortune, Buck."

"We need food."

"We gotta wait until we get to San Francisco. Jane will help us sell the stuff. She can get the *good* prices for it. You said so yourself. Sol wouldn't know what they are worth."

Buck groaned and slowly collapsed on the floor. He rolled over and stared at the ceiling. Then he rolled back over and took the pile of Rita's job slips off the stack of books by the bed and spread them out. "We're going to have to go to work," Buck said. "Jesus, I never thought it would come to this."

Mordecai went back into the kitchen. The flame was under the pan, the water was in the pan, but the water was not boiling. Mordecai watched it closely.

"Floor therapy," Buck said.

"What?"

"Floor therapy. We could install tiny therapeutic squares of mystic hardwoods in every house in America, or at least in California. Cool hardwood squares, bare of any rugs. For the sick, for the weak, Mordecai, for the infirm of body and mind."

Mordecai stared at the water in the pan. The water was resisting the fire underneath it. The pan was resisting the fire. The water was *not close enough* to the fire. Mordecai tried to figure out how the water could be put *directly* on the fire.

"*Lie down and be healed,*" Buck said. "That would be our slogan. Yes, people in California would turn away, Mordecai, from the false gods of Gestalt, group therapy, encounter groups, and flock to our . . . . *Our floors of perception.*"

Mordecai looked up from the gas range at the grey fog drifting in over the Presidio. "Coffee," he prayed, "please let there be coffee."

— 2 —

From her apartment porch in San Francisco Jane James looked down the flight of stairs at Buck and Mordecai. "Where the *hell* have you been? My god, I had to put off my airline reservations, my whole bloody life is screwed up royally because of you. You said you'd be here four days ago. Four days. What *happened?*"

"Now Jane," Buck said, starting up the stairs, "this can all be explained."

"Bloody fuck, it better be explained. I got the packing crates. Had them delivered. I have packing crates up and down my hall, in my living room, packing crates all over the goddamn place, it's been like living in a warehouse."

"Jane, this is really a nice place you have here." Buck turned and looked out over the bay toward Oakland. "We'll get you back home to Missouri in time."

"Balls you will," Jane said, pushing Buck off the porch. Buck reeled back down the stairs, almost knocking Mordecai down. "I called up *last* week! You said you'd be leaving the *next* day! I got tickets, I got packing crates, I got reservations, but *no Buck!'*

"Wait, Jane, let me show you something." Buck walked down to Mariposa Street and began to rummage in the cardboard boxes in the back of the Grey Ghost.

"Who are *you?*" Jane snapped.

"I'm Buck's partner, remember me, I'm Mordecai, we met at Beer Springs? Look, we had to help this old Portuguese fisherman move." Mordecai decided against telling her about the day spent trying to budge the bellbuoy. "Then we had to help Ethel, the bartender down at Beer Springs, you remember her? she had a pile of stuff in her corral out in Carmel Valley and the Grey Ghost got stuck in the mud there, with this load of fence posts on, so we had to offload them into a neighbor's truck and that got stuck." Mordecai paused. He looked up into Jane's face and smiled. "Then these two twins came by and offered to take Buck to get a tow truck," Mordecai said, mentally eliminating the day Buck spent with the blonde Invoglio twins at the side of a swimming pool in Carmel Valley, stranding Mordecai at Ethel's house. "And by the time he got back it was dark."

"What the *hell* is he looking for down there?" Jane snapped.

Mordecai turned. Buck pulled the silk kimono out of a box. Buck began walking up the stairs and talking. "Now Jane, you're a woman of taste, let me show you some of the scores we got. Now this is a kimono from the China Estate. We're having it appraised at the De Young Museum here in town." Buck came up the stairs, the kimono draped over his shoulder, his hands out in peace, smiling at Jane. "What do you think this is worth?"

"Don't confuse *me* with your low rent pickups, Buck. I'm not impressed. You can take that kimono and shove it where the sun don't shine." She whirled around and went in her apartment, slamming the door behind her.

Mordecai looked at Buck. Buck started laughing. "Holy mother of god," he said.

"Buck, I think it's time for me to have a melanoia attack. Gimme twenty."

Buck took out his wallet and handed Mordecai the money. "You're right, you better let me handle this," he said. "Take a stroll around the neighborhood. Pet your disease a little. See if it purrs. I'll get Jane straightened around. We need her pretensions to sell the China Estate for us. We don't want to get ripped off."

Mordecai moved down the stairs. "See you later," he said. "And Buck, good luck."

"Nothing to it, Mordecai," Buck said. "I've seen Jane like this before. Trust me. She's not really angry, if she was, she'd start talking Missouri drawl, instead of stage British."

"Really?" Mordecai said. "She's from Missouri?"

"Oh yeah, you ought to hear her between the sheets," Buck switched into a Southern accent. "Oh yeeah, yore jist doin' me to deayth!" Buck snorted and looked at the front door. "Nothing makes Jane more angry than the fact that you can't get good help any more." Buck smiled confidently. "I know the kind of help she really needs," he said. "Leave this to the President."

— 3 —

Phonebook Phil was a red-haired guy who had only one trick in life, but like the hedgehog's single act, it was a good one.

Phonebook Phil would go into a bar that had a piano and act a little drunk. This was not difficult, because Phonebook Phil was either entering or leaving drunkenness normally, and had an excellent short term memory of that state. Then he would challenge a bozo at the bar. "I betcha I cun ... cun play the ... the *phonebook!*" If the bozo bit for the act, then Phonebook Phil would stagger over and make a big show of fumbling with the San Francisco phonebook, letting it fall off, propping it back up .... Then he would squint at the phonebook, do a plink and a plunk, before launching into something dear to the hearts of the assembled lushes, *September Song, Autumn Leaves, Send in the Clowns.*

Mordecai hooked up with Phonebook Phil in a bar on 16th and Alabama, where Phonebook Phil had just dazzled some longshoremen with *Red Sails in the Sunset.* Mordecai liked Phonebook Phil because when he followed Phil from bar to bar, he was sent free drinks. Mordecai didn't mind imitation melanoia. Phonebook Phil liked Mordecai because he knew Hack Wilson's lifetime batting average and because he thought Nellie Fox should be in baseball's Hall of Fame (or at least Nellie's famous right cheek, stretched taut and shiny over possibly the largest chaw of tobacco in baseball history). Phonebook Phil was a refugee from Chicago where Nellie Fox had played. Phil and Mordecai made the tour of the bars from the Sunset to North Beach. Mordecai enjoyed the city life as seen from Phonebook Phil's 1964 Valiant and inside middleclass bars. As long as Phonebook Phil didn't get too drunk and imagine that he was Thelonius Monk, banging out weird chords, the drinks kept coming.

Mordecai enjoyed Phonebook Phil's eloquent *Hands* soliloquy. "You see these hands?" Phil would say, holding up his mitts. "These hands once could have played with ... *any symphony in the United States.*" Then Phonebook Phil would turn the hands palms up and slowly clench them, "But, just before I graduated from UCLA," he'd whisper.

Mordecai like it that with each new bar the schools Phil attended also changed, depending on what college basketball team was playing on TV. Mordecai had a bossa nova approach toward his past, and he admired anyone else who could improvise as eloquently as Phonebook Phil did.

The two of them did not return to Jane's on Mariposa street

until two days later. Mordecai had told Phonebook Phil all about Buck and the China Estate. When Mordecai knocked on the door to Jane's apartment, she opened it. "Who?" she said. "Oh, him? He's in the basement!" And then she slammed the door. Mordecai and Phonebook Phil turned around and walked back ·down the stairs and into the basement.

"Jesus," Phonebook Phil said, looking around, "and this guy you say just *scored*? I'd hate to see where he lives when he's broke."

"Well, it's completely carpeted," Mordecai said, surveying the basement. The floor, the walls and the ceiling had all been covered with carpet samples. It gave the room a curious patchwork look. "It's a little sparsely furnished," Mordecai continued. He stepped over to the lone bare mattress on the floor and looked down at the tiny transistor radio propped up next to it. "I wonder where the China Estate is," Mordecai said. There was no sign of it in the carpeted cave.

— 4 —

When Mordecai checked back after four more days with Phonebook Phil, he saw that Buck had moved up in the world: upstairs into Jane's top floor apartment. Buck buzzed him in and he shouted down to Mordecai, "I'm going to the can, make yourself comfortable." Mordecai climbed up to a large landing at the top of the stairs. Pine packing crates were stacked up there, full of Jane's goods. There was a small door to the left that let into the apartment. Buck had also pulled back the double doors that opened out onto the landing, creating the space that Buck seemed to require. The false wall which had once covered the doors lay in splinters at the end of the landing. "Only two days in and already remodeling," Mordecai murmured to himself. Buck was notorious in Monterey for tearing out walls in his houses. The landing and bathroom had been a dining room in the good old days before the house was remodeled into two apartments. Mordecai was pleased to see a bottle of Grand Marnier on the kitchen table. It was a possible signal that Buck had scored on the China Estate. Mordecai sat down facing the window overlooking the bay. Buck came back from the john.

"Get The Money movers may be a thing of the past," Buck said, pouring some Grand Marnier into a glass of orange juice and handing it to Mordecai. He poured one for himself. "I felt that I should consult with my Vice President first. You wouldn't believe it," Buck said. " The phone started falling off the hook and I had to go out on a few job calls."

"Job calls? You put in an ad in the *Chronicle*?"

"My roommate did, Jesse, Jesse James. A fine lad, he had the phone switched over in his name too."

"Jane's brother," Mordecai said, looking out the double doors at the packing crates stencilled with Jane James' name and her Missouri address.

"Yes, no deposit, since Jane kept her bills paid while living here with Jesse. The Ma Bell folks thought Jesse was a good credit risk." Buck smiled. "It's good to know the phone company still respects *family*. An old honored Missouri family. So, anyway, Mordecai—after the phone fell off the hook for a few days, and I went out and did some moving jobs with the Grey Ghost, I thought that perhaps we should change the name of our company to meet the needs of the modern single apartment dwellers here in San Francisco." Buck leaned back and closed his eyes. "How about this," he said, holding up his hands as if framing a sign,

"HEARTBREAK HAULING
TWO TO MOVE & ONE
TO CONSOLE"

"Goddamn, Mordecai, you have no idea how many divorce cases that GTM has handled while you were gone. Not only divorcing Jane here, but all over the city. One hundred and fifty dollars a crack, about two hours moving, half a single apartment usually, hell . . . . I've had two, three jobs a day," Buck said. He looked at Mordecai's orange juice. "You want some champagne in that?" Mordecai nodded. Buck leaned back, opened the refrigerator, and pulled out an opened bottle of Mumm's champagne from among the white doggie cartons of Chinese food. "I've been eating good. Had to keep my strength up while I was divorcing Jane. God in heaven, Mordecai, I was sorely tried.

Buck, can you do this; Buck, can you do that. No one to powder her ass, wipe her nose. Well, she's back in Missouri and the family riding academy now." Buck added some orange juice and Grand Marnier to Mordecai's champagne. "You hungry?" Buck said. "Heat up some of that chink food, if you want."

"What about the China Estate?"

"Oh, that's taken care of." Buck picked up a record of Handel's *Water Music*. "We got the right stuff."

Mordecai didn't like the sound of that. "You took it to the De Young Museum?"

"Certainly . . . and they said it was the genuine stuff, only they didn't want it. They said the mandalas were 19th Century, could have been produced by any number of monasteries. They couldn't date or authenticate any of the paintings. So, they didn't want to buy them."

"But they put a price on them?"

"Well," Buck said, slipping the record on the stereo. "No."

"So did you sell the stuff?" Mordecai began to imagine Beer Springs filling up with Buck's angry creditors and investors in the China Estate.

"Oh, before I forget," Buck said, "I saw Steve Wire the other day. You remember him, carpenter friend of Tom Soper? He's living over in the Haight. He said he'd like to see you."

"Sure, fine," Mordecai said. "But what *happened*? Did Jane sell the stuff?"

"Oh shit, *Jane,* you know what *Jane* said once the word came down from the De Young. She wouldn't have anything more to *do* with the China Estate once she knew that. Wouldn't touch it. Don't worry, they'll be sold." Buck turned up the Handel. "It'll just take time."

"You put an ad in the paper?"

"Oh no, I'm not that stupid. Why, anyone could come by, look at it, and then break in later, steal it. No way."

Mordecai was slightly mollified. "I never thought of that. So, where is everything?"

"They're on commission. In a shop."

Mordecai began to imagine the people in Beer Springs coming up to him. *Where's my money? What happened to the China Estate?* "What shop?"

"Well, it's on . . . it's uh . . . over by Clement Street. See, we were coming back from the De Young . . . . you should have seen the bastard, he was probably from Nebraska, turn up his nose at the China Estate—*rawthur poor stuff*—I thought Jane was going to back up and piss on his boots, she got so excited by his total disdain and English accent. And after we went to a couple of antique-creepy stores, we stopped to get a bite to eat, Jane and I had a little spat, crazy bitch dumped a plate of oyster sauce beef down my front and left, . . . and then I saw all these shops, and so . . . ."

"What kind of a shop?"

"Well . . . . it's a . . . an Armenian rug shop."

"*An Armenian rug shop?*"

"They were the only ones who would take the stuff. I lugged the stuff around to all the high class ones and they wouldn't touch them. Toney bastards."

Mordecai looked at Buck. He was wearing jeans, a torn t-shirt, and hiking boots. Mordecai imagined how the scenario had unfolded: it had been hot, Buck sweating with a good shirt on in the De Young fronted by Jane. Next Buck with Jane and with his good shirt unbuttoned in the ritzy antique shops. And finally Buck in a food-stained t-shirt, without Jane, busted down to dealing with Armenian flea market dealers.

"I don't think you should criticize the business decisions of your partner without knowing the facts," Buck said.

Mordecai's mind traveled back to Monterey again, the winks of Widow Lazarchuk, her smile, her little whisper, *he's a con man, isn't he?* . . . . "She did it to you, didn't she?"

"Who? Jane?"

"No, The Widow Lazarchuk. That kindly old woman who greased you up for the big one."

"Oh, we'll get our money back! Don't worry about that!"

"Sure you will. How much outfront money did you get from the Armenians?"

Buck looked uncomfortable. "Eighty bucks. But that was up-front, before they sold any of it! And sixty-forty for the rest."

Mordecai put down his drink and began to rub his eyes. "Does your roommate still have his guns?"

"Who?"

"Jesse, Jesse James," Mordecai said. "Because the only way GTM is going to come out ahead of any Armenian rug dealers is to hold them up. And he better bring his brothers."

— 5 —

Steve Wire was a skinny Southern boy, an Alabaman just like Buck. Unlike Buck, however, Steve was a small-town gossip. He doted on the sin, weirdness and perdition of his California neighbors. At this time Steve was living in the Haight district with Angie Reuss, a feisty young woman from Oregon, who was studying painting. Steve met Angie in Monterey after his divorce. When Angie transferred to the Art Institute, he moved to San Francisco with her. Steve worked as a carpenter for the Bay Area Rapid Transit line, building forms in the tunnel under Market Street. When Mordecai showed up at their flat, Steve delighted in detailing for him the messes that he had seen. "You should see this job I got, Mordecai. Talk about crooked? Our crew goes down there in the morning, punches in, and then we all split. Ride back up to Market Street, fall out in a 24-hour movie house. Then about 3 or so we filter back down and put in for overtime. Whew! I'm making doubletime every goddamn day! You know how much money that is? I am ashamed to say."

Having discharged his tale of civic corruption, Steve pumped Mordecai for news about Buck, the China Estate, Jane, and who was doing what to whom down in Monterey. Mordecai told Steve about his disease. But he didn't say that he had decided to stay away from Buck for a few weeks.

Steve was pleased to hear about Mordecai's melanoia. Steve joked about mental diseases being an admission of weakness and backsliding. Nothing pleased Steve more than, as he said, *a friend in mortal trouble.* Mordecai liked Steve Wire because he was always dealing with such things, rather than suppressing them, and it made good theater. Mordecai had some hope that Steve would get over these Baptist flashbacks. But also, Steve's routines made him a little nostalgic about his own small-town Lutheran upbringing in the Northwest.

Once Angie sensed that Mordecai was upset after the China

Estate fiasco, she was concerned about him. It didn't escape her that Buck kept calling up, but Mordecai always found some excuse not to go over. One night after a pleasant Italian meal and much red wine, she got Mordecai to talking.

Mordecai related again how they came to the city with high hopes and how badly things turned out. "I don't know, maybe it's pride."

"Pride goeth before the fall. I know my Bible, it was either that or a licking."

"Oh quiet, Steve. We know you were raised razor strap Baptist," Angie said.

"I guess I thought that my disease could pull us through this. I don't want to go back to Monterey and tell everyone at Beer Springs that it came to zilch."

"A man's gotta take pride in what he does best," Steve said. "Even if it's being mentally sick."

"Steve, you don't have to *rank* Mordecai."

"I'm just joshing him, Angie."

"You think everyone is signifying. You think mental disease is just another modern coverup for sin. Shutup for a minute. Now, Mordecai, it's that your melanoia *looks* like it doesn't always work, is that what bothers you most?"

"Well, yeah, but I think this is not a case where appearances deceive."

"Just because you're sick with a wonderful disease," Angie scolded him, "doesn't mean everything's going to turn out for the better. Events may be changed by it, but you can't change human nature."

Mordecai considered that for a moment. "I guess so."

"Yeah, but if you got that, then what's Buck got?" Steve said. Steve always envied Buck's good time life, mainly because he couldn't live that way.

"Buck? Buck has primal optimism."

"That's a great way to describe Buck," Steve said. "Primal optimism. Maybe original optimism."

"Well, it sure does put my melanoia to the test," Mordecai said.

"Yeah, but then why are *you* with Buck, anyway?"

"I'm with Buck because no matter what my melanoia gives him, he tries to turn it into something better; I got to admire that." The whole adventure started to seem funny to him again. "Stresses, warps and plain old fuckups galore. I don't know if I'm ready to go back to it."

"He's been calling nearly every day. He says he's had so many jobs that he's had to hire a friend of yours, Phonebook Phil, as his helper. He didn't seem to think this guy was working out. Who's Phonebook Phil?"

— 6 —

Even with Angie's pep talk, Mordecai delayed going back to Buck. He knew that no matter how much money Buck piled up, he would spend it within a day or two and none of it would get back to Monterey. "Oh look, Mordecai, how much could he have borrowed?" Angie said. "Maybe twenty-five dollars per person? People love to grumble about it just like a mildly bad vacation, but secretly they would have spent that money on some other thing that they'd forget about right away, so this is probably an excellent return for their money. Besides, anyone who hands Buck money knows that it will be spent on whoopee, food, drink and music, and if they don't know *that*, they deserve to have their money taken away from them anyway."

"I know, but I've got to work some things out."

So Mordecai went for long walks in Golden Gate Park and thought about his melanoia. It did seem to be a process completely separate from his life, a sort of alternate universe that he carried along with him. He felt it *within* himself, but yet it seemed to exist independent of his will.

It's still like my old Army jacket. Melanoia allows me to be myself when I'm at my best, Mordecai thought, *and maybe I ought to be content with that. Trying to direct it to produce results is possibly just another way to be unhappy.*

Mordecai wondered what would happen if he lost it. *It was probably more likely that he would give it away.*

Since his melanoia guaranteed that there was always more coming, Mordecai felt no need to hold onto anything. Mordecai drifted in and out of the city's whirlpools, parks and people and architecture; whirlpools that were spiced with light, salt air and fogs and served with side orders of Japanese, Chinese and Spanish. He had no apprehensions that he would get sucked under but let whatever current there was take him. Sooner or later, he bobbed back up and eddied out to the side where he would steer himself back to Steve's apartment and fall in bed for a day or two, drying out from these cultural deluges. Mordecai found it easy to kick back at Steve and Angie's apartment. Essentially without anything more than an attitude to his name, Mordecai felt his ability to trust his melanoia grow in the diverse tides of the city; at the same time he recognized the potential for exhaustion—the darker dangers of his appetite for the ebb and flows of San Francisco days.

When Mordecai felt that he had got back in tune with himself, he decided to go back to Jane James' apartment and see how the moving business was going. Steve had kept monitoring Buck's movements and reported back that he was still in the money and eating three or four times a day, usually at different restaurants.

—7—

"Holy Mother of god, I sure am glad to have you back, Mordecai. Did you get that disease of yours all petted back into place? I hope so, your feathers looked a little ruffled last time you left. Gawdamn boy! That drinking pal of yours, Phonebook Phil, he's a weird one, isn't he? Where do you dig these people up, anyway? Those are truffles, Mordecai, ever had them? Here, eat a few. Might as well swallow gold flakes with what they cost, but truffles taste a lot better. So this is how it works. We got a gold mine here. The Teamster moving companies charge around two-fifty a half day minimum. Most of the urban citizens don't own enough to fill a goddamn pickup truck and so they end up paying these Teamster fellas to sit on their butt." Buck pulled out a roll of bills and stuffed two twenties in Mordecai's pocket. "That's Chateauneuf du Pape, try some. There's some 64 Meursalt in the fridge if you want white. Rabbit pate, put some truffles on that. Okay, where was I? So we bid under the two-fifty, move them out and in, takes maybe an hour each way, and it's Veal Parmesan at Vanessi's in the afternoon, if you want. And how do you like the view?"

Buck waved at the open double doors. A stack of seven television sets all tuned to the same channel lined the landing. With the sound turned off, the TVs all showed the empty halls of the Senate building and a man with a microphone talking. "That goddamn Watergate is totally addicting. Shoot, Mordecai, did you see that Dean testify? No sight like a Republican bagman in full flight, a bunch of 3-piece pheasants, fat as pigs, flapping their wings and trying to fly. Ha! they forgot if you pork up, it's hard to get off the ground when you're flushed. Sitting ducks. How about some smoked duck, speaking of duck. In the white carton there."

Mordecai followed the tangle of extension cords from the TVs to where they disappeared ominously into the far wall, under a pried up board.

"People moving away from the city, they dump their stuff. I got a basement full of refrigerators, gas ranges, you name it. We'll have a garage sale right before we leave. Hmmmmmm, come to think of it, the landlord came by and we'll have to have that garage sale in a few weeks. I did a little work for him, so we have an extension on the two months rent, we could sit here and harvest the gold, baby, rent-free. Where do you want to eat tonight? Chinese? Italian? Thai?"

—8—

After he returned to Buck, it occurred to Mordecai that perhaps it was lucky that the China Estate *was* sold off in dribs and drabs. If they had gotten a big wad of money, Buck would have eaten and drunk himself to death inside a week. As for the customer relations, the new prosperity of GTM affected them, too. Buck began to get a shade abrupt with those jobs that promised any complications. *Any steps?* add another fifty. *A hideaway bed?* double the bid. *A 24 inch entry way?* forget it, lady.

And their moving methods became a bit slipshod, too. The recent run of work had left the Grey Ghost a little tattered. GTM had lost their tailgate when an unlashed water heater had rolled out the back, taking the tailgate with it. They had been doing fifty down the Great Highway when the water heater had caroomed off the back end.

During this time Buck had been reading Jane's collection of Jung. Later, over cognac, Buck theorized that the water heater's journey was an example of *primordial aquatic longing,* since it had hit the sand dunes in a furious roll and had disappeared from sight in a whirlwind of sand, heading toward the ocean.

A less theoretical view of the event was taken by the drivers behind them.

Some of the customers balked once they saw the Grey Ghost. They had been expecting a little grander truck, at least one with a tailgate instead of a frayed piece of rope. One customer, upon declining GTM service, suggested that the Grey Ghost be donated to the Park Service as a malarial control device because of the clouds of oily smoke that surrounded the truck upon take-off.

A return call was a rare event, as most customers shied away from repeating the GTM experience. However, that summer they did get *one* repeat call from Rosey. The first time they moved Rosey it was on spec. Rosey was, as she said, "stoney broke." She claimed that she had a job in the future. Rosey was moving into Edna's apartment and Edna had arranged for her to start work later that month at the same warehouse where she worked. They were both "big old gals," as they called themselves, and Buck liked them enough to move Rosey for free. A few weeks later, Buck began to get twenty-five dollar installments on the move until it was paid off. Then Rosey and Edna got a chance for the top floor flat of the apartment house in front of their small, rather dark, house in the back of the lot. They called up GTM. "We're moving to sunlight. Come on back, boys."

Rosey greeted them at the door. "Edna's at work, but I can give you boys a hand." Rosey had on a pair of grey chino pants and a blue work shirt, her hair done up in a grey bun. She weighed about 200 pounds. "Got a new helper, hey Buck? What happened to that other guy, who said he slept with vaseline all over his hands and wearing gloves. Weird bird, wasn't he? Never heard of a moving man who played for symphonies before." Rosey waved at the front room. "It all goes, so just start picking it up and setting it down. Top floor," she pointed out the open door, "you can use the front door or the back, the front steps are a skinny and a stiff climb but the back stairs are a bit twisty. Take your pick."

Mordecai and Buck were rocky after a night of cognac but with

Rosey doing some of the work, nearly most of the organizing, and all the talking, they managed to sweat and disperse the poisons. At 1 o'clock there was only Edna's red sofa left. Rosey was confident that things were well enough in hand to go back to work. "You boys want a drink before I go? Sun's over the yard-arm."

When Rosey said that Buck and Mordecai were standing by the door, each holding one end of a red mohair sofa. Since they didn't want to pick it up in the first place, they set it back down and sat on it as Rosey fixed them a drink. Rosey didn't fuss around with a drink, she poured a waterglass full of bourbon and asked if they wanted ice. "You boys look a little peaked, this will pick you up. Ha-ha-ha, know how you feel, know how you feel. Here. You two look better on that sofa than under it. Ha. Now that's Edna's mother's sofa. She won't part with it, so treat it nice. I've got to get back to work. Leave the glasses in the sink." Rosey paused. "Buck, I can pay you off in a lump sum, how about that?" She handed Buck the cash. "So long, boys."

Buck and Mordecai sat on the sofa. They sipped their drinks in silence. There was a long quiet pause. "Well, that gal don't slow down much, does she?" Buck said. "My ears are damn near talked off." They drank their whiskey slowly and stared out the door at the narrow, steep flight of stairs going up to the top floor flat.

After Buck and Mordecai put their empty glasses in the sink, they found that the sofa had grown underneath them. Wasn't just a small growth, either. They found that now the mohair sofa was huge. When they first picked it up, the sofa looked like it would go right through the front door. But now they couldn't get it through the front door. After Buck took the door off its hinges, they laid the sofa on its side, wrangled one end through, stood it up, dragged, pulled and strained, until Buck lost his temper and crowbarred off part of the doorjamb. Then they carried the sofa out through the passageway to the front apartment stairs and up the steps to the top flat. The sofa seemed to like the exercise because it grew again while they were carrying it up. The stairs seemed to narrow too, as the neighbor's roof jutted out at the top of the stairs right before the porch landing, cramping the available space. By the time Buck and Mordecai got the sofa up the steep stairs, one end had grown enough to fill up the entire porch. Half of it was hanging over the stairs. There wasn't enough room to turn the sofa, because the front porch walls and the neighbor's overhanging roof blocked that, let alone enough space to get it through the door. Buck decided that they weren't thinking right. "*Forget* about doors," Buck said. He went around and hiked up the back way and took out the front room window above the stairs.

While Buck sweated and cursed and jimmied the window out of its frame, Mordecai sat on a box, still poleaxed by whiskey and looked out over the urban vista. He noticed that the fog was coming in over the neighbor's roof.

Buck leaned the window against the front room wall. Then he went down the back stairs and came up the front stairs and lifted the end of the sofa above his head. From the front porch landing, Mordecai picked up his end and eased the sofa towards Buck. The stairs were so steep that Buck had to go up on his tiptoes, balancing the sofa above his head, while Mordecai tried to turn his end so the sofa would go in the window. Buck stretched to his full six foot two inch height, holding the sofa above him, as Mordecai eased one corner of the sofa onto the empty window frame. Then Mordecai ran around inside the apartment to pull the sofa in.

"Goddamnit, hurry up, Mordecai! I can't hold this damn thing much longer!" Buck yelled. Inside the apartment Mordecai grabbed the end of the sofa and shouted, "Heave-ho!" Buck was thrown off-balance by Mordecai's move and he began to fall down the stairs. In a spectacular show of strength, Buck threw the sofa toward the window. Mordecai tried to guide the flying sofa in, but it hit the window frame, bounced completely out of control, flipped over and then jammed down between the window frame and the overhanging roof of the neighbor's house.

Across the upside-down sofa Mordecai could see the fog coming closer. "You okay, Buck?" Underneath the sofa he heard Buck panting. Mordecai tried to move the sofa from inside the apartment. It was firmly wedged. "Buck, can you get it from the bottom?" Mordecai asked. He saw the fog racing across the rooftops toward them. "Buck? You okay, Buck?"

The fog soon overtook GTM, filling the apartment with white

mist. After a few minutes, Mordecai could not see out the window to the other end of the sofa. Buck couldn't budge it from underneath, the stairs were too steep to get a good push on it, and Mordecai couldn't do anything from inside. They heard the sofa growing larger out in the fog, swelling up with water, growing heavier. They decided that they needed another man.

"Well, hell," Buck said, "all we need is *one more good man*." He peered at the upside-down sofa lurking outside the window like a red mohair nightmare. They locked up the apartment and walked under the sofa down the stairs to the Grey Ghost. At the bottom Mordecai looked back but the fog had covered it up.

They only needed one more good man to finish this job. The phrase reminded Buck of a friend of his who lived nearby. She had an interest in good men. They stopped by. Her name was Sadie. "But everyone calls me Strawberry," she said to Mordecai. She was a skinny woman with frizzy red-blonde hair and a friendly smile. "I don't have an extra good man around," she said, "but I'll tell you what I'm hungry for. Hot crab and cold gin. I've been up for three days on a speed run, designing a graphics project. Nothing but coffee and pills, I feel like my hair is vibrating off my head. I need to get *grounded*, Buck, and just looking at you two, gives me the idea that I'm at ground zero. Come on, I'm hungry! Treat this woman good!"

Buck and Mordecai took Sadie to lunch out at the Cliff House. Buck decided they needed a stiff ocean breeze to clear the whiskey cobwebs out of their minds. At the Cliff House the fog was still coming in. They ordered up all the hot crab and cold gin Sadie wanted. The fog continued to roll in. The Golden Gate Bridge was blanketed with it. Mordecai was on his third gin and tonic when he felt a tiny *ping*. He walked outside the Cliff House and began to stroll toward the beach. *Ping*. He never saw who he was following because of the fog. When he got back from the beach, Buck's truck was gone. Mordecai walked into the bar and met a man who looked like the actor, Andy Devine.

Jingles! Wild Bill Hickok! Sugar Frosted Flakes! Mordecai thought, awash in television nostalgia. He walked up to the man and said, "*Wait for me, Wild Bill!*" The man laughed. His big belly shook as he laughed, just like Jingle's belly shook when he laughed at something Wild Bill did. He bought Mordecai a drink. He had just sold his family's house in Marin and he was drinking up some of the profit. He also was a painter. He said that he wanted to draw Mordecai's chin.

— 9 —

The painter's name was Eric. He lived in one of the strangest houses that Mordecai had ever seen. The house faced the Great Highway and the Pacific Ocean. It was a nondescript one story shingled building between two tall stucco duplexes. But inside it was miraculous. Some ship captain had built the place so he would feel at home. The ceiling was formed from a ship's ribbed vaulting. The supports were stained oak and the ceiling itself painted red. Living in the house was like living in the captain's cabin on a schooner.

Mordecai was so delighted with the outcome of his latest melanoia attack, he stayed there a week, modeling for Eric as he painted what he called *The Saga of Wild Bill's Chin*. While Mordecai posed, Eric and he traded stories. Eric said that he had sold the family house in Marin to support his painting career. If he didn't make any money in another six months, he'd damn well sell this house. He was determined to make a go of it.

Eric said that recently he had to sell his four-wheel truck. He was still pissed about it. None of the money went for his painting career, it all went to the US government.

"What for?"

"I was arrested for bombing a swamp," Eric said.

"Bombing a swamp?"

"Yeah, turn a little to the right, will ya, Mordecai? Chin up now."

"Is that what you were charged with? Bombing a swamp?"

"Naw, it was destroying a wildlife preserve. They fined me twenty-two hundred bucks." Eric turned and pointed at the television. Mordecai was watching the Watergate news. "Think those Republicans are going to pay that much for abusing our trust?"

"How'd it happen?"

"It wasn't my fault. I took a fall for a buddy. I was out in my fourwheeler and pulled off the road. I had decided to hike up a trail on foot and when I came back, all four of my tires were slashed. Some National Park vandals or something. I don't know. Anyway, there I was, sitting on four flats beside this swamp, so I got on my CB amd I contacted a trucker. He was 40 miles off, straight down the canyon, passing on the highway there. He put in a call to my good buddy Dogleg that I needed four hoops. So I was setting there, looking down the road and hoping that Dogleg'd make it before dark when I heard this plane. Well, it was Dogleg, somehow he requisitioned a Cessna. That's why I never brought his name up in court."

"You don't know how he got it."

"That's right. Enough trouble as it is. Besides, it was my business and he was just doing me a turn. Well, the Cessna dipped once and then they came right back up the canyon and I saw the door open and four hoops stacked up there. The pilot leaned it over and I saw Dogleg kick them hoops out the door."

"No," Mordecai said.

"Yeah, kicked them right out the door. You should have seen it. Boy it was something. Tires raining down from heaven. Ha! One hit the road and damn near bounced into the next county! That was some road test. Didn't bust, either. But the other three, they hit the swamp."

"Big splash?"

"Naw, there weren't that much water up there then. Only one stayed up, it didn't sink in the mud, but the other two . . . they was gone, let me tell you."

"What'd you do?"

"I got out an idiot stick from the truck and I went into the swamp to dig them up. Well, I was mucking one of the tires out when along came the Game Warden and asked me what I was digging for. I said tires and he got all hot and arrested me on the spot. Hell, maybe we flattened a frog or two but how can you hurt a swamp? Besides it was an emergency and my life was in danger."

"How was your life in danger?"

"Mordecai, you ever heard of . . . California Bat Mosquitos? No? If I hadn't seen them, I wouldn't have believed it. Got the face of a mouse, but moves like a mosquito."

When he wasn't hearing stories like this from Eric, Mordecai took walks along the ocean. He kept having brief flashes of melanoia, moments when a figure down the beach seemed like someone he was following, but these moments never did bloom into an outbreak of riotous good fortune. Then, one day, Mordecai was coming back from the beach, feeling nostalgic for Monterey, when he heard the first *ping*. The faintness of the *ping* made Mordecai think this was another false alarm, but as he got closer to Eric's house, the *pings* grew louder. He picked up the mail and went in the house. Eric was in his studio. Mordecai told him that he was in the middle of a melanoia attack.

"Really?" Eric said, taking the letters. He began to sort through the mail. "Hmmm, a letter from New York." He opened it up and found an advance for eleven hundred dollars and a list of paintings that a certain lawyer, Mr. Price T. Dunn, wished to buy. "Goddamn, I sent those slides to the gallery ten months ago," Eric said. "This guy wants all eleven of them. Look at this!" He showed Mordecai the list of eleven names. "So he's putting a hundred down on all eleven!" Eric frowned.

"What's the matter?" Mordecai said.

"This is embarrassing," Eric said, holding up the list. "I wonder what the hell is *Alphabet Polyp*?"

"You mean you don't know?"

"Hell no, I don't know! When I sent them off, it was just a lark. The paintings didn't have any names. I named them whatever came into my head. They're all abstractions. Let's go back in the warehouse and see if we can figure out which ones are which."

"Don't you have the slides?"

"Naw, it was the only set. I don't even know where I put the negatives. I told you, it was a lark. That gallery hadn't sold diddley for me, I was about to dump them."

Mordecai and Eric spent the next two days viewing his abstractions, trying to figure out what names seemed right. They never did figure out what work the name "*St. Sinus*" referred to. After they packed the paintings and shipped them east, Eric booked a flight to New York and left, taking down Mordecai's address at Beer Springs before he departed. At the Airline bus terminal in downtown San Francisco early that morning, he gave Mordecai $200 for modeling fees and for helping crate up the paintings. He also gave him the key to his house, in case Mordecai ever needed a place to stay. When Eric left, Mordecai decided to spend the day in Chinatown.

With a wake of *pings* trailing behind him, he began following an old Chinese man with a dime in his left ear down Grant Street toward Columbus. Then Mordecai decided he was hungry. Eric and he had gotten up so early to catch the bus to the airport that there had been no breakfast. Mordecai turned into a Chinese bakery, his mind awash in the sea of spoken Chinese around him. He was concentrating on what was being said, conscious that his Chinese vocabulary had eroded over the past few years from lack of practice, so he paid no attention to the woman walking out of the back of the shop with a large pink carton in her hand. She had on sunglasses, a marine blue scarf, and a large fur coat. Mordecai was staring at the various pastries, saying their names over and over, so he wouldn't embarrass himself with poor pronunication, when he felt someone standing very close behind him. He looked up, his mind full of Chinese sounds, and glanced back.

"Hello, Mordecai," Francine said.

— 10 —

Francine was staying in some friends' apartment on Upper Broadway. It commanded a view of rooftops and the Bay Bridge. Below it was a children's playground. Francine explained that her fantasy for that day was that she was Greta Garbo's maid, picking up Chinese pastry. Mordecai and Francine sat on white iron chairs on the deck, eating Chinese pastries and drinking green tea. On the table was a stunning array of flowers in a big clear glass vase, orchids, a bird of paradise, green bamboo stalks. "They arrive every week," Francine said. "I have no idea why. I suppose my friends have some sort of arrangement with a neighborhood nursery."

"This place is a change from what I'm used to," Mordecai said. "I've been living in three different houses the last month or so. It's nice to have flowers around."

Francine got up and went into the kitchen. "So what else have you been doing?" She held up a casaba melon and looked a question at Mordecai.

Mordecai nodded that the melon was okay. "I've been getting edgy," Mordecai said. "Not exactly bored, but more like sated."

"You don't like being pleased?" Francine said. She held down the melon on the counter and sliced it in two. Pale green juice ran all over her hands.

"Oh no, I like being pleased, okay, but not all the time. It was nice living with Eric. We ate really simple food and I went for walks on the beach. Buck's cuisine got a bit heavy on me, and the only exercise we got was moving furniture. That's exercise, okay, but it was Eggs Benedict and champagne and orange juice for breakfast that got to me."

Francine came back to the deck with a white plate decorated with melon slices wrapped in proscuitto. "How unfortunate," she murmured. "Would you like me to throw these off the deck?"

After brunch Mordecai and Francine decided to go through the closets of the apartment and try on the clothes they found there. "I have no idea what my friends have hanging around here," she said. "You are looking a little scruffy, Mordecai, so why don't you pick out a new pair of pants from the lot here and get rid of those. Those are the ones I saw in Monterey, aren't they?"

"I wasn't in them all that much if you remember."

Francine put on a pair of red sparkling high heels and viewed them in the mirror. "Oh I haven't forgotten," she said. "So really, Mordecai, what are you going to do, enter a monastery or something? If you're having this rash of good luck, and your friends are having it too, right and left, whenever you show up, jetting off to New York to collect the cash, what can you do about it?"

"I don't know," Mordecai said, "I'm not sure that's the right question." He found a pair of hiking pants with many pockets and took off his old jeans and put them on.

"Those are about your size," Francine said, "but they need a bit of taking in at the waist. And don't worry, my friends won't miss them. Her husband hardly ventures outside of his favorite bars, let alone into nature." She peeled off her blouse and stripped her jeans off, kicking the high heels into a corner. She held up a skimpy blue velvet evening gown. "This must have been from someone's hippy days," she said. "Go on, Mordecai."

"Well, it seems to me that it's fine if my friends, such as Buck, get what they want, because of my disease. And I guess it's none of my business if what they want sends their lives into total disorder and chaos . . . .but there's got to be more to melanoia than just satiation of desire. I mean," Mordecai shrugged, "they only wake up wanting more or mad because the more they got wasn't really good enough."

Mordecai thought about what he had just said. "I don't know. It seems like Buck and me have gone into a real confusing time, right now. I don't know what the hell is happening, except we went to the big city to make our fortune, and somehow ended up with everything on consignment with a bunch of rug merchants."

Mordecai looked at Francine as she put the high heels back on and stood admiring herself in the mirror. "Take off that shirt and put on that pilot's jacket," she said. "Then I'll take in the waist of those pants." Mordecai did what she said. The leather felt funny on his bare shoulders.

"The trouble with you, Mordecai, is that you're so easygoing it seems as if this menaloia of yours doesn't mean that much to you. You never really have told me why you need it."

"Hey, how can I need it? It's here, in me, from time to time, and . . . well, look, I guess I have the idea that this could be catching, you know, like paranoia is catching. Or that other people might get contact melanoia—like people get contact highs," Mordecai said. "But this city life eats up good luck too fast. Hardly have time to savor anything before something else happens. And I begin to feel like I'm surrounded by speed freaks, I mean, people addicted to velocity."

"Then you like it slow?" She came over to him and ran her hands down his bare chest. "You're getting a little paunchy," she said. She knelt and began to pinch the waistband of his pants on either side, her warm breath hitting his stomach.

"So what are you doing in San Francisco, Francine? You disappeared."

"Me? I'm hiding out."

"From what?"

"A bogeyman, Mr. Pogson. A mean old man named Mr. Pogson is trying to catch me. It's part of my Greta Garbo role."

Out the plate glass window Mordecai could see down into the children's playground. Two Chinese children were starting some game in the sand, moving with the perfect gravity of children at serious play.

— 11 —

By nature Buck was a generous man, but he was only generous with his pleasures—not his problems. When he invited Steve and Mordecai over to a Potrero Hill cafe for a drink, Moredecai noticed that Buck was very somber. Mordecai wondered what was up. Then, over a chilled bottle of Pouilly Fuisse, Buck began talking about his fight to give up smoking. "I've been waking up not feeling too well and I think it's the smoking."

"Well, you've been eating kind of rich, too, haven't you?" Mordecai said. "What'd you have for breakfast this morning?"

"Lox, cream cheese, a couple bagels and a side of ham," Buck said. "And I cleaned up last night's lasagna while the ham was cooking. Naw, that's just good food. I think it's the smoking."

"Good thinking, Buck," Mordecai said. "Now that you've got the good life here in the city, you better make sure it doesn't kill you."

"You know how I quit smoking," Steve said, "I bought a half pound of Colombian gold. Whenever I wanted to smoke, I had to smoke pot. See, then I had to think whether or not I could afford to smoke pot, because I might have to work as a carpenter and need all my faculties. So far it's working out great. I haven't smoked any tobacco for two weeks and I haven't worked either." Steve smiled at Buck and Mordecai. "And not working lessens the tension, so I don't want to smoke as much."

"Just laying around stoned avoiding tobacco and work, huh?" Mordecai said, lighting up a cigarette. "I don't know if I could stand the strain of that."

Buck ordered up a bottle of Pouilly Fuisse and said that he thought maybe a pipe would do. "That would slowly wean me off my habit, see." Buck stared off at the traffic crawling by on the street.

Mordecai had never seen Buck so thoughtful before. "Yes, a pipe," Buck said, "but it would have to be a beautiful corncob pipe, . . one as fine and shiny and solid as jade. A pipe to end all nicotine habits, . . . in a deep purple velvet case."

"Yes," Mordecai said, "and on the side would be the words, in gold script, *For Oral Emergencies Only.*"

Buck was only half-listening to anything anyone else said, but the collision of the words *For Oral Emergencies Only*, with the wine, the strain of quitting smoking, and the good-looking waitress bringing their second bottle of wine, all conspired to bump him off onto the real subject of the afternoon.

"Well," Buck said, "you ever have a girl who is frigid?"

Mordecai looked at Steve. They both pulled up their chairs a little closer. The waitress carefully put the Pouilly Fuisse down between them and looked at Buck. Buck was staring off out the window. "I don't know what to do," Buck said. He looked at the waitress. "And a cognac for me," he said, dismissing her. "I think you met her, Mordecai. The girl downstairs in the lower apartment. Julie the Nympho's roomie, goes by the name of Carrie?"

"I've seen her," Mordecai said. "But you mainly talked about Julie, if you remember. How she used to shout down to you, when you were living in the basement, every time her lover left." Mordecai imitated Julie's voice. *"That was Eddy, Buck. Isn't he crazy?"*

"Wait a minute," Steve said. "She used to ball guys over your head and then yell down to you in the basement about how they did?"

"Oh yeah, a running commentary, so to speak. Well, Julie's roommate, Carrie the Radcliffe girl, she's the problem," Buck began, "she got involved with Larry, Larry the Revolutionary. It was my fault, really, when Mordecai disappeared, I needed someone to help, so I hired Larry. Bad move on my part, he only worked a week with me before he wanted to share the profits, 50-50." Buck snorted. "Well, turns out that Larry's father owns a chocolate factory in Boston. I asked him if he was going to share *that* with his revolutionary party 50-50 when he inherited it. Ha! you should have seen his face! *Nooooooo,* he says."

"Wait a minute," Steve said. "Where's this revolutionary party?"

"Out at San Francisco State, where Larry is majoring in modern dance. Anyway, I got to know this bunch of squirrels when I invited them all up to watch Watergate on my seven television sets. So, I moved Larry down to the basement, set him up living there, because he got evicted from his old place for a rent strike. He romanced Carrie and moved up into the lower apartment. The first night he moves in, he and Carrie get in a big fight and he punches her in the eye and liberates her room."

"So who's frigid?" Steve said.

"I'm getting to that," Buck said. "So Carrie goes out sobbing and forlorn and the next day she comes by to beg a place to stay." Buck paused, picking up two creased bills and giving them to the waitress with a big smile as she set a cognac down. She smiled back. "Where was I?" Buck asked.

"Carrie left and came back," Steve said. He tried a smile with the waitress but she turned and left.

"I wasn't going to go out of my way. I said she could sleep on the couch. Make herself at home. I was busy crating up Jane's books that night. So you see I wasn't going to make any moves."

"And?" Mordecai said.

"But I could tell . . .that she wanted a little more than a place to stay. But I wasn't going to make a move, not one."

"Why not?" Steve said.

Buck regarded Steve with disbelief. "Why, you never force your attentions on a woman," Buck said.

"Oh," Steve said. "I was just asking."

"Well, I gave her some blankets and said goodnight and went to bed. I was in there reading when she said she was cold. I got out a sleeping bag and gave it to her. About twenty minutes later she said she still was cold. I told her to get a drink of brandy, put her right to sleep."

Buck paused and took another sip of cognac, letting it roll around in his mouth, savoring it. "And?" Steve said.

"So, she said she was still cold and asked if she could come in there with me, where the heater was. I said sure, and put the mattress and sleeping bag on the floor and she came in and crawled in bed with me."

Buck took another mouthful of cognac, signaled to the waitress for a refill, and then went into a long revery. Mordecai and Steve watched him. Buck seemed to forget what he was saying. "And?" Mordecai gently prodded.

"Well, she didn't seem to know what to do with what she found there. Jesus, I don't know what they're teaching those girls at Radcliffe anymore," Buck said.

Buck then got his second cognac, giving the waitress a little hug when she brought it, which didn't seem to surprise her.

"Wait a minute now," Steve said, watching the waitress walk away. "She crawled into bed with you, and then didn't . . . .?"

"Oh yeah, but it wasn't any good."

Intrigued, Mordecai and Steve then reconstructed the story. Carrie had been forced out of her apartment. She had been given a black eye. She had wandered around the city all night. She'd gone to work at Blum's candy store. And then she had come back to Buck's asking for shelter.

"Well Jesus, Buck, no wonder she had trouble with her responses!" Steve said. "She was probably completely exhausted. Black eye, lord. Now this is what you gotta do."

By this time Buck was only paying sporadic attention to either of them. He was watching the waitress walk around the cafe. When she brought his third cognac, he had asked her when she got off work. Steve was busy recalling other cases of frigidity which he had heard about. He was deep into his small town Southern gossip when Buck let it slip that today was Carrie's birthday.

"Well my god, and you call yourself a Southern lover. Come on Buck!" Steve announced. "What that girl needs is a little tenderness! a little *romance*! Champagne! Strawberries! Whipped cream! Steaks! A little bill and coo! Come on, boy! Surprise her! Whoopee!"

Mordecai and Steve drank the last of the wine and discussed where to buy the roses. "A night of champagne, why not roses?" Mordecai said. Steve and Mordecai got so carried away with the project that they didn't notice Buck's intoxicated condition until they were out in the Grey Ghost and Buck let out the handbrake and the Grey Ghost started to roll away from the curb.

— 12 —

Eddie DeAvila was checking the dumpster behind the M. Sowl Import firm for aluminum cans. He always stopped by there on Saturday as he had discovered that the firm usually had an office party Friday evenings. Eddie took out the leather gloves from his overcoat pockets and put them on. He hiked up his gabardine overcoat, put his foot on the welded loop at the bottom of the dumpster, a gloved hand on the top and hiked himself up to have a look. Down in the rats nest of paper and excelsior and strapping tape at the bottom of the dumpster were a pile of aluminum beer cans, all Budweiser. Eddie regarded them. Then he gauged the distance from the top to the bottom. He climbed back down and looked around the alley. There was an empty 5 gallon paint can jammed between the bottom of the dumpster and the wall. Eddie gave the dumpster a shove and pulled the can out. Then he dropped it in the dumpster, picked up his burlap sack and climbed in. He got all the cans bagged up in a few minutes and then he placed the paint can on a pile of wooden slats and stood on it as he lowered the bag of aluminum cans to the sidewalk. He was about to climb out of the dumpster when he heard a car horn honking. He looked that way and saw a grey Chevy truck come flying through a red light at the bottom of the hill. A white car on the right swerved. The grey truck skidded around the front of the white car and then slid up on the sidewalk. Eddie watched as the grey truck came fishtailing down the sidewalk at the dumpster. "AYA!" he screamed. The grey truck straightened out at the last moment and swerved back out into the street, catching the burlap bag of cans on its bumper and sending them flying up against a brick wall. There was a hollow *pulp* sound as the cans flattened inside the bag. The grey truck careened in behind a car coming up the street, turned left at the next intersection and disappeared. Eddie looked down. His legs were shaking so badly the paper and packing tape and excelsior were rattling around his feet.

— 13 —

Buck's hand were claws around the steering wheel. His mouth was hanging open and his eyes were blank. Steve opened the door. "You guys stay here, okay? I'll be right back. Don't move. I'll bring coffee. Turn off the engine. Buck? You hear me? Stay here. Okay? I'll be right back." And then he wobbled off on his shaking legs.

Buck was talking to himself. "Jesus . . . I . . . didn't . . . what . . . the hell . . . ." But somehow there wasn't an excuse for what had just happened. When Steve returned with three cups of ugly coffee, Mordecai was still shaking so badly, he spilled most of it on his pants. But the burning was better than the caffeine.

Steve walked around the front of the truck as Buck drank his coffee. "Move over, I'll drive us some place for a quick sobering up." Steve drove them to his ex-wife's house in the Mission district. She had left Steve after their first two months in Monterey, accusing him of turning hippy. Steve said she now lived with a batik designer. Mordecai was still in shock from almost permanently losing his melanoia when Steve led them up the stairs into the front room of the apartment. Steve had a short discussion with his ex before she left. Soon there was the sound of frying things and boiling water.

Buck and Mordecai sat in the dark front room. They had forgotten to turn on the light when they came in. Buck was mumbling to himself. "Er . . .didn't see the light change . . . who . . . haven't . . . what the hell . . . missed . . . never saw . . . . lost control hmmmm."

Steve's daughter came in and sat down and began drawing a portrait of Buck with crayons. She didn't mind that the room was dark or that she hadn't seen Buck in months. She was looking for something to draw and Buck was it. She kept lookng closely at Buck and drawing until she finished her work. She did a fine job. In her drawing Buck had seven heads and they were all wavering.

Buck and Mordecai could probably have sat there for the rest of the day, letting the alcohol and the adrenalin leach out of their systems, if the Devil hadn't walked in. He was wearing a tie-dyed t-shirt with dirty jeans. The Devil sat down next to Buck and brought out a small leather bag. In it was a corncob pipe and some Thunderweed. He stuffed the corncob pipe full of the weed, said something that sounded like, "hey man, how's it going?" and lit the pipe and handed it to Buck.

Mordecai knew that this was the Devil. He knew this was a bad thing to happen. But all Mordecai had left were his eyes. Shock and fear had taken words far away from him. He watched helplessly as Buck discovered there was a pipe in his hand.

Of course Buck knew whose pipe it was. It was his. It was the pipe that was going to lead Buck out of his nicotine habit. Perhaps even out of those habits which lead a man to career down hills, skidding through two intersections, lust and alcohol and tobacco clouding his mind. Buck stuck the pipe in his mouth and began to puff.

After awhile, the Devil got pissed off. He made a move to take the pipe back out of Buck's hand. Buck gave off such a savage grunt that the Devil jumped up and walked out of the room. "Hey, man, if that's the way you want it, *fine!* I'm not going to hassle you, man."

Mordecai watched Buck smoke the pipe until his mouth stopped making the proper motions to smoke and the pipe was held forgotten in his right hand. Mordecai reached over and gently took it.

Steve came in, sniffed, and said, "Oh, no, did *her* roommate just come in?" Then he saw the pipe in Mordecai's hand. "You're not *smoking* that, are you?" Steve took the pipe away from him and handed him a bowl. Mordecai looked in the bowl. It was full of half-burnt potatoes. Steve left and then returned. He became even more offended when Mordecai didn't eat. "How you gonna get sober acting like that?" he snapped. He handed Buck a cup of coffee. Buck, stoned as he was, made human motions and tried to drink the coffee. Mordecai could see that Steve didn't realize how stoned Buck was, but he couldn't talk either. Steve was even fooled enough to let Buck drive the Grey Ghost again when they left to go shopping for Carrie's birthday party. Buck drove very carefully. He took each turn as if the truck were made of glass.

Meanwhile Steve was jabbering. "We're going to give Carrie the best birthday party that girl has ever had. A bottle of Mumm's, and maybe a little bottle of cognac, not a large one, for you two later, after we've gone. Turn here, Buck." Steve pointed. Buck turned the truck. "We're going to give this girl a party she will never forget. I'll be right back, doublepark."

When the Grey Ghost arrived at her place of work, Carrie was standing in the doorway of the candy store. She was wearing a pale blue frock and a round grey hat, her skin a delicate white around the shiner she was sporting on her left eye. She waved at them and started to walk towards the truck. Steve pushed the bouqet of flowers into Buck's lap and gave him a nudge. "Go on," he said. "Mmmfurf," Buck said. Carrie came up to the truck. "Flowers!" she said. "For *me?*" She reached in and picked them up off the steering wheel. "Thank you, Buck!" She leaned and kissed him on the cheek. Steve elbowed Mordecai. "See?" he whispered. "Ummmm," Buck went. "Mmmfurmur."

"Happy Birthday, Carrie. Get in," Steve said. "I'm Steve Wire."

Mordecai got out of the truck. "I'll ride in back," he said. Carrie came around to his side. "No," she said. "I'll squeeze in on someone's lap. You're Mordecai, right?"

Carrie sat on Steve's lap, clutching her flowers. Steve and Mordecai sang Happy Birthday to her and Buck drove. She began bubbling when she saw the goodies in the shopping bags in back. "Oh Buck," she said, "you didn't have to do all that! How nice of you! Look at all that! Is that champagne? Oh, and strawberries, I see strawberries, too."

"We'll put them in the champagne!" Steve said. "Won't we, Buck?"

Buck looked over at Steve and then noticed that Carrie was sitting on Steve's lap. "Arbggarrrhhh," he grunted. "Mmmerow." Carrie laughed at Buck, thinking he was putting her on with his imitation of Cro-Magnon man.

"Buck said it was your birthday and that we ought to do something special," Steve said.

"Oh, that's just what I needed," Carrie said. "My god, it's so nice to find someone here in San Francisco who isn't a total airhead. What I've been *through* these past few days. When I came to San Francisco, I thought it would be a change from the East Coast, but not the way it's *been*. Even the people I know who have moved here are all ... well, they've just .... I mean, they've *changed*, they all used to be so ... you know, charged *up* about things, and now flat-tire city, like they're on *inertia pills* or something, I hardly know what to *say* to them, ... But it's so nice of you, Buck, to do this."

"Murmmeninz," Buck said. "Getsa ... mursendsaman ... errrr." Carrie leaned across and gave Buck a kiss. "Mursendsman to you too," she cooed at him. Buck began to look from her to Steve and back again.

When they got to Buck's apartment, Steve got busy firing up the grill for the steaks and popping the champagne top and cleaning the strawberries. Buck collapsed in a chair and turned on all seven of his television sets to the Watergate reruns as Carrie took a quick shower and changed her clothes. She came out bubbling. "Here, me the birthday girl gets some champagne. Buck, get out of that chair!" Carrie met Buck with a glass in each hand, gave him one and they clicked glasses and Buck drank it down. "Mmmerr," Buck said. Carrie wrapped her arm around his waist. "To my birthday!" She laughed. "No more blackeyes!"

Mordecai and Steve both sang Happy Birthday to her again and they toasted the happy couple as she and Buck sank down on the couch. After two more glasses of champagne with strawberries in them and extravagant toasts to the future, Mordecai suddenly had the urge to sit down on the floor. The champagne, once inside him, had turned surprisingly heavy. Steve looked at Mordecai, and then he, too, sat down on the floor. The two of them sat together and neither seemed to have any energy. "Jesus," Steve said, "those three glasses got me totally bombed again."

And that was when Buck and Carrie came in to check on the steaks. Both Mordecai and Steve sat there and watched them as they "fixed the steaks." It seemed to involve a lot of highly non-verbal rubbing up against each other. Then Buck tickled Carrie and she ran into the next room. Buck chased her past the seven TV sets and around the landing and then in the bedroom door and back out into the living room and into the bedroom, all the while making animal noises and high trills of pleasure. Mordecai and Steve had stopped watching when the two lovers had circled the landing for the first time. They both stared at the grill and the smells coming out of it. They were dead drunk again. "If we don't get something to eat," Steve kept repeating, "we are all going to go crazy." He said this over and over until he stopped.

About that time Carrie and Buck danced back into the kitchen and took out the steaks. Depositing one each in two bowls, Buck handed the steaks to Mordecai and Steve. They began gnawing on them. When they had finished with their steaks, they raised themselves off the floor and stumbled into the living room where they collapsed on the couch. Steve looked at Mordecai. Mordecai looked in at the kitchen. Buck and Carrie were feeding each other bits of steak with one hand while they fiddled with each other under the table.

Steve swallowed once, coughed, and then looked, too. "I don't think that our presence is required," Mordecai said slowly, "for this case of frigidity any longer."

And with that, both of them got up and wobbled down to the street. Once there, Steve and Mordecai realized that they were both broke, all their money spent on Carrie's birthday party. They also realized that they had no car and that a horrible, crushing champagne hangover was only minutes away.

Steve and Mordecai stood there in silence, thinking their situation over. Then Steve turned to Mordecai. He looked up at the apartment. "Do you suppose," Steve said, "that Buck could have been *mistaken* about her?"

— 14 —

There is nothing to say when someone's soul is overcome with melancholy. San Francisco, that shining and sappy city by the bay, has a darker side, a side of fogs and muddy dawns and dark overcast days where nothing good is going to happen. When the San Francisco summer fogs set in for good, Mordecai began to feel foggy too. He began to feel his melanoia slip. His disease deserted him for entire days. He wandered around following no one, not even an illusion of someone. No one gave him anything. He began to feel that he had made a mistake coming to San Francisco. Mordecai rarely felt that anything in his life was a mistake. He speculated that the wild ride down Potrero Hill might have jarred his melanoia loose from his soul. He knew that it wasn't Buck's fault. Buck was only pursuing his own propensity for outlandish bliss.

One day, he was feeling so blue, Mordecai put a call in to the apartment on Broadway. A few days before Francine had called and left the number with Angie. "Hello, hi there, yes?" a woman's voice said. "Who? No, Francine's not here, you must have the wrong number. What? Yes, I'm the owner of this apartment. No, there's no Francine here. Don't even know anyone named Francine. Sorry, wrong number. Ta." There had been a false, nervous tone to the woman's conversation.

Since Buck had embarked on a honeymoon with Carrie, Mordecai hung around Steve's apartment. But the episode with Buck and Carrie had turned Steve's head around and his Southern Baptist upbringing began to surface. Steve was also making too much money working overtime on BART. Things were going too good for him, Mordecai could see that. "How many women do you think Buck has bedded since he came here?" Steve asked Mordecai after dinner. Mordecai said he hadn't kept count. "Umm," Steve said. "Sure gets around." Angie came into the room. "What do you suppose it is about Buck," Steve said. "He's always got women around."

Angie settled down on the couch with a glass of wine and a copy of Margaret Drabble's *The Garrett Year*. "I think it was generous of Buck to let you pay for his latest honeymoon," Angie said. She laughed. "You should have heard him *complain*, Mordecai." She switched into an approximation of Steve's accent. "I bought him everythin' and he doesn't even say thank you, just jumps to it. No shame t'all." She shook her head and went back to her book.

"What do you think it is?" Steve said. "You're a woman. You've seen Buck in action."

Angie raised her head from her book. "Buck?" she said. "Oh Buck is only good for a roll in the hay. No sane woman would want to marry him. It'd be like marrying a peach orchard bull. You know that expression, wild as a peach orchard bull? It's an old Oregon saying. Bull gets into a ripe peach orchard and eats the fruit, ferments in its stomach and the bull gets crazy drunk."

"I know that," Steve said. "Don't have to tell me about that. But what about Buck. How come he always scores?"

"Oh he's just a good time daddy. Anyway, no woman in her right mind would take Buck home to show off to her mother." Angie looked down and turned the page of her book. "She might pass him on to her sister," she commented under her breath, going back to reading.

"Mmmmm," Steve said. He sniffed. "I've never met your sister."

Angie continued reading. Steve sat there chewing on his lip. He picked up a toothpick. He chewed on it. Then Steve opened up a bottle of brandy.

Mordecai decided that he needed a pack of cigarettes. He left. He had seen Steve's routines before. They rotated on a six month basis: for six months Steve would work, be happy, get along with his girlfriend and working buddies, do everything right. Mordecai liked being around him for those times. Then, Steve started talking about how other people didn't deserve it, whatever *it* was. He skipped a few days on his job, calling in sick. He started drinking brandy in the morning with his coffee. Usually during these spells he tried to change something about his life, like smoking.

His pot reduction cure did not work out. Steve was either spaced or irritable. He spent hours staring out the window and recalling his Alabama childhood. Soon, all that he could talk about was how life was lived back home, how much he disliked it, and how much better he was now. Finally, one night, with a bottle of brandy as a friend, he decided to go back down South and prove to them just how much happier he was, and face those ghosts from his past. The next day, without telling Angie, he registered with a drive-away car agency. Two days later they called up and said they had a car going to Georgia.

"Come on, Mordecai, let's go drive around a little. Maybe we'll take a trip to Monterey and see if we can flush out your melanoia while we're at it."

"Shouldn't you say something to Angie?" Mordecai said.

"I'll leave a note," Steve said. "She knows I've been thinking of taking a few weeks off."

"But to drive to Atlanta?"

"I've got seven days to get the car to Atlanta, starting tomorrow. Really eight, counting today. We can waste one, right?"

As Steve shaved and put on a clean shirt and a sports coat, Mordecai watched John Erlichman equivocate on the Watergate hearings. Then they took the 7 Haight bus down to the Driveaway agency. Mordecai hid around the corner while Steve went in to pick up his car. Mordecai was smoking a cigarette and watching the light bounce off an office building's windows when a sleek red Mercedes pulled up next to the curb and honked. Mordecai ignored it. The horn honked again. Mordecai leaned down and looked in. Steve was sitting in the driver's seat, a big grin on his face. "Hey, let's go get Buck," Steve said, "see if he wants to go down to Monterey. How about this, Mordecai? You ever rode in a Mercedes before? How's your melanoia feeling? Huh? Whooooo-weee!" They drove over to Buck's place. When Buck heard that they were going down to Monterey, he handed Mordecai a hundred and fifty dollars from the latest China Estate check to pay off some of his debts and stuffed a fifty in Mordecai's pocket for his own fun. He was busy with Carrie but he wished them well. Steve and Mordecai got in the Mercedes and hit the coast highway. A few miles outside of Santa Cruz, Mordecai heard a familiar sound inside his head. *Ping.* As the Mercedes rounded the bend and Mordecai saw Monterey Bay, the *pings* leveled out into a low hum in his head.

— 15 —

Four days later, Mordecai was back in San Francisco. Buck poured out a little more Chateau de Safeway cooking sherry for Mordecai. *"Yes, the honeymoon is over,"* Buck said. Mordecai agreed, holding the sherry up to the light flooding out of the seven TV sets. He toasted Buck. There was deep wisdom in his face.

"I can see the deep wisdom in your face," Mordecai said.

"A ten year marriage in ten days. Modern life is such a whirlwind."

"Why do things have to end in these ways, Buck?"

"It turned out she wanted strawberries and champagne every day, that's why."

"Maybe *that's* what they taught her at Radcliffe."

"Yeah, but when the money ran out, . . . it was back to Daddy in Detroit. Another lesson from Radcliffe."

"What happened to Carrie's job?"

"You have to get out of bed to go to work," Buck said. He smiled. "But she certainly made a remarkable recovery from that small problem she had."

"She'll never forget you, Buck," Mordecai said. "I bet you were a real trip for her."

Buck grimaced. "Well, there was that too. I think she came to San Francisco about seven years too late. I really can't talk hippie talk anymore. I've been thinking, Mordecai, people seem to come out here from the East to get laid, find out if they're gay, or dabble in radical politics. We're the quickchange capital of America. Speaking of trips, how'd the Monterey jaunt go, anyway?"

"Our trip? Well, it was a disaster from the minute we got down to Monterey," Mordecai said. "It started out okay, whizzing down the coast in a Mercedes. And Tom and Duane were happy with the money, let me tell you. They never thought they would see that again."

"Fortunate that the Armenians paid some off right before you left with that squirrel Steve." Buck waved at the TV sets. "I haven't done a lick of work ever since that slimeball Erlichman came on TV. I sit in front of these TV sets, this Watergate junk. Totally addicting. So what happened in Monterey?"

"We were only supposed to be there one day and then Steve was going to drive down South through Arizona to Georgia. Well, we got to Beer Springs and all hell broke loose. I paid off some of your debts and the next thing I knew we were down in Big Sur at a party. Steve got picked up by those twins, the Invoglio sisters?"

"Ah yes," Buck said, "the Carmel pool cuties."

"Yeah, he went for twins, once he heard you'd had a turn with them. And then we ended up out at Ethel's place in Carmel Valley. Steve was only going to drop me off there. But my melanoia was working before that, got my first *ping* outside of Santa Cruz, and it paid off at the party in Big Sur. Some guy gave me this fake fur coat, all black, synthetic stuff, and that was when my luck ran out, let me tell you. As we were driving into Ethel's place, one of the twins dropped a match in my lap—the whole front of the coat caught on fire. Pouf! just like that. Steve panicked and floored the Mercedes, trying to drive right up to the watering trough inside the corral. You remember that corral, the mud pit that we got stuck in last time we were there? So, as the Mercedes sailed into the corral with me, the living flash fire in the back seat, the tires sunk down in the mud and the back end bottomed out on the cattle guard, scraped the muffler right off the damn thing. Sounded like Godzilla's tooth removal, let me tell you. I piled out of the Mercedes and rolled on the ground, put out the fire. The girls and Steve, they were all so stoned, they got in a mud fight. I ended up sleeping in the back seat of the Mercedes in the corral. The twins and Steve ended up in Ethel's guest house. Well, the next morning when she came in there and found them all naked and muddy and snoring after some drunken orgy, Ethel threw them out. Mud all over the place. Took us two days to get that Mercedes hauled out of the mud, Steve and I stayed at the twins. Then we drove the Mercedes back here."

Buck turned up the sound on one of the TV sets. A TV

commentator was rehashing the previous day of testimony. "You been listening to Senator Sam?"

"Yeah, that's all anyone's talking about," Mordecai said. "So we came back at four in the morning with that Mercedes sounding like it was a WWII bomber, no muffler on it, big burn spot in the ceiling liner from that damn coat. Steve dropped the keys into the drive-away agency mail slot and we snuck off. So much for his trip back to Alabama. I can imagine what the drive-away people thought when they came back that morning and found their client's Mercedes."

"Oh shit, Mordecai, Steve gets that Southern guilt trip going, nothing will do but to have a car wreck, trash a bar, or break up with the wife."

"I think Steve's going for the grand tour, all three," Mordecai said. "When we got back, Angie was not too happy with Steve. She didn't know where the hell we went. He said he left a note, but he didn't. She was worried as hell, and then pissed off, I mean, *real* pissed off. You know Angie. I decided to come over here and let them have it out."

"Here they come," Buck said, and he turned back to the TVs and watched as the Senators trooped into the room. Mordecai stayed there with Buck all day and returned back to Steve and Angie's apartment late. All was quiet there, both Steve and Angie in bed. Mordecai hoped that Steve had weathered the storm okay. He went to bed.

In the morning Mordecai came into the dining room and Steve smiled at him, so he thought everything was fine. Then Angie came in and put a plate of fried eggs down in front of Steve. The eggs were sunnyside up with a matching pair of razor blades in each yolk as garnish.

Angie walked back out into the kitchen. Mordecai looked at the eggs and then looked up at Steve.

"Hey, what's this?" Steve said.

"Oh I just thought that maybe you would like to *eat* razor blades as long as you're pissing them."

"Jesus, honey, I told you I was *drunk.*"

Steve looked sheepishly at Mordecai as the back door slammed. They heard the sound of Angie's footsteps going down the stairs.

"You didn't tell me you had the clap," Mordecai said.

"Why should I tell *you?*"

Mordecai left. He decided that he didn't need breakfast. He waited for the bus to take him back over to Buck's place. His life was beginning to yoyo. He hoped that he could get Buck off the TV sets and back to work.

But Mordecai's yoyo continued. Buck was broke and he was addicted to Watergate. The bland venality, absolute corruption and sheer chutzpah of the conspirators addled Buck's brain until he was awash in all of it. His Southern love of righteousness was fueled by Senator Sam Ervin and this corresponded to the decline of any inclination to work, the fudge of Southern rhetoric fattening Buck's self-image until he viewed such notions with august disdain. In front of a mirror he practiced lines from Senator Ervin: "Because I can understand the English language. It is my mother tongue." While he was doing this, Mordecai spent some time at Buck's place repacking and nailing up all of Jane's crates. She had called up in a fury, demanding her books and records arrive in Missouri instantly. Buck had never even found out how the crates could be shipped. He only broke into them and sampled the contents. So he fobbed the job off on Mordecai.

This work was preferrable to the job of counseling Steve or Angie. Each time Mordecai returned to their apartment, more household items were broken and new empty brandy bottles were piled up on the back porch. Mordecai's yoyo continued between Buck and Steve, neither household on the rise, both decaying in slow motion. Finally Mordecai returned to Eric's house and stayed there, but Eric had not returned from New York and it was too lonely so he went back to Buck's place.

Buck and Mordecai battled the crates down to the Grey Ghost for the ride to the shippers. A day later Mordecai came back to Buck's apartment and found the crates still on the truck. Jane had sent Buck some money for shipping but it wasn't enough. Buck said that the shippers would not do a C.O.D. number with that many crates. He was very crabby so Mordecai circled back to Steve. That night Angie did not come home. Steve broke open a new bottle, and at four o'clock that morning, Mordecai woke up to Steve stitching all her clothes to the closet wall with his staple gun. The next day Mordecai returned to Buck's place to find all the crates on the Grey Ghost were now empty. Buck claimed he had to sell Jane's books and records because there was no other way to get the crates off the truck and he needed the truck to go to work. However, since he had some money now, Buck had stayed home to watch Watergate and the jobs also slipped away. "The hydrocephalic bagman, Haldeman, is testifying now, Mordecai, you know he used to work for Walt Disney? He looks like one of the Seven Dwarfs. I can't wait til Senator Sam bites into him," Buck began buying the *New York Times* so he could read about the criminals in depth.

After filling Steve's tool chest with expoxy, Angie verbally threw Steve out of the apartment. Steve moved into a new apartment, unfurnished and low rent, out by Buck's place. Mordecai and Steve went over to Buck's to select items from the GTM garage sale in the basement for refurnishing. Not much selecting got done. Buck had done a small moving job. Back in the chips Buck had fronted Steve to some cash which he spent on cognac. That night Steve slept in an empty packing crate and Mordecai slept on the couch. In honor of their situation Mordecai composed a new lyrics to the tune of *Old Man River:*

> Old man attrition,
> He jus' keep rollin' along.

— 16 —

It was about noon when Buck came back from a job. In the kitchen Steve was complaining. Mordecai was staring at the end of his cigarette. Steve said that what he needed was a stove. He was horribly hungover and he needed a stove. Mordecai was hungover and he wanted Steve to have a stove. Just the thought of a stove, something white and heavy and large, was enough to crush any other plans for the day. Nothing could be done until Steve had a stove for his new apartment.

"Hell, I've got a stove," Buck said. "I've got money, too. While you two lounge lizards were laying around here letting your brains scab over, I was working. GTM is back in business. What a night, though. Sadie Honeydew Strawberry. Mmm-mmm. Last night I took her out for din-din. She's been working too hard, designing a poster for these hippie capitalists. Poor girl's chewing her cheeks. Hardly ate at all. Anyway, this morning my customers gave me some stuff, left it in their apartment. All we have to do is go over and pick it up! Come on!"

· Steve and Mordecai allowed themselves to be herded down to the Grey Ghost. Both of them clammed up. There was no way to dampen Buck's enthusiasm.

"You should have seen this job this morning. Whooo-wee! Boy, there was this big old Texas bullfrog." Buck roughened his voice until it sounded like a cross between a bullhorn and a steel wool pad.

"Come on ovah heah, don't mind her (his wife), want a drink? Just clear all this shee-it out of here and we'll get the rest later."

"Nine o'clock in the morning and he was drinking Jack Daniels and she was drinking beer. You boys would have loved it."

Both Steve and Mordecai were too sick with the swing and sway of the Grey Ghost to reply.

"They had lived in that rathole for twenty years. Big ole Texas bullfrog hunkering down and drinking Doctor Jack. I was about halfway through the job when their daughter showed up. She *said* she was a painter but really she was a Teamster truck driver. Leather jacket, face like a bulldog. I nicknamed her Leather Buns. Anyhow, she began harping on the old man and she had about as deep and froggy a voice as he did. Straight out of Tennessee Williams, let me tell you. I thought I'd wandered into a time warp, New Orleans, 1956. I ever tell you about when as a young innocent boy I entered a sleaze bar down there and met Tennessee Williams and Truman Capote in drag? Well, Leather Buns got the bullfrog all worked up and split, letting her mother take the brunt of it. I had just loaded up the truck and there he was, beating the crap out of his old lady. He had turned her face into a replica of his: all purple and lopsided. He laid off her when he saw me coming. He pushed her in the car and flipped me the key. *Fuck it,* he says, *if you want any of this shee-it, it's your'n."*

Buck smiled over at Steve and Mordecai. "Then he couldn't get his car started and she reached over and knee capped him with a beer bottle." Steve and Mordecai were white from the waltz of the Grey Ghost. "We'll go over there and pick it up."

"What?" Steve croaked.

"Why the gas range, your stove!"

Just pick it up. Buck's optimism was not catching that morning. Steve and Mordecai both felt as if their nerves should be taken out for dry cleaning. When they got to the Texas bullfrog's apartment, inside it looked like an Alcoholics Anonymous display about the effects of spilt beer and piss on a human environment. The apartment was a stinking yellow greasy hole.

"Buck, thanks a lot," Mordecai gagged, looking around the living room. "Just what we need this morning."

Buck led Steve into the kitchen. There was a huge, greasy gas range with four burners and a griddle and a trash burner. Buck began to disconnect it while Steve looked on. Mordecai stayed in the living room, charting the route for the gas range — down one flight of stairs to a landing, then a right turn and down the second flight of stairs to the first floor entry. Then Mordecai looked up and saw the painting.

The painting was hanging above the molding circling the ceiling like a strip of greasy putty. It was a painting of two swans.

The swans were greasy white. One of them looked as if it had swallowed a coathanger. The artist had tried to depict the swans billing and cooing, but had only succeeded in showing one coathanger swan trying to hang itself on another bird's neck.

"Like that?" Buck said, walking past with a handful of greasy stove parts. "Leather Buns did that. You want it, Mordecai?"

"Want it? I've got to *have* it! It's the ugliest painting I've ever seen.

"Sort of reminds me of French poetry," Buck said. "Mallarmé, Valéry, all them frogs wrote about swans."

When Mordecai returned from depositing the daughter's painting in the Grey Ghost, he saw that GTM was having some difficulties with the gas range. Steve and Buck tried to get it through the door into the living room but it had fallen over. That was when they discovered that the trashburner on the side had not been cleaned. Ashes and broken beer bottles and scorched aluminum foil fell out on the floor. Buck decided that this was the most stable position for the gas range. They tried to slide it across the floor. The gas range did not cooperate.

"Ah, we'll use an Oklahoma moving dolly." Buck went back

into the kitchen and got a broom. "Just tip one end up and I'll put the straw end of the broom under it and we'll ease it across the floor."

With one end of the gas range up on the broom, the other end dug into the floor. By the time they lugged the gas range to the front door, there were twin gouges in a trail of ashes and trash across the living room floor.

But Buck had no time for the past once they got to the stairs. "The best way is to carry it," Buck said. He took the front end and Mordecai and Steve took the back end. They lifted. Then they set it down. "Hell, let's *skid* it. You two guys aren't any help at all. Ready, heave-ho."

Mordecai was so deprived of oxygen from the first lift, what happened next never was too clear. At one point Buck yelled that they should "flip" the gas range around the corner of the landing. Buck lifted up the front of it and began to ease it around.

Somehow the gas range turned upside-down. But even more seriously, one corner of the gas range was buried in the hallway wall. The other end balanced on the corner post of the landing bannister. The gas range was about three feet above the nearest step and upside-down, its huge iron legs pointing up.

Once it got there, the sight of a gas range precariously balancing above the next flight of stairs seemed rather artistic. "That's got tension," Mordecai commented. "A kind of *menacing tension*, that isn't often seen in some of the most expensive and famous kinds of art." He was still thinking about the swan painting by the Teamster daughter.

"Jesus, Buck, maybe we better call up the museum right now," Steve added. "Have them come down and buy our new sculpture, STOVE IN FLIGHT.".

Buck bristled under Steve's sarcasm. "We'll get it out of there," he said.

"How?"

"Well, we can do two things."

"Yeah, we can walk or run away from it," Steve said. "That thing's buried in the wall, we can't budge it."

"Naw," Buck said, eyeing the range. "We can kick out the bannister and let it *drop* down to the ground floor ... or ...," Buck paused, giving it some mature consideration. "Or we can *tip* it over and let it *bounce* down the stairs."

— 17 —

Cleveon Hoover doubleparked her rig outside the Clipper Street apartment. She climbed down out of her Peterbilt semi and walked up to the front steps. She noticed a thin trail of plaster and ashes down the steps. She hefted her bulk up the stairs and tried the front door. It was locked. Cleveon reached back to her massive thigh and plucked the key ring off the wire holder hung on her leather belt. Then she selected the key and opened the front door. The first thing she saw was the bannister hanging down from the top landing like wooden bunting.

The bannister posts along the first flight of stairs were bent this way and that in tortured angles as if some massive wind had bashed them around, sending the top railings flying down to the front hallway.

The plaster wall had a huge crescent gouge in it, the lathing ripped out from underneath, and the broken slats poked out like demented wooden teeth. The top two stairs were crushed, flattened like balsa wood into a mashed nest.

Cleveon regarded this and then started up the stairs, kicking plaster and splintered wood out of her way with her polished Wellington boots. She stopped at the top landing and inspected the twin rips in the floor that led under the front door. Cleveon grunted and selected a key from her ring. She opened the front door.

On the floor in a pile of ashes and broken beer bottles and charred aluminum was a broom, its bristles parted in a vicious crease, the end of the bristles pointed straight up in a twisted thatch. Cleveon stared at this a moment, sniffed, and kicked the broom out of her way, sending a cloud of ashes swirling over the floor. Then she looked up.

Below the moulding where her painting had been there was only a pale yellow square in the dark greased wall. "Well, kiss my ass," Cleveon rumbled. "Those assholes stole mah painting."

—18—

Mordecai was in the kitchen when Buck got a phone call that evening. It was very short. Mordecai heard the phone ring, Buck answered it, and after saying, "No," once, he listened for a minute and then hung up. Mordecai kept drinking from a Falstaff quart as Buck came in with a cardboard box. He stopped at the kitchen counter, swept all the pots and pans off it into the box and then walked back out the double doors to the landing. He dropped the box, picked up another empty one, and came back to the sink for the dishes.

"What's up?" Mordecai said.

"We're breaking camp," Buck said. "Why don't you go down and get one of those packing crates from the basement? And hurry."

There was a certain urgency in Buck's voice. Mordecai hustled down to the basement and extracted one of Jane's packing crates from in front of the appliances. "What about the TVs and stuff?" Mordecai asked.

"Fuck em," Buck said grimly. He pulled out the drawers from the dresser and emptied his clothes into the packing crate. Then he took a Safeway bag and filled it full of the food in the refrigerator. "Let's go," he said. They swept out of Jane's apartment down to the truck, Mordecai dragging the packing crate behind him while hugging his quart of beer. Buck carried the two cardboard boxes with his pots and pans and dishes. They put them in the back of the Grey Ghost and got in the truck. Buck let the truck coast down the hill a half a block, popped the clutch, and they were off.

Mordecai watched as Buck kept glancing in the rear view mirror until they got out on the Great Highway heading for Santa Cruz. Then he seemed to relax for a moment. "We'll have to stop and call Steve or Sadie, have them sell off all that stuff for us," Buck said.

"Who called?"

"I don't know."

"What'd they say?"

"Nothing much," Buck said. "Just asked me a question."

"And it was?"

"Wanted to know if GTM belonged to the Teamster's union."

"Oh, and you said no. And then what did they say?"

"That it was hard to move furniture from a hospital bed."

Mordecai nodded. "I see," he said.

Buck looked out at the Pacific Ocean. "Then he said something funny. He said once we were in the hospital we'd have a long time to look at pictures."

"Why'd he say that?" Mordecai said. "What pictures?"

"Got me," Buck said. He swerved around a corner and started down the grade of Devil's Slide. Across the road there was a huge black bump of new asphalt from last winter's repairs. The Grey Ghost bounced over it, the back end flying up. An upside-down picture frame sailed out of the Grey Ghost, barely missing the green Toyota behind it, clipping only the radio antenna before the painting kited over the edge of the cliff and waffled down in the updraft toward the rocks below.

The Toyota honked its horn. Buck looked in the side view mirror. "Wonder what *he's* all shook up about?" he muttered. "Crazy knucklehead."

Book Three
Monterey/Big Sur
Autumn
1973

SIX O'CLOCK IN THE MORN-
ing and the sun was up flooding the ice plant with light. The waxy
green plants with their pink and yellow flowers followed the path
around the rocks toward the ocean. Mordecai walked along the
path, his head pleasantly out of synch with last night's talk and
smoke and drink. Mordecai felt as if he were only half there.
Although he was back in Monterey, his mind was still running
movies of San Francisco, the city scenes alternating with scenes
from last night.

Mordecai stared at one rock, noticing how the pebbles had
fallen out of it in such a perfect circular fashion that the rock now
resembled a grey wet head of Buddha with African bead scarifi-
cation—a disjointed notion that amused him greatly.

Up ahead a dark figure seemed to appear in the wind. Mordecai began walking out toward Asilomar. At each turn in the
rocks, he expected to see this someone down on the beach, but no
one was there.

Mordecai drew even with the cemetary when he felt a small
shiver come out of his mind. As if from a long distance away, he

heard a soft *ping* with its thin bell of sound. He looked down and in a small tide pool below him was a newspaper rack.

Its plastic hood was raised up as if it were some animal yawning. Below it the cardboard placard was half-eaten away, leaving a big

W A T E R G A

fading into the pulpy white paper. Between the rack's rusted white steel legs foam rushed, the kelp bobbed and disappeared like diving ducks as the ocean whirled and plunged and drained away.

Up the beach he stopped at a bench and sat down, feeling pleased and empty save for the word *ocean* in his head. He looked out at the ocean for awhile, and then he saw a small girl sitting below him, on a single rock in a big stretch of wet grey sand. Mordecai watched her. She was looking down at something in her hand. Mordecai walked down the rocks toward her.

Around the edges of the blue parka top her blonde hair waved in the wind. She had on white tennis shoes, salt and peppered with the sand, and a pair of streaked dirty jeans. She was hunched over, looking intently at her hand. She didn't notice as Mordecai eased up a few feet behind her on a high rock and looked down over her shoulder. Held in her two cupped hands was a round mirror. In her mirror she was watching the long soft white roll of a cloud stretching up into the blue sky.

As Mordecai continued around the tip of the peninsula he saw a camper parked on a turnout. Mordecai walked past it and then looked back down and saw its probable owner, an old fellow with a khaki wool hat and faded Army jacket sitting before an easel above some tide pools. Mordecai picked his way down the rocks until he was behind the man. On the easel was a painting of the corner of a tide pool. The man was patiently trying to get the shade of green-grey-black rocks right. Mordecai sat down and watched as the painter worked on this. He looked from the rocks to the man's painting. Each time the water slipped up over the rock, its color changed. Each time the painter added a daub of this or that color the painted rocks changed. Mordecai watched as neither was ever the same.

—2—

A blind old man in a battered leather jacket was standing in a circle of calla lilies in front of a Victorian Pacific Grove house on 17th Street. The front porch had a long bank of windows trimmed with rain-stained white gingerbread moldings. Its garden was a botanical riot of grass, calla lilies, camellias, hydrangeas, fuschias and two unpruned black oak trees. On his head the man had a white carpenter's hat with a burned slash up the right side. He was leaning on a pitchfork stuck in a pile of dead grass. His right eye looked up at a black oak branch teasing out above his head and his left eye pointed towards the white picket fence encircling the house. "Hello," he called out as he heard Mordecai's footsteps. Mordecai stopped.

"Nice day, isn't it?" the man tested.

"Smells great," Mordecai agreed. He heard a loud *ping* inside his head.

"What are *you* doing here today?" the man said, shifting slightly so that his body was now facing toward Mordecai.

"Walking."

"That's good, good morning for a stroll." The man seemed to relax. "I like that. Not many people bother any more with strolls. What's your name? I like your voice."

"Mordecai. What's yours?"

"Mr. Glimping," he said. "*Evan* Glimping. Used to be the town clerk here."

"Really? How long?"

"More years than I care to remember. Then my sight went all cattywumpus."

Mordecai came closer and looked at the man's eyes. They were milky with cataracts. "You working, Mordecai?" Mr. Glimping asked.

"Working at it."

Mr. Glimping laughed. "That's it. Thatta boy. Life's too short to worry, right? Well, if you're not doing anything, you want a job?"

"Sure," Mordecai said, "what's the job?"

"Washing my windows," the blind man said.

Mr. Glimping took Mordecai around the back porch and up

the steps. There he kicked a row of wash buckets a few times until he heard the one he wanted. "People keep moving these *around*," he grumbled. "Don't know where the right one is." He handed Mordecai a steel bucket and a sponge.

A big clumsy-looking man came to the back porch door. This man's eyes were closed almost completely, his eyelids half-lowered so it appeared he was looking down in a sleepy, happy way. He had a huge square head with a slash of brown hair coming down over his forehead. He was dressed in a white shirt and a black leather vest, with dark coarse workman's pants and blunt-toed, thick soled work boots. "Evan?" he said.

"Yes, Borton?"

"I heard you talking."

"Yes, Borton, I found a young man to do our windows."

"Good," Borton said. He nodded slowly. "That's good." Borton stepped back a few feet to let them both into the house.

Mordecai walked in between Borton and the table. "I'm Mordecai," he said. "Pleased to meet you," Borton said. "I'm Borton Akard." Mr. Glimping went over to the sink and ran some water. "It'll get hot in a minute. The ammonia's under here."

"Don't forget the squeegee," Borton said.

"He's got the sponge," Mr. Glimping said.

"How about the squeegee? Some people use sponges for the house windows, too," Borton said, "but the professionals use squeegees."

An old woman stepped into the doorway. She was wearing dark glasses, a brown faded frock, and pink fuzzy slippers. "He'll need the newspapers," she said. She let go of the doorway and walked past Borton. "I'll get them."

"Get the chamois, while you're at it," Borton said.

"He won't need a chamois, if he has a sponge," Mr. Glimping said, turning off the water, "even if he uses the squeegee. He can wipe the squeegee off on the sponge."

"Newspapers are best," the blind woman said. "I'm Mrs. Knauth, Mordecai. I overheard the introductions. Don't listen to these two, I've washed more windows than I care to mention." She held up her arm in Mordecai's direction. A large fresh ragged scar traversed the lower part of her arm.

"Is she showing you her scar?" Borton said. "She always shows people that. She got it punching out her windows, trying to wash them. She used to be our housekeeper until she did that."

"If I still was, I'd do the windows right. We haven't been able to keep anyone," she said. "I hope you work out. You have to get used to *these* two kitbitzers." Mrs. Knauth came back from the porch with a handful of folded *Monterey Heralds*. She pushed them out until Mordecai took them. "Use these on my room," she said. "I don't care what you do for *their* rooms."

"You don't need them, if you have a sponge," Mr. Glimping said. "Once they made the sponges square, why they fit windows perfectly."

"Chamois and a squeegee's all you *really* need," Borton said. "The pros will tell you that. You look at pro window washers, they have a chamois hanging off their safety belts and a squeegee somewhere near."

"Pros, shmoos," Mrs. Knauth said. "We didn't need them in the Depression and we don't need them now. Newspapers."

"Uh, look, folks," Mordecai said, "how about I'll use whatever anyone wants for each of *their* rooms and we'll flip for the front room and the front porch windows." Mordecai paused. Mr. Glimping was pouring the ammonia into the bucket. "Agreed?" Mordecai looked from one blind person to the next.

Borton shook his head slowly. "I think the front windows will streak if you use newspaper," he said. "They're much too big. It's hard to get an even pull with wadded up newspaper. With a squeegee you get that nice and even pull."

— 3 —

A couple hours later Buck and Mordecai were having a cup of coffee on Buck's "patio" beside his house on Alice Street. Facing a line of oak trees at the edge of the Presidio, this hodgepodge of two-by-fours and plywood sheets had an old spindly table set down on it next to two folding chairs. The Chemex was sending up a spiral of coffee breath into the morning air. Mordecai walked to his shed in back of Buck's house and looked up at the mare's tails streaking the sky out over the ocean. Then he looked back East, towards the Gavilan mountains. Over there the clouds were forming two bands of little scalloped pockets. Those scalloped pockets of clouds always reminded Mordecai of an illustration of the caterpillar's belly in *Alice in Wonderland.* Mordecai walked back to Buck. "I don't know why the hell we ever went to San Francisco. How could we have been so fooled, Buck?"

"Ah my son," Buck said. "It was the primordial urge to light our cigars with hundred dollar bills. But damn, smell the air down here, it's thick enough to eat." Buck leaned back in his chair, closed his eyes and breathed deep.

Mordecai took his cup of coffee and walked back to his shed on a path of marble children's tombstones. Buck had found them scattered in a tangle of blackberries on an old landslide hill in Big Sur. Mordecai walked inside and surveyed his room. A narrow bed lined the opposite wall next to a table. The table had once had four legs and twice the table top, but now had only two legs and half a top. This half a table was nailed to the wall.

He opened his footlocker and began to sort through his treasures. He took out his volume of Chuang Tzu. A snaplock plastic baggie containing an inch of white sand hung out of the book as a bookmark. He put the book on the half a table. Then he took out his copy of The Book Of Songs. He wrote out new translations in calligraphy and went out and pinned the sheets by the door. "Got new poems," Mordecai shouted to Buck. Buck came over to read the first one.

> He knocks over the willow fence
> Crazy & in a hurry
> If he's not early
> He's an hour late

"Hey I know that guy," Buck said. "I shave him every morning. Beautiful poetry, Mordecai, keep it coming. How's your melanoia this morning? Got it all petted and soothed?"

"Oh yeah, a pretty good attack this morning."

"What'd you get?"

"Oh, the ocean, then the sky, then a bunch of rocks."

"Wow, that's *groovy*, Mordecai," Buck snorted, "but uh, we can't eat any of those. Did you bring back any *lunch*?"

Mordecai took out the two fives from the window washing job

for the Three Blind Mice. "Ah, a little score. Hmmmm. Keep petting it, Mordecai, nice poems." Buck held the money and sighed and looked up at the sky. "It looks like another beautiful California day. Why don't we go down and check in on Jasmine? You want to go to Big Sur?" Buck said. "Got enough here for gas and a good burgundy. Whatta ya say, let's go watch the whales punch in on the old biological time clock! Let's piss off a cliff? hey?"

— 4 —

Once down in Big Sur, Buck decided that his biological time clock needed a punch or two. Jasmine didn't mind working the swing shift, and so Mordecai went for a tour of the trout pond. The pond was full of trout, fingerlings growing fat and lively. The feed shed was on the north side of the pond. The feeding troughs were on the east, lined up two abreast under the scrub oak trees. There were ten troughs in all and they followed the feeder stream coming out of the pond down to the creek.

Mordecai sat on a mossy rock and watched the trout rise. He tried to figure out if there was a spring in the rocks behind the pond, or whether the pond merely collected the runoff from the two canyons which opened up in the thick brush behind it.

Mordecai was idly speculating on the size of the feeder stream beyond the pond, when something drew his attention back to the troughs. Behind the troughs was a mass of manzanita and poison oak and dead limbs with a background of tan dirt and dull reddish gray crumbled rock. Mordecai suddenly saw two large yellow eyes. From out of the background a two hundred pound mountain lion emerged, just sitting there and watching him. Moradecai rose up in slow motion and began walking backwards. "Nice kitty," he crooned, "that's a real nice kitty, stay were you are, I'm leaving, really I am . . . ."

By the time Mordecai got down the creek to the beach, adrenalin was still rushing around his body. He was having a quiet talk with himself about fear, and why fear was a valuable emotion to have. *There's alive,* Mordecai thought, *and then there's fear.*

He found a comfortable niche in some volcanic rock from

which to watch the waves roll in. To his side was one end of a large battered log, the other end tapered off out of Mordecai's sight up in the sand dunes above him. Mordecai began a complicated dialogue with himself about the nature of fear, listing the things he had been raised to fear as a child. He had been afraid of food. He had been afraid of cars and streets and electric fences around pastures. For several years Mordecai had been afraid of his mother's poppies. He had been told that a dangerous drug was in them. When he saw white stuff leaking out of their hairy fat green heads, he had nightmares for years about poppies biting him like snakes and infecting him. He had also been afraid of fish hooks because they were hard to get out of his skin, and germs and atom bombs and polio. When Mordecai had become a teen-ager, his fears seemed to multiply like lizards and dart and vanish in and out of his life with bewildering speed. At one point Mordecai could remember being afraid of his knees. They were hurting so bad that he knew that if they grew any more, his knees would burst like struck cantaloupes and leave him a hopeless cripple. As Mordecai began to tote up the circus acts of his previous fears, he was struck by how many were merely practice runs. He decided that human society was largely a staged rehearsal for real fears—fear of being eaten, for example.

Mordecai looked out at the surf and thought about this notion. He tried to list what he thought were the really elemental fears, the ones which could jack him up so high that every second seemed clear and clean and huge. It occurred to Mordecai that he had grown up with more unnecessary fears than necessary ones.

Then he saw the big driftwood log shake slightly in front of him. Mordecai turned and looked up at the sand dune above him. He heard some young voices. Then two boys about age ten came walking down the log, balancing on it. They both were wearing the blue blazers, white shirts and creased blue shorts of a Catholic grammar school, only they were barefoot. The boy in front was talking as he came into Mordecai's sight.

" . . . and that was Jesus Potato," the boy said. He held out both his arms and walked expertly down the log toward the sand.

"That's right," the boy behind him said, imitating his balancing motions, "Jesus Potato died for our sins and then they put mustard on him and ate him."

— 5 —

So Mordecai slipped back, smooth and clean, into the Monterey life and the strange workings of his disease. He continued his Three Blind Mice maintenance job and lived in the little shed behind Buck's Alice Street house, rent-free.

Buck spent more and more time down at Jasmine's in Big Sur until the end of September. Jasmine and her neighbor Larry managed to protect their Afghanistan herb garden up in the canyon from deer and other predators and sold the entire crop. With the money they were both going to Hawaii. Buck moved into Jasmine's house and took over the trout-tending duties.

"I am now the headmaster for several thousand unruly teenage trout. Nothing to it," Buck told Mordecai. "Every now and then I go down there and crack a fly line over them and scare the little buggers to death."

Buck now had a house with cheap rent (75 dollars a month), a few hundred sacks of fish food, some small troughs full of trout, and a hundred fog-shrouded mornings in which to meditate on the meaning and direction of life until Jasmine returned. "There's even an attic for the Vice-President, if he feels like retiring to the pleasures of the country."

"No, I think I'll stay here on Alice Street."

"What's the matter, darling, is it time for a trial separation?"

"Hey, Buck, I'm on a roll. Non-stop melanoia. I'm enjoying Monterey so much, it's better I stay here. Besides, I think my melanoia might get a *dark tinge* down in the canyon."

"A dark tinge? What's your melanoia going to get down in Beer Springs? A lounge lizard tan? Ah, just kidding, Mordecai, I understand you need the company. You hold down the Alice Street fort for me. All our jobs will be here in Monterey and I'll always know where to find you."

Buck moved his books and records down to Big Sur, leaving his waterbed and household utensils at the Alice Street house for any overnight runs into Monterey. Moving closer to the primitive gods of Big Sur almost immediately caused Buck to intrepret this change as part of a master plan. "Caretaking a trout farm and having a house in the country was just a *sign*," Buck told Mordecai. In recognition of fate's re-organization of his life (and in case the Teamsters local had been alerted), GTM was formally changed into

BLUE WHALE MOVERS

When Buck gave his new card to Ethel to pin next to the pay phone at Beer Springs, he explained the name. "Now the blue stands for the sky, because the sky's the limit when it comes to American business."

"And the whale?" Duane asked. "What the hell has a whale got to do with moving, Buck?"

"The whale is the logical and biological end of raising trout fingerlings," Buck said. "Yes, what you are witnessing, friends, is the rebirth of the American dream on a little trout farm in Big Sur."

"Nice card," Ethel said. "Who designed it?"

"Jasmine," Buck said. "My little helpmate in our American dream."

Buck did not mention to the Beer Springs Chorus that to complement this dream, he had taken on a spiritual roommate, William Bonney, a.k.a. Billy the Kid. A phone had been installed in Big Sur under Billy's name. Jasmine had been prudent enough to have her phone service discontinued. But before she left for Hawaii, Jasmine designed their business card putting Billy the Kid's phone number under the picture of a cavorting Moby Dick, tastefully shaded blue.

After this Buck borrowed some money from Mordecai and placed an ad for moving/hauling in the *Monterey Herald*, also under Mr. Bonney's name. And this was how, in the fall of 1973, Blue Whale Movers rose like a fishy phoenix from the ashes of GTM.

— 6 —

Blue Whale's first job was in Carmel Valley. The address turned
out to be a ranch house down a long eucalyptus lined lane. The
house was surrounded by a high privet hedge. Buck parked the
Grey Ghost out of sight behind a row of eucalyptus trees. The
house was low and elegant with an ornate bonsai garden around
it. A black Mercedes and a pale silver Porsche coupe stood in the
driveway. Buck and Mordecai surveyed the landscape.

"Mmmm, not our usual run of customer," Mordecai said. "I
wonder why they called Blue Whale?"

"Well, our client, Dr. Verog, said that they had to move out by
today," Buck said. "Heavy fines. They sold the house. The regular moving company pulled out on them, left them high and
dry."

"Well, ours is not to reason why . . ." Mordecai said, getting out
of the truck.

"Yes, for Dr. Verog, I believe the bid will be *flexible*."

"And I believe I'm having a melanoia attack, Buck." Mordecai
was imagining himself following someone circling the house.

They walked up to the polished mahogany door. "Is that so?"
Buck said, eyeing the door. "This house is probably the *birthplace*
of melanoia. Look at that door. Behind doors like that big money
subdivides." Buck let the brass knocker fall once.

A tall blonde woman in a brown silk dress opened the door.
She had high cheek bones and clear blue eyes. She regarded
Buck for a moment, then her eyes moved off him to Mordecai.
"Yes?" she said.

"Hmmmmm." Buck stepped back into her vision. "Why hello.
Mrs. Verog? We're your moving men." He smiled. "We're right
on time, too," he said.

Mrs. Verog stepped back into the house. "Come in," she said.
"I'll get my husband Ed." She turned and started to walk away.
Buck watched her walk and then smiled back at Mordecai. "Fringe
benefits," Buck predicted.

Twenty minutes later in Dr. Verog's study, Buck put two
hundred dollars worth of crisp fifties in his wallet. Mordecai
watched Buck's hands shake. The tentative bid of twelve hundred dollars had been accepted without a qualm. Mordecai could

see Buck was thinking of many things: lunch of canelloni at the Thunderbird bookstore and restaurant, a late harvest Zinfandel, the teenage girls standing around in their tennis whites outside the restaurant, idle, bored . . . Buck quaked with unresolved urges and plans for the money. Mordecai could already feel that this was potentially an unfinished piece of work for Blue Whale.

Buck tucked his wallet in his ripped jeans and went back to Dr. Verog. He was standing at the end of the hall, back lit by a huge white window, a study in apprehension. "Oh no," Buck said as he walked down the hall, "Dr. Verog, no problems with your couch. We'll take it right out the sliding glass doors in your study."

Mordecai peered out the sliding glass doors at the Grey Ghost, masked behind the row of young eucalyptus. Neither of the Verogs had seen their truck yet. Mordecai turned to see Buck eyeing Hilda Verog's shapely back as she sashayed down the hall.

Dr. Verog slipped past Buck into his study and looked from the couch to the sliding glass doors and back again, as if he didn't see how it could be done. He had the sideways glance of a nervous bird. He was a tight bundle of moving day anxiety. "What do you think you'll take first?" he said. He eyed the rows of books and the desk and the various file cabinets. "There's so *much*," he murmured. "I wouldn't know where to start." Dr. Verog picked up a pencil and examined it closely before sliding open a drawer and placing it just so, in a tray with several other pencils, all placed with their lead points in the same direction. Mordecai looked at this display and then shifted uneasily. He was still having pings but all he could rationally foresee was disaster. Dr. Verog put three fingers up to his right cheek and began to knead his cheekbone with them, pushing down into his jaw in rapid flicks, as if he were on a cheekchewing amphetamine run. Mordecai went in search of Buck.

Buck was following Hilda around the kitchen. "And this goes," she said, easing a pale hand across the dishwasher. "Oh, we'll move it right," Buck said, his eyes far from the dishwasher.

"Buck," Mordecai said. "There's something you ought to know."

"In a *minute*, Mordecai. Can't you see I'm specing the job."

Mordecai retired to the patio outside the study and contemplated his melanoia. No use saying anything, he decided. He sat on the painted white iron chairs and remembered a line from his favorite Chinese philosopher, Chuang Tzu: *words are like wind and waves, actions gain and lose.*

Dr. Verog's big breakdown came during the clearing of his studio. When Buck began to unscrew the legs from the Doctor's work table—while neglecting to remove anything from the top, causing files and papers to go slip-sliding away—Dr. Verog blanched and retreated to the hall bathroom. But he came back, unable to resist the fascination of random action on his carefully ordered study. Dr. Verog was watching from the hall doorway when Buck picked up a file cabinet and slung it over his shoulder, producing a paper avalanche inside. Dr. Verog's face went white. He bolted down the hall. Buck and Mordecai finished loading up the study furniture when Hilda drifted in, dressed for her morning tennis lesson. "Where's Ed?" she said.

"The Doc? I don't know where he is. He was here a minute ago," Buck said. He smiled. "Anything I can do to help?"

"I saw him go in the bathroom," Mordecai said.

"Oh god, not *that* again!" Hilda whirled around and marched down the hall. "Ed!" she yelled, pounding on the door. "Ed, are you in there again?"

Buck and Mordecai leaned out from the study and looked down the hall. Buck sighed as he saw the side view of Hilda, all in white tennis gear, backlit by the window at the end of the hall. "Ah sport," Buck said, padding down the hall toward her.

"Ed, the movers want to go!"

Silence.

"Maybe you should talk to him alone," Buck said, trying out a fatherly tone.

Hilda ignored him. It was obvious that she did not need a father. "Ed? I won't *have* this again!"

Mordecai had a low tolerance for family psychodrama so he moved out to the living room and located a pack of Dunhills. He lit up a cigarette and timed his pings. They were coming faster and faster. Through the four huge picture windows he contemplated the Grey Ghost in the driveway behind the Mercedes and the Porsche. With all the upsidedown chair legs sticking up over the sideboards and the ropes trailing off this way and that across the asphalt, it looked like Oklahoma had finally settled in among the bonsai.

Better Homes and Wrecking Yards.

"You won't believe it," Buck hooted, coming into the room. He laughed. "Oh lord, I can't believe it. Our client, Dr. Verog? I got a peek when he let Hilda in the bathroom. You know what he's doing? He's sitting in the bathtub and *sucking his thumb*." Buck collapsed with laughter on the couch.

"Primal therapy," Mordecai guessed.

"Well, *whatever*," Buck wheezed. "Squirrel time where the big money subdivides. Well, it looks like Hilda is going to miss her tennis lesson. We're going to have to follow her over to the new house, high in the hills above Monterey." Buck sniffed the air delicately. He sat down next to Mordecai and began to stroke the polished redwood burl slab table. "She's calling in a colleague of Dr. Verog's to take care of him. He's likely to be tucked away for a week or more this time, intensive therapy, Hilda said. Mmmm, sad case this, what? Just have to do, ..." Buck paused. "Mmmm, without him."

— 7 —

Mordecai screwed a leg on Dr. Verog's work table. He heard Hilda's high happy shriek followed by a loud splash. Mordecai picked up another leg and began to screw that on. "And now I'm coming in to get you!" Buck yelled from the pool patio outside. There was another splash, followed by delighted shrieks. Mordecai finished assembling the work table and turned it up on its legs. On the patio the stereo began booming out Creedence Clearwater Revival's *Out My Back Door*. Mordecai returned to the den. His melanoia was still working, slow but steady.

There was a long redwood bar there. Mordecai went behind it and located the hard liquor and helped himself to his second drink of Jack Daniels. Then he went back into the study and set up the various file cabinets in their proper order.

Finishing his drink, Mordecai moseyed out to the patio. Two pools of water were drying off on the other side of the swimming pool where Buck and Hilda had sat in front of the guest house. The guest house screen door was open, swaying slightly in the breeze. Buck's jeans and shirt were on the cement under the patio table. Mordecai took out the wallet and helped himself to

one of Buck's fifties. *Ping.* In his mind he began to see someone
walking down Alvarado Street in Monterey. *Ping.* He went back
into the house and found a carton of St. Moritz cigarettes on top
of the refrigerator and took a pack. From the driveway there was
a clear view of the bay and Monterey. The red tile roofs of the
City Hall and library looked soft and chalky in the dusk. Just then
the street lights of Monterey were turned on, glowing in the soft
evening light. The street light outside the driveway flicked on,
turning the leaves of the catalpa into golden red furry hearts.
Mordecai began to saunter down the driveway, heading for the
city.

— 8 —

Mordecai stopped at the entrance to the boat landing and looked
at the memo pad paper that Ethel had given him at Beer Springs.
"*Slip 19*". Mordecai walked down the dock, looking for the numbers painted on the truck tire rinds that were nailed to the edge
of the dock. *Ping-ping-ping.* Slip 19 turned out to be the one
closest to the bay, out at the end of the dock. A one-story houseboat was rocking with the waves in Slip 19. The houseboat was
shingled and had a large skylight funnel sticking out over the
front door facing East. Up in it Mordecai could see the faint light
of an electric bulb. Mordecai turned and faced the bay. The night
was dark and around the gray hump of Presidio hill lines of car
headlights appeared and disappeared in slow precision.
Mordecai stepped off the dock onto the front step of the houseboat and knocked.

There was a slight click and the door swung open. "Hello
Francine," Mordecai said. "Got your note."

— 9 —

Francine was wearing cut-off jeans and a dirty white sweatshirt
top, the neck stretched and tattered. She was barefoot. She idly
ran the big toe of her left foot up the wooden creases of the old
1940s radio cabinet as she twirled on the knobs with her left

hand. "They wouldn't tell you," she said, "even if I had been there."

"I thought it was something like that," Mordecai said. He was about to say something when *Your Mother's Son-in-Law* came out of the speakers behind Francine's back. The radio didn't work, a speaker inside was hooked up to the tape deck in the bookshelf. Mordecai listened to Billie Holliday for a few moments. "I was disappointed," he added.

"Were you?" Francine said. "How sad. But you've recovered?"

"I had no choice, I'm a *sick* man," Mordecai said.

"Ah. And how is your disease coming?"

"Seems to be almost up to gale force," Mordecai said. "It started early this morning and never quit all day."

Francine turned and regarded the lights on Fisherman's Wharf through the window. She leaned an elbow on the round top of the radio. A breeze came through the screen door and the heavy wood front door creaked as the houseboat shifted. From his seat Mordecai could see a man come out of the boat in the opposite slip, one landing over. He was wearing a pair of white pants and a dark windbreaker. He brought his right arm up and checked his watch. He started to look over at the house boat when Mordecai got up and walked in behind Francine. He put a hand on either side of her, touching the radio's polished top.

The Billie Holliday song ended on the tape. "It'd be nice if the next tune were *Red Sails In The Sunset*, wouldn't it?" Mordecai said to the back of her neck. He was not touching her.

"Sunset was a long time ago," Francine said. "Moonlight would be more appropriate." She brought her other arm up and folded both her arms across the radio top. She leaned forward. Mordecai could see her collar bone as her sweatshirt top bloused out. There was a pearl shine to the skin over the bone.

The next tune started, *Let's Burn Down The Cornfield* by Randy Newman. Mordecai eased up to Francine and his arms closed around her shoulders. She bent forward from her waist, pressing her chest against the radio top. She brought down both arms in front of her and undid the top button on her jeans. Then, with a brisk twist of her hips, she shed her cutoffs and let them fall on the floor with a loud *flap*.

— 10 —

The next morning around 10 a.m., Mordecai and Francine were lying on the boat house deck, drinking orange juice through straws. "I missed Monterey. San Francisco was okay, but there were reasons to come back," Francine said as she sat up and spun around, facing the other way, so that her legs were beside Mordecai's head.

"I'm glad you left the message at the bar. The grocery store was all boarded up when I went past. I figured you weren't there."

"There's a back entrance," Francine said. "I'm surprised you didn't know about it."

Mordecai rested his chin on his fist, watched the waves lapping on the dock, and thought about that for a moment. Sometimes Francine could give him such great pleasure with her comments.

"A penny for your thoughts," she said.

"Look, I don't mean to pry, but I get the idea that someone might be looking for you. Your friend in San Francisco was real clumsy covering for you. *Real clumsy.*" Mordecai shrugged. "I'm not snooping. I like being right here and that's good enough for me, if you get my meaning."

Francine didn't say anything for a moment. "Good," she said. She put her hands behind her head and did a slow bend forward, touching her knees with her elbows, and then she leaned back, all the way down. She came up once more in a situp and leaned back down again, her feet coming up off the deck as she stretched her legs.

Mordecai brought his glass of orange juice closer and sipped some through his straw. The morning sun was warming up the boards. The salt water smell came up through the cracks in the slats and mixed with the smell of the drying wood. He raised his head and leaned forward until his face was next to Francine's shoes. Then he scooted down a bit and licked the top of her instep, the small stiff hair at the top of her ankle registering on his tongue like tiny bristles.

Then he did it again. He was working on her knee when he heard a loudspeaker voice say, "AND TO THE RIGHT IS ONE OF MONTEREY'S FOREMOST INDUSTRIES."

Francine jerked, her knee whacking Mordecai in the cheek. When Mordecai's head cleared, he saw a sightseer's boat chug by, a row of tourists on the top deck, all looking out toward the fishing boats coming back into the bay from the morning fishing run.

Mordecai burst out laughing. "Jesus, I thought it was the police," he said, turning to Francine. But Francine was gone. "Francine?" Mordecai said. She looked around the corner of the houseboat. Mordecai laughed at her big eyes. "Well, who'd *you* think it was?" he said.

Francine stepped back out on the deck and pushed both hands across her face, holding her hair back. Then she looked out at the guide boat and the bay. "I didn't know who it was," she said.

— 11 —

About noon Mordecai straggled up the driveway to Dr. Verog's new house. The Grey Ghost was still there, the ropes trailing off it. Hilda's Porsche was gone. Inside he could hear the Rolling Stones' *Wild Horses*. No one answered his knock. The door was locked. Mordecai walked around to the side and opened the gate to the backyard and went in. Buck was sitting by the pool in a director's chair. On the small yellow table with a blue tile top beside him stood a tall Bloody Mary. He had on someone's white bathing suit. "Good morning, Doctor," Buck said, opening an eye. "And how is the patient today?"

Mordecai eyed Buck's Bloody Mary. "You look like the dog drug you in," Buck said. "Go ahead, have some."

"You know," Buck said, squinting up at the sky, "it's strange how people only have that one little burst of poetry in their lives."

Mordecai took another drink of the Bloody Mary. "Really?" he said.

"Yes, it always amazes me. Christ, the one little burst of poetry," Buck continued, "at around seventeen or so. Women have it early sometimes, but everybody does have one."

"I take it you heard Hilda's life story last night."

"Oh yeah, Mordecai. That one burst of poetry, then some shy away from it. Others get nervous and then shy. They don't know if it can go on, they don't know what to do if it does go on, and they get nervous and clamp down on it. It never occurs to them that it may not ever come back."

"And in this case," Mordecai prompted him.

"A trip to Europe at age sixteen and a brief Vespa motor scooter tour with beach ball bikini whoopee with a dark Spaniard. And then she returned to Dr. Ed with his primal arms outspread." Buck paused and shrugged. "I don't know why I'm talking to you about this. You never get mixed up with women." Buck laughed. "Lord, and she thinks she's old." Buck laughed again, musing on it. "She thinks she's *old*."

Buck sighed and stood up and slipped off the bathing trunks. He stood there nude and kicked them up into his hand and sent them sailing out into the middle of the swimming pool. The white swim trunks slowly soaked through and began to sink down into the shiny aquamarine water. For a vodka-deranged moment, Mordecai thought Buck was about to go to work in the nude. *I am tired*, Mordecai thought.

Buck went into the guest house and dressed. Then they went back out to the Grey Ghost. Instead of driving back to Carmel Valley to finish the moving job, though, Buck drove to his house and picked up his chainsaw. They continued on into Pebble Beach where Buck located two wooded lots. They were twin lots, located between a modern red-shingled ranch house and an older two-story white colonial house. The lots had been partially cleared of the Monterey pines. There was a set of tire tracks in the smashed and flattened brush under the pines where the crew had been set up to work. "Now you see," Buck explained, surveying the lot, "all this wood is ours. All we've got to do is get it out of there. Then we can knock down those pines over there on that side and the ones on the other side, cut them up and sell them!"

"What happened to the people who were doing it before?"

"They just took off," Buck said scornfully, "and didn't even finish the job. They sure left Hilda in the lurch. She inherited this property from her Granny. Why we've got a gold mine here, Mordecai. A hundred dollars a cord, maybe one twenty, why we've got over thirty cords here."

"Looks like all the hard ones are left," Mordecai said. "All the easy ones in the middle of the lots have been dropped."

"Ah, naw," Buck said. "Just drop the ones on the side in the middle. Easy job."

"I think they're leaning the wrong way, Buck. Besides, shouldn't we finish moving Dr. Verog *first*?"

"Hell, Mordecai, we'll hire some college kids to do *that*! Subcontract! That's the ticket. This is *real* money, Mordecai, pay for the winter gloom. From now on it's Blue Whale Logging company! You ever do any tree work before?"

Ever do any tree work before?

— 12 —

As he sat in his front room with an old copy of *Yachting* on his lap, Fellows Nearson heard the sound of a chainsaw. He sniffed once and went back to reading. A few moments later he heard a loud rending crash. Fellows brought his head up, then peered out the window through the line of madrones to the street beyond. He could see the nose of a grey truck at the edge of the neighboring lot. He leaned forward and brought up a pair of naval binoculars from the lamp stand beside the easy chair. He focused it in on the truck. The truck seemed to have been painted with a paint brush—a large paint brush. There were *lines* running through the paint from the brush bristles. The chainsaw started again. After a few moments, the front end of the truck was obscured by a falling tree top.

"Ur, . . . see what those fellows are up to," Fellows Nearson said to himself. "Looks like they almost dropped that tree on their truck." He put down his binoculars on the bronze-colored shag rug and looked around for his slippers. He located them under the footrest and put them on. Then he took hold of the arm rests and launched himself into a standing position.

He shuffled over to the front door and found his tam o'shanter hanging on the brass hat rack. Then he put his muffler around his neck and selected his bamboo cane from the artillery shell holder. He started off for the door to the garage.

The chainsaw was running when he stepped down into the garage. Through the window above his garage work bench, he could see a young man in an Army jacket standing with a rope in his hand, looking up in the direction of the chainsaw.

Fellows Nearson pressed a black button above the bench and the automatic garage door began to whine and clank. The chain caught hold and the door jerked once, and then began to rise. As it opened up, the roar of the chainsaw grew louder. He started off at an angle for the madrone trees lining his property so he could view the work next door. Then he remembered that he had forgotten to get the paper. He walked down the other side of the driveway lined with camellias, stopping to look backwards at the tree cutters from time to time. All he could see was the young man with blond hair in an Army jacket holding a rope that went up at an angle toward one of the trees on the south side of his house. Fellows could not see the man with the chainsaw until he got to the end of his driveway by the paperbox. The man with the chainsaw was standing on a tall stump, cutting into a big Monterey pine. The guide rope from the man in the Army coat was tied to a tree limb another six feet up the tree trunk. Fellows took out his copy of the *Monterey Herald* from the paper box, turned and looked back at the neighboring lot.

Just then there was a crack and the tree went over. Fellows Nearson saw that the tree was heading for his garage. Then the tree twisted to the left as it snapped free of the stump. The man holding the rope was dragged forward as the tree sliced down through the limbs of the other pines. The trunk hit another pine tree and bounced back to the right, tearing off big limbs and scattering them, some flying out to the road.

The tree top came smashing down about five feet away from the corner of the garage, and one of its top branches caught a madrona tree and bent it over in a circle, its roots pulling free from the ground in a groaning crackle, and then the tree was slingshoted up into the air, dirt, roots and all.

The madrona landed on Fellows Nearson's garage roof upside down and then settled in on the peak. The tree sat there with its roots in the air as the brown dust cloud drifted slowly through the camellias on the other side of the driveway.

The man on the stump turned off his chainsaw. "Hey, Mordecai," he yelled to the man picking himself up off the ground. "That one *twisted* on us a little, didn't it?"

— 13 —

When Hilda called that night, Buck and Mordecai were cleaning up the last of a large roast beef dinner. "Why hello, Hilda. How are you . . . what?" Buck listened. "What did he call me? A wild man? Me? Why that old fart is nothing but a walking granny gland. Granny gland, granny gland, you know the gland that goes squeak and leaks when you get petty." Buck listened again. "Hell no we didn't hurt Mr. Nearson's house! Aw we dropped a pine and it flipped one little bush up on . . . mmmmmm? Now listen. I was raised in Alabama and if I don't know how to drop a pine over, why I don't know who does. Mmmmmm? I'm just having dinner. Sure, we'll drop by. Uh-huh, well—you just have the gin and tonics ready. You heard me. We'll talk about moving and our other business then. Uh-huh by the side of the pool. I'm going to need some cash in advance to get this tree job done right. You heard me. Okay. I'll be there."

An hour later, while Hilda and Buck discussed the financial arrangements over some gin and tonics out by the pool, Mordecai wandered around Dr. Verog's new house. The house was no longer so bare. Dr. Verog's own psychiatrist had recommended that, except for the study, the house in Carmel Valley be left as it was. So Hilda had rented furniture for the front room. "I don't want to add to Ed's trauma," Hilda said. "And the people who were supposed to move in are going to be two weeks late anyway."

Mordecai stayed in Dr. Verog's study and watched Dr. Verog's assistant Ed Willits work on straightening up. He was a tall, serious young man who had his orders to make sure the study was exactly the same as the day Blue Whale Movers first made their beachhead on its propriety. Dr. Verog had taken some Polaroids of his book shelves so that the books could be replaced in the exact same order. Ed Willits consulted the Polaroids before inserting the various volumes in their right places.

Buck came in the study to tell Mordecai he wasn't needed any longer. "Boy, the Doc really has a giant granny gland, doesn't he?" Buck said, checking out the Polaroids on the desk. Mordecai introduced Ed Willits to Buck. "You're his assistant? Why don't you tell Ed about your disease, Mordecai? Mordecai's got a rare mental disease."

Mordecai explained his melanoia as Ed finished arranging the books.

"I've never heard of it," Ed Willits said. "Are you sure a doctor told you this?"

"Doctor, smocktor, it works," Buck chimed in. "In fact, it's probably working right now, isn't it, Mordecai? Melanoia needs the bright lights," he said, pointing down at the city of Monterey. "Why don't you two go hit the bright spots? Take Ed out on an introductory melanoia spree?"

Buck peeled off a fifty and handed it to Mordecai as Ed went to get his coat from the hallway closet. "You won't believe," Buck called after Ed, "just how powerful melanoia can be."

Mordecai looked over Buck's shoulder at Hilda out on the patio beside the pool. "Another swimming party tonight?"

"The Verog's have an *open marriage*," Buck said in a lowered voice, turning away from Ed. "But Hilda is not sure this is known to her husband's assistant." Buck began escorting Mordecai to the door. "Have a good one, boys."

Ed Willits fixed his gaze on Mordecai. "Now, you mean you don't feel any *compulsion* to do these things? Do you feel as if you have a *choice*? Or do you have to do this . . . following? Or is it a *conspiracy* to make you feel . . . mmmm, *optimistic*. And you don't *really* want to feel . . . fine."

— 14 —

In the El Condor bar on Alvarado Street Mordecai was providing details of his melanoia past when a lumber salesman by the name of Sean LaBaron sat down by them. "I'm divorcing the bitch," he announced. "What're you boys drinking? I just cleaned out the safety deposit box, cancelled the credit cards, and had the movers in and the whole shebang carted away. She's at her mother's. It's my pre-emptive strike. If our weasel President can do it, so can I."

This was the start of a melanoid spree that amazed even Mordecai. Before Sean left Ed and Mordecai, he gave Mordecai a large silver bracelet with a piece of triangular turquoise set in it in honor of Mordecai's knowing Goose Goslin's lifetime batting average. From the El Condor club they waffled along the railroad tracks into New Monterey and ended up at Chino's where they had a snack of the free tiny hot dogs on the grill there and Mordecai explained how he first found out about his melanoia. By then Mordecai had traded the bracelet for a portable TV, suitable for use in his tool shed up at Buck's house, along with a Kay guitar with two strings missing. Once they had eaten their fill of free tiny hot dogs, they moved back down the street to Beer Springs where the Kay guitar changed into a buck knife and a pair of binoculars. Mordecai was looking through the binoculars when he noticed a fellow in a beige sports jacket having a beer back by the pool table.

"Follow me, Ed," Mordecai said. "I guess you might as well see this, too." He walked over to the guy and sat down. Ed pulled up a chair. "You're the new guy?" Mordecai said to the man in the beige jacket.

"Oh yeah," the guy said. "I'm new to this bar. My name's Bret."

"This is Ed Willits," Mordecai said. "He's studying me too." Bret smiled nervously and picked up his beer to drink. He was left-handed. Mordecai waited until his arm was up and then he reached over and pulled open the right side of Bret's beige jacket, exposing a pistol in a holster.

"Don't do that in here," Bret said.

Ed Willits looked from Bret to Mordecai and back again. "What's going on?"

"Bret's doing some field work too, tonight. You want to talk to me?" Mordecai asked him.

"Oh no, no, just checking in," Bret said.

"You don't exactly fit in at Beer Springs. The last guy they sent stood out like a sore thumb, too."

Bret smiled again. "Gotta run," he said. He got up and left Beer Springs. He was clearly nettled.

"What was that all about?" Ed said. "He a cop?"

"No," Mordecai said, "government."

"Government?"

"Yup. CIA."

"CIA? What's he doing in a dump like this?"

"Checking up on me. I used to work for them, sorta, when I was in the Army," Mordecai said. "I guess you might as well know this too. I was a listener. I listened to what the Red Chinese pilots said over the radio and wrote it down. That's what I was trained to do. It was boring, really. So when I decided that I had enough of it, I went crazy a little bit so they could discharge me. Wasn't really anything much but they fell for it."

"Why does this guy show up now?"

"Well, they were sure I was a spy. Or counterspy. See, when I went crazy there, they put me in a hospital and they went through my things. You really want to hear this?"

"Of course I want to hear this," Ed snapped. He was about half drunk but he had begun *observing* Mordecai again.

"They found this drawing. They brought it to me. They said what's this. I told them. They didn't believe me."

"What was it?"

"It was a drawing of a harbor in Korea. I had a girlfriend there and I was studying a rare form of Japanese mathematics just for fun. It was like chess. I was waiting for my girl and I drew a picture of the harbor above the math, you know, just doodling, and they thought it was some kind of code."

"Didn't you tell them?"

"Sure I did. They didn't believe me. Then they found the sand and . . . ."

"Sand?"

"Yeah, white sand from Carmel Beach. I just love that sand. I took a baggie and put some sand in it when I went overseas. They found it and analyzed it and re-analyzed it and tested it and then they came to me and said what is this? I told them. They didn't believe me. They thought it was part of the code."

"What did you know that was so important?"

"I don't know. They have real precise tests. Before you become a monitor, they test you so they know just how much information you can process before you start putting together a pattern. Anyway, I was a monitor but apparently I pulled the wrong time to go on my crazy routine."

"So, why are they checking up on you now?"

"Oh just to see if I make my move. Get my gold out of the bank in Switzerland, who knows? Who cares?"

"Christ, don't you see? You reversed the tables on them. You should have been paranoid but instead you turned it into this imaginary disease of yours. Don't you see? That's the *answer!*"

"What answer?"

"The answer to your disease!"

"My disease is not a question," Mordecai said.

"Well, now we can help you make an adjustment."

"*Adjustment?* what the hell are you talking about?"

"So you can understand it," Ed corrected himself. "Understand how it works, I mean."

Mordecai was silent. Ed took out a small notebook and began to write down things in it. Mordecai watched him. "You know what you are?" he said. "You're an understanding addict. You think that understanding is some kind of magic. You think it's real hard to understand something and you have to work at it for a long time and then the magic works. Actually that keeps moving you farther and farther away from what you're trying to see."

Ed stopped scribbling. "I don't see what you're saying. Understanding isn't an addiction."

Mordecai pointed at Ed's beer. "You understand that drink there?"

"Sure I do." Ed looked up from his writing at the beer. "It's so much alcohol and so much water and so much malt and hops, whatever. I know the effect it has on my body and I know how much it costs and its color . . . ."

"What's it called?"

"It's called a beer."

"What's it called before you think of its name?"

"Nothing."

"Is that so?" Mordecai said. "So you think nothing or do you understand that nothing?" Ed shrugged, meaning either would do. "So you understand nothing," Mordecai continued. "It's gotta be an addiction if you bother to do that."

— 15 —

The night proceeded with Mordecai and Ed circling through several Pacific Grove houses in search of minor parties. By then Ed Willits had stopped drinking and was busy taking covert notes. Mordecai traded the binoculars for a bag of junk including a flare gun set. The night ended on a beach somewhere out near Fort Ord. Mordecai and Ed were sitting in the sand in a hollow formed by two sand dunes along with Roy Smirle. They were waiting for the sun to rise. Roy was passed out, with one arm around a gallon jug of rose wine with cocktail fruit floating in it.

"Jesus was I glad to get out of *there*," Ed said to Mordecai, looking up from his notes. He had a pencil flashlight on the pad.

"Out of where?" Mordecai said. He was examining the flare gun. He hadn't seen one of them since Army basic training.

"Back there in that last house in Seaside. Didn't you see what was going on?"

"No, what?"

"I walked into the front room and some guy had just pulled a knife. Christ, I thought we were all going to get killed!"

"Really?"

"I was goddamn paralyzed. I think it was some kind of a drug deal. We could have been in bad trouble." Ed rubbed his eyes. "Does this happen to you every night?"

"Well every night my melanoia is working something like this happens. Maybe not so frantic. I've never noticed anything being *exactly* the same, have you?" Mordecai looked up from his flare gun but Ed was not aware that Mordecai was having a bit of fun with him.

"Either you've got the disease or you're goddamn charmed. I've never . . . what's that?"

"What's what?"

"That. There. That . . . *whump*."

Mordecai was inspecting the flare gun cartridge. He stopped and listened. He didn't hear any *whump*. He was beginning to get bored by Ed. Listening to him was like listening to a record skip. "That's just Ford Ord. We're right below it, I think." Mordecai looked back at the sun rising above the brown hills behind them. "About time for them to start."

"Well . . . I . . . ." And Ed blinked at another, closer *whump*. A shower of sand suddenly flew over them. Ed's mouth opened wide. "Where the fuck are we? Where'd this asshole take us, anyway? Wake him up!" Ed jumped to his feet and began to kick Roy Smirle in his leg.

Whump! There was another shower of sand. Ed clambered up

to the top of the dune above them and peeked over the crest. Then he came tumbling back down.

"We're on the fucking mortar range!" Ed screamed. He seized Roy Smirle's limp left arm and began to drag him down the hollow toward the sea.

Whump! A clot of eelgrass flew over Ed like a green witch. He screamed and flattened himself on the sand. "How do we get *out* of here?" he moaned.

Mordecai loaded the flare gun and cocked it. He held it over his head and pulled the trigger. "See?" he said to Ed. Over their heads a red column of smoke was heading inland and then it burst at the top in a flash of fire. From it parachutes of smoke and fire began falling.

"No problem," Mordecai said.

On the drive back to Monterey, Ed had calmed down enough to piece together the results of his night's research. "I don't know exactly how this works, but I think you ought to come down to Stanford with me and we'll run you through some tests."

"What good would it do to get melanoid in a laboratory?"

"I'd like to make some studies of you under more *formal* arrangements."

"I'm not sure this is a formal mental disease," Mordecai said. "I'm not sure this works under any arrangements. In fact, I'm sure I wouldn't want to."

"Why not? We'll pay you."

"I don't see any point in getting melanoid for science. What will you guys do with it once you've pinned it down? Isolate some hormone and have everybody following each other once they get a shot? I've got nothing against science but I think it would just turn into another control mechanism, Ed, and who needs any *more* of those?"

— 16 —

Buck sold the wood from his truck, parking the Grey Ghost downtown with a sign: *Firewood For Sale*. By the third day of Blue Whale's logging operations, Buck was selling *"English cords"*.

"Well, now, you see," Buck explained to their customers,

"English cords are a *little bit shorter* than American cords. That's kind of strange because English gallons are a little bit larger than American ones. but a cord of wood in America is 4×4×8 feet. That's why we're only charging ninety bucks a cord. Regular American cords are one hundred-twenty dollars."

Mordecai added such items to Buck's legend at Beer Springs. The regulars enjoyed hearing the logical progression from American cords to English cords. "The first day of work Buck was selling American cords," Mordecai told the Beer Spring chorus, "but then he found out how much work it took to cut and split an American cord."

"But that's *wet* wood," Tom Soper put in. "That won't burn for six months."

"Oh, Buck had an answer for that. You should have heard him, he sounded like an old Pall Mall cigarette ad. *Its longer length filters the smoke and makes it mild.* Remember that on television?" Mordecai went into his imitation of Buck. "Using the unpatented Blue Whale method of driving *slowly* and letting the air *rush* over the wood, the cords of wood are cured *and dry* by the time they arrive at their destination."

With the money from the English Cords for financing, Buck decided that a new phone at Alice Street and a Blue Whale firewood ad in the newspaper were needed. Keeping with the English style of Blue Whale's operations, Buck gave Mordecai a new roommate: Commander Ralph B. Gory.

Commander Gory had the phone installed in his name. The phone company thought nothing odd in that; Monterey was a sea port; lots of military people live there. "The Commander almost had a RET (retired) put after his name," Mordecai explained, "but then . . . he left with the fleet, unable to control his Mad Dog English wanderlust."

The Blue Whale Logging Company's actual *physical* operations remained in the hands of the founding fathers exactly three days. After the first three days of cutting and selling wood, Buck retroactively instituted a three day work week. Blue Whale rested for four days. Next, Buck reversed the order of the work week so they rested for four more days.

Then, one Saturday morning, while Buck and Mordecai were buttering their croissants and discussing the difference between

Kenyan and Jamaican coffee, a battered red Saab pulled up in the driveway. In it was Sadie Strawberry from San Francisco with Steve Wire.

Sadie got out of the Saab. She still had that red blonde halo of frizzy hair but she looked frail and wan. "Lord, girl, what is wrong with you?" Buck said. He went up and gave her a hug.

Steve got out of the driver's side. "Hard times in the city," he said. "We're fleeing to the country."

"Hepatitis," Sadie said. "I lost my job and got evicted from my apartment." She held out her arms and turned around. She was thin as a reed. "So here I am."

"Well, you're welcome," Buck said. "You can stay here, hell— you can have the *whole* house, I'm living in the country these days. Damnit, Sadie, I told you not to work so hard, take all that crank. Well, come on in."

They went in the house and swapped stories. Sadie admitted that she had burned out on coffee and dex and then, as Buck had predicted, her hippie poster moguls had fired her. Steve was relocating in Monterey. He had put in overtime on the BART carpentry job and saved plenty of money, plus he had unemployment benefits coming until he got settled. He also had brought Buck the money from the GTM garage sale. "Me and Sadie sorted it out and sold almost all of it."

Mordecai suspected another reason for Steve stopping by with Sadie. When Buck offered to put Sadie up in the Alice Street house, Mordecai noticed the speed with which Steve disappeared. Mordecai knew that Sadie had filled in for the loss of Angie in Steve's life, and Steve for the loss of Buck in her life, but when she got sick and lost her job, Steve more or less dumped her with Buck. Of course, Buck barely noticed Steve's behavior, concerned as he was with Sadie. He took up nursing Sadie. Buck had tried to give Steve a commission for the GTM garage sale, but Steve gave it to Sadie for her immediate medical expenses. Mordecai regarded this as another sign of his guilt.

As it turned out, Sadie was more sick than they first thought. Buck and Mordecai took turns taking care of her. This left the Blue Whale Logging operations in the lurch. But one day Mordecai was out on a melanoia run and he met two unemployed Mendecino brothers named Joe and Seth Raeth at Beer Springs.

The Raeth brothers were coming back from a trip to Mexico. Their bankroll was low. They already had chainsaws and a truck and they were ready to go to work. Mordecai took them up the hill to the Blue Whale headquarters. Buck overlooked their drunkenness and hired them on the spot. Cords of split wood began to pile up in the Alice Street front yard. Mordecai handled the phone calls for firewood and stacked the wood in the Grey Ghost for delivery. To make his money, Buck had only to dump the firewood in the right driveways and collect the customer's cash. Buck revived his sawed off Nash Metropolitan with a new engine. He commuted from Big Sur when he wasn't nursing Sadie. The Raeth brothers worked too fast to pile up a large weekly wage, doing more work in a three hour day than Buck and Mordecai could do in three days. Buck tacked up envelopes of money nearly every day on Mordecai's poem board outside his shed door.

About then Buck did something that amazed Mordecai. Buck's hatred of bureaucracy was monumental but he spent close to a week in the welfare office, filling out forms so that Sadie could get on Medi-Cal. She was too sick to do it herself. Until Medi-Cal kicked in, he paid her bills. Slowly Sadie began to mend. The sunny days of Monterey autumn seemed endless.

— 17 —

Mordecai went back to the houseboat during Sadie's convalescence at Alice Street. Through the window the place looked clean and deserted. Francine had done another disappearing act. He walked back to Beer Springs, then returned to the Aurelia Market. Francine had claimed there was a back entrance but all Mordecai found was an impenetrable mass of blackberries and old cherry plum trees. For three days Mordecai haunted the boat landing.

He reran their meeting over and over in his mind. Something about it was bothering Mordecai. On the fourth day he tried the houseboat again. He tried remembering exactly the night that he spent with Francine. He pretended that a scrap of paper in his pocket was the one with Slip 19 written on it. He took it out of his pocket to look at as he stepped out on the float, just as he had the night he first came there.

He knocked on the door. He looked up at the funnel skylight above the front door. He tried to remember how Francine an-·swered the door. Then he leaned against the door and thought it all out, what she said when he came in, what they drank and what they did after that. The houseboat rocked in the waves of a passing powerboat as Mordecai thought his way up to the inelegant, yet satisfying *flap* of Francine's cutoffs hitting the floor. Then his mind dissolved into the riot of pleasant sensations of their communion over the radio.

Mordecai reran the sequence, trying not to rush to the sex. When he came out of his thought, he found himself staring at the empty slip across from the houseboat. He remembered the boat that had been there that night, then the indistinct figure of the man coming out of the boat. Mordecai recalled the gesture as the man checked the time just before Mordecai moved out of view behind Francine.

Mordecai spent three days searching Monterey. He borrowed Buck's hacksawed Nash Metropolitan and canvassed the beach front and Carmel and Cannery Row. He was alternating nursing assignments with Buck up until then, but he got Buck to take his shift with Sadie while he made his search. On the afternoon of the third day, Mordecai parked down by Lovers Point and watched the surfers waiting out in the water for a high wave. He took a stroll by the parked cars, looking for the Metro van. At the parking lot by the railroad tracks he spotted it. Through the windshield of a grungy grey Metro van he saw Francine's head poking up over the top of a large easy chair in back. He knocked on the glass. "Francine," he said.

— 18 —

"I can't tell you any more than that someone wants to find me, not for me, for something else," Francine said. "I can't say who. I left the houseboat. I had an intuition. It was sort of like that *ping* you talk about. I cleared out right after you left and I located Gary, my surfer friend." She waved out at the figures in the waves. "He knows nothing except I need a place to stay."

"If it's government," Mordecai said, "there's some things you have to know about me." Mordecai gave a brief history of his past. Francine didn't say anything. Then Mordecai explained how his run-in with the agent at Beer Springs had occurred. "It was maybe chance, maybe not. But let's say he sailed down on vacation from San Francisco, maybe to keep tabs on me, or maybe just saw my picture as part of his routine work. He's the new man here in Northern California, or at least he said that at Beer Springs. Then he may have got curious and checked about you." Mordecai waited for her to say something about that but Francine only nodded. "That's how they work," Mordecai continued, "but this Bret guy did not ask me anything about you. And I didn't notice anyone watching the houseboat when I went back."

"When did you go back?"

"Yesterday, but there was no one there that I saw." Mordecai paused. "Don't worry, it's impossible to follow me, I take short-cuts. I would have noticed anyone behind me. You don't have to tell me what's going on. I don't want to know."

Francine nodded. "Good," she said. "What I need now is to get out of this van. I found out one thing, I'm not eighteen any more. What I need is a place no one knows about."

"I have just the place," Mordecai said. "No one knows about it. I haven't been there since I saw you or the guy in Beer Springs that night. And I've never said anything to anyone about it, even my friend Buck. You'll like it."

"It's got to be a place where no one sees me," Francine said.

"If that's what you want, then you'll love this place, the Three Blind Mice live there."

— 19 —

"This is my friend, Francine Fingers," Mordecai said. Francine looked from Evan to Borton to Mrs. Knauth. "I'd like you to meet Evan Glimping, Borton Akard, and Mrs. Knauth."

Evan nodded from his chair. Borton eased around the table and turned his head to one side so he could listen with his good ear. Mrs. Knauth was reading a Braille book. "Hello," Francine said. "It is so kind of you to put me up."

"Any friend of Mordecai's is a friend of ours," Borton said.

"That's right," Mrs. Knauth said. "What part of the country did you say you were from?"

Francine looked at Mordecai. "Colorado, originally."

"I thought I heard that in your voice," Mrs. Knauth said.

"I would have guessed Maryland, Virginia," Evan said.

"I . . . I lived there for a time," Francine said. "Some of that talk must have rubbed off."

"Mordecai will show you to your room, he knows where it is, we've been trying to get him to move in for weeks," Mrs. Knauth said, pointing back in the direction of the stairs.

— 20 —

Francine lifted the quilt off the bed and let it fall back on top. It was a wonderful shade of yellow with ink red flowers. Then she pulled out the black afghan from the end of the bed and examined the little white centers of the rectangular pattern. "One of the Three Blind Mice did this?" Mordecai nodded yes. Francine went over to the knickknack shelf. There were yellow and black and rust red ceramic cats of different sizes. She picked one up. "It gives you a funny feeling to know that no one here sees these."

"Yeah, they only feel them," Mordecai said.

"It's sort of like breaking into a tomb or something," Francine said. She picked up a plaster replica of an Egyptian tomb cat, long neck with stylized eyes. "Human eyes have not seen these things since they were put here," she said, using a Boris Karloff lisp.

Mordecai sat down on the bed. He was suddenly tired. Francine went into the bathroom. Mordecai heard the water running. "I'm going to take a shower. Do you want to join me?"

"In a minute, let me finish this smoke." Mordecai stretched out on the bed, first taking a green pippin apple out of his Army jacket. Then he took off all his clothes. He put his cigarette in an ashtray, leaned back on the bed, yawned and fell asleep. When he woke up, he felt the soft abrasion of wool being wrapped around him. "What?" he said. He opened his eyes and a checkerboard of light and dark was covering his sight. Then Francine was on top of him. "I've got you captured."

"You do?" Mordecai said dreamily. "Who am I?"

"You're the Creature from the Black Afghan." Mordecai could feel her breath through the woolen cords of the afghan over his face. "Oh," he said. He began to get a warm rising sensation.

"What's this?" Francine said, rolling to one side. "The creature is alive!" She tugged at the afghan which was wrapped around Mordecai in a long woolly cocoon. Then Mordecai had a peculiar sensation of tight wool and cool air. "Mmmmmm," he said.

"I believe," Francine whispered through the wool, "that this creature is wearing the world's largest crochetted cock ring." Mordecai glanced over at dresser mirror and through a hole he saw himself on the bed as a black and white hump with only his erect cock sticking up out of it. As she rolled back on top of him, she smelled of bath and shampoo and soap. Mordecai felt incredibly weak and lightheaded. She got on top of him and her knees dug into his ribs, her legs clasping his thighs. She brought her face down until through the stretched hole of the white center he felt the tip of her tongue slowly running its wet edge along the bridge of his nose. She lowered herself down on him. Her mouth covered his and a small piece of apple entered his mouth. Mordecai transferred it back into her mouth with a sudden fierce sense that he was giving her something more than just an apple.

— 21 —

Sadie Strawberry and Buck talked about Mordecai over a small brunch out on Buck's patio. "Must have been some party," Buck said. "Mordecai's been gone for a week now."

"Most likely just a party of two," Sadie said, sipping her ginseng.

"Mordecai and a woman? Naw, Mordecai's a juicer, Sadie, he's everybody's uncle down there at Beer Springs. Mordecai probably knows more secrets that aren't worth telling than anybody in Monterey. But Mordecai and a woman? No way."

Sadie crumbled off a little salmon and smeared it on a torn crescent of bagel. "I swear, Buck, sometimes you got more blind spots than a slug."

Buck was offended. "Me?"

She pointed at him with her salmon bagel. "You." She walked over to Mordecai's shed and tore off a piece of paper from beside the door. "What about this?" She read the poem.

> Blue your collar
> blue my heart
> You go to town you come
> back
> The day I don't see you
> is three months long

"Ah that's just another Chinese poem he's translated."

"I'd bet my whole roll of Medi-Cal stickers that he's been at something that's more fun than a bottle." Sadie looked off for a moment. "You must have had a love affair like that once, Buck. Day and night."

"Agnes Lee Saroux, daughter of a Southern senator."

"Really? Agnes Lee. Southern girl, hmmmm? What was she like?"

"A filly. Big brown eyes, little overbite, thin face, small lisp, long auburn hair . . . a little crazy but my, my."

"How'd you meet her?" Sadie asked.

"Met her in North Beach at a poetry reading. Oh, we had a whirlwind romance. We were married exactly one day after her great aunt's trust fund came into her hands." Buck sighed. "Flew from San Francisco for six months of riotous living in New Orleans. Lord, we ate! Hotels all the way."

"How did it end?"

"Badly," Buck said. "An honest mistake on my part. After the trust fund evaporated, we returned to the family manse. Always a mistake to go back to Daddy. The Saroux family lived in a dry county, that was how her daddy, Colonel Saroux, had got the cash to buy the county up, selling some of the smoothest whiskey a man ever laid his tongue on. He had his brother, Agnes called him Uncle JW, who made the whiskey up in the hills. Well, one day the Colonel decided to put me to work and I was given the family car, a pink and white Chrysler, and sent up to Uncle JW's for a load of the hooch. I was supposed to give it to the Sheriff for delivery. The police delivered the liquor in the Colonel's county, just to make sure there were no problems. So, the Sheriff and I met down at the river to make the exchange. A call come in while we were sampling the whiskey there to make sure it was the right stuff. Some time later I got the idea that Daddy's Chrysler needed a wash job. I couldn't consult with the Sheriff since he had passed out in the back seat, and so I was left to my own imagination about how to get the job done." Buck paused, recalling with a smile the incident. "So I drove it into the the river for a start, figuring the car had to be wet before I could wash it. The deputy in town happened by about then. He had never met me—didn't know who I was. When he saw me crawling out of the Chrysler sitting half under water on a sand bar in the river, why he jumped to the conclusion that I had stolen the Colonel's car, got drunk, and ran it in the drink. Oh he was talking *mean* to me, too. I had lost most of my accent being out here in California, so he thought I was a Northern boy trying to pass."

Buck laughed. "You should have seen him. He was saying things like, *you stole the wrong car, heah? This is the onliest pink and white Chrysler in the county! We're not going to throw you into the jail, we're gonna throw you under it!*"

"And just as he was about to break my head open in defense of the Colonel's Chrysler, up sat the Sheriff in the back seat. Water woke him, I guess." Buck laughed again. "You should have seen that deputy's eyes! *Gaaawdamn*, he says, *it's the Sheriff!* So that was the final straw and the family tucked Agnes away—I guess marrying me was proof enough of insanity. The family threatened me and I had to split. I circled back but I couldn't get near her. I was so broken up, I came back to San Francisco and tried to drink North Beach dry. But every time I taste hot file gumbo, I think of Agnes Lee, . . . she was a pistol."

"What a love story, Buck," Sadie said. "Sometime you'll have to tell me something about *her*."

— 22 —

When Sadie was well enough to travel, Buck took her down to Big Sur for a vacation in the country. She was able to feed the trout and keep house for herself by this time. Buck also put her to work answering Billy the Kid's phone for any quickie moving jobs to supplement the cash flow from the Blue Whale Logging operation. For the firewood sales Mordecai manned Commander Gory's phone in Monterey. Buck leisurely commuted between Big Sur and the Alice Street house. This easy money fueled his notions about remodeling the Alice Street house.

Physically, the house was merely a converted garage. Two rooms had been fashioned in it by a dividing wall down the center. A small telephone booth-sized bathroom was to the right of the front door, set up on a slab of cement about two feet above the floor. It contained a toilet and a very compact shower stall. Buck hated that stall.

Buck always wanted a tub in the house to soak his aches and pains from his jobs. When a seven foot bathtub was given to Blue Whale on a hauling job, Buck placed it next to the patio on the side of the house, so he would see it constantly and plan its eventual installation. As the weather turned cool, Buck's imagination wrestled with the size of the cast-iron tub, the size of his bathroom, the bathroom's elevation from the floor, and the proximity of the front door to the bathroom door. All of these should have been enough to cancel the project.

However, one night after a particularly good ham dinner with a bottle of BV Pinot Noir, followed by a short nap and then several cups of brain wowser coffee chased by some Calvados, Buck wanted a hot bath. *No use being antsy about it, grab a root and growl,* he thought. He got out his crowbar and set to work.

— 23 —

Mordecai and Francine were sitting in the Three Blind Mice's backyard, next to a white metal table on the brick patio. Beside the patio were two old twisted oak trees with a twine hammock suspended between them. Behind the trees was a square patch of lawn with a sprinkler set in the middle of the grass.

Mordecai was wearing his shorts. His Army jacket, sweatshirt, pants and shoes were in a pile beside the trunk of one of the oak trees. Mordecai was meditating on his sock, which hung from the hammock, caught in the twist of the twine.

Francine had her legs up on the table. She was wearing a white tennis outfit, short skirt and cotton shirt. She was contemplating her right knee. In her left hand was a tall clear glass, half full of papaya juice.

Mordecai said something in Chinese. "What?" Francine asked.

"Nothing, just a poem," Mordecai said. "I've been working on some lately. It's better if I carry them around in my head and then say them now and again."

"What did you say?"

"Oh, it goes something like this," Mordecai said. He recited the poem in English.

> The East wind comes again & again
> Even on the mountain top it whirls
> Not one blade of grass that isn't dying
> Not one tree blooming
> I was good to you & you
> Remember my small mistakes

"It's a complaining song then," Francine said.

"Yes. Could be just the facts though."

"Sometimes facts are complaints I suppose."

"Just the facts, ma'am," Mordecai said.

Francine returned to contemplating her knee. She took a sip of her juice.

"I mean it's great, Francine," Mordecai said. "All these decorator fucks, but when do we get to the facts?"

"What do you want to know?"

"What you want to tell me."

Francine regarded the weathered redwood fence surrounding the yard. She took another sip of her juice. She shrugged. "I'm not really ready for the facts myself."

"Why not?" Mordecai said. "What difference is any of it going to make in my life? Hey, I'm not exactly connected to any *authorities*. I don't have a pipeline to anything but poverty and the gypsy life. I'm the world's greatest vacationeer. And I'm *happy* to be along for the ride. But when does the timer go beep and when do we get to exchange home addresses so we can always write?"

Francine shook her head. "I don't know."

"Well, I'm not going to change," Mordecai said. "So as far as I'm concerned it might as well be now."

"It won't be," Francine said.

"Okay," Mordecai said. He stood up and took off his shorts. He walked over to the sprinkler hose on the lawn and stretched out on the grass. "Turn on the water and wash my sins away for me, will you Francine?"

—24—

The next morning, when Mordecai opened the front door of the Alice Street house, the door smacked up against something hard. Mordecai peered in around the door. He found himself looking over the end of a bathtub. Mordecai shut the door and looked back around the side of the house. In the high grass to the side of the Plywood Swamp there was only a patch of dead brown weeds to mark the spot where the bathtub used to be. "Must be the same bathtub," Mordecai said. He opened the door again and studied the arrangement. The back end of the tub was sticking out of the destroyed shower stall wall and blocking the passageway. The only way into Buck's house was to crawl under the bathtub. It was too high to climb over. Crawling under it looked tough, as there were big blocks of wood jammed under the bathtub's gold painted griffin's feet, limiting the crawl space.

For a moment Mordecai crossed the whole thing off as a waking nightmare. He started to close the door. But he wanted a cup of coffee and there was no other way into the house so he got down on his knees, pushed the door open again as far as it would go, and began to crawl for his coffee.

"If things had stayed right there," Mordecai later told the Beer Springs regulars, "maybe it all would have turned out different. Looks like the damn tub torpedoed the goddamn shower stall. Splintered wood all over the floor, look at my bleeding elbows."

But Buck was not yet done. Shortly after the torpedoing of the shower stall by the tub, Buck went into the Pacific Grove market and saw that the owners had taken out a huge steel frame double window and replaced it with several smaller windows. Getting the old window was no problem—the owners were only too happy to have someone take it away. The problem was getting it home. Buck had tipped the window into his truck and then driven up the Forest Avenue hill. Old Jasper was walking his dog so he witnessed this event. "That Chevy of Buck's was leaning so far sideways with the weight of that window frame—it looked like a drunk sailor with an anchor tied to his ass," Jasper said. "You could *hear* the rubber being scraped off the tires on the right side of the truck as it went up the hill. That truck was walking sideways like a crab, damnest thing I ever saw. And the smoke! Looked like a German gas attack. He musta burned out what was left of that engine."

Buck backed the Grey Ghost up to the edge of the Alice Street house and eased the window frame off, letting it lean against the house corner. That night he cut a hole in the roof directly over the kitchen sink.

When Mordecai came home at night, he saw the window frame but he did not notice the hole in the roof until the next morning, when he was climbing in the kitchen window above the sink to make his coffee and noticed a downdraft.

"For my skylight," Buck said later. He put out both his hands and lifted the huge steel frame up in his imagination and placed it over the hole in the roof. "Lay it right up there, *easy*."

While Buck was figuring out how to defeat gravity, he put a sheet of plastic over the hole in his roof. Then the autumn storms began. The plastic flapped. The plastic stretched. The plastic filled with rain until it hung down above the kitchen sink, the water a liverish yellow, like a rain god's condom. Buck grew tired of seeing it first thing in the morning. In a pique he jabbed it with a steak knife. That night the winds came again. The plastic tore. Rain drizzled down into the sink, washing the dirty dishes.

Meanwhile, what with nursing Sadie and remodeling, Buck did not have time to maintain the lines of communication to Hilda Verog. This caused Hilda to go out to her lots in Pebble Beach and see how the lot clearing was coming along. Hilda found that Joe and Seth Raeth's idea of her property was considerably wider than the official version.

Hilda dropped by the Blue Whale offices unannounced that same afternoon. Buck and Mordecai were playing chess over an amusing Cote du Rhone, 1963. Buck looked up to see Hilda standing in the doorway, peering over the bathtub at him.

"What's this?" Hilda said, pointing to the bathtub.

"Hilda! that's my new bathtub. The bathroom's not finished yet."

Hilda looked around the house. "How do I get in?"

"I'll come out," Buck said. "I've got to cut a new door in back for the patio." Buck climbed over the bathtub and walked out the door.

Hilda stood by the side of the house, staring at the plywood patio, which, because of the rains, was now a wavy sea of unglued sheets. Hilda looked up. "Why did you cut a hole in the roof?"

"That's for my skylight," Buck said. "This is the glass that's going up there." He pointed to the huge frame leaning against the corner of the house and showed her with his hands how the window frame would be placed up on the roof over the hole. Hilda looked at the hole and then she looked at the window. They were not the same size.

Mordecai watched the episode from the kitchen window. "That's when I knew Buck was in trouble," Mordecai said later, "when she saw that the hole in the roof had no relationship to the size of that window frame. I could see in her eyes a revision of Buck's capabilities suddenly taking place."

"Maybe you better stop work out at Pebble Beach," Hilda told Buck. "I've got to run, I'll call."

Hilda might have given Blue Whale a call too, but one day there was an ominous snuffling at the other end of the phone line. Sadie had been free with her long distance phone calls while recuperating. She needed some sympathy from distant friends. Sadie had a lot of friends in faraway places. The phone rang one morning and it was the Nose, closing in on Commander Ralph B. Gory.

"Commander Ralph? No, he's not here," Buck said to the Nose. "I'm sorry to tell you that he is now officially Missing in Action. Yes, in Vietnam. Hmmm? I'm his brother, Standand B. Gory. My brother is one of our MIA's, ma'am. We think he is in a Vietcong prison camp but we don't know. We are all praying for his safe return."

Buck leaned the phone away from his ear so Mordecai could hear the Nose too. " . . . *even if he is in a Vietcong prison camp, he has to pay his phone bill,*" the Nose was saying. "*Surely there is some way for the Navy to pay for it while he's away.*"

— 25 —

In Beer Springs it was a regular Saturday evening. The afternoon college football games were over on TV. The crowd had thinned. Those who had no home cooking to look forward to were planning a walk down to Ace's Pizza across from Lighthouse Liquors. Ethel had come on duty. She was placing the clean glasses on the back counter. Mordecai and Sal and Jasper were waiting for Tom Soper and Duane to finish their pool game. Mordecai had won a bet on a University of Washington game (his alma mater, he called it, having spent two years there before the Army) and he was feeling flush. When the three of them got up to leave for their pizza, Ethel turned the TV down. "See you in a bit," she said. "I'm going to watch the news. Bring me back a slice of pizza."

Duane and Tom put on their coats and left with Mordecai and the gang. Ethel checked the remaining drinkers for refills, then stepped back by the pay phone and worked at her bar tabs. She glanced up at the TV and saw a man yammering into a microphone. Even with the sound off, Ethel could tell the announcer was babbling as fast as he could. Ethel reached over and adjusted the remote control. She listened to the announcer. Slowly the bar chatter died out as the announcer continued his rapid-fire delivery.

Mordecai and Jasper and Sal returned to Beer Springs. "Jesus, holy hell broke loose in Ace's pizza. The cook came out swearing in Spanish, and nobody got served any beer because the waitress went back to the kitchen to listen. Is it true?" Mordecai said.

"Yeah, our President did it again," Ethel said. "He fired the goddamn guy who was investigating Watergate."

"What the hell do you expect? He's been lying through his teeth ever since this started. He's done. He's finished. They'll impeach the bastard." Sal said. "That shyster's through."

The three of them sat down at the bar and slowly the bar filled with people coming off the street to find out what was happening. When Mordecai looked around, the bar was three deep with people, all looking up at the TV and listening to the news commentators. "He's gone," Jasper croaked to Mordecai, shaking his head. "Nothing can stop it now. Stupid bastard. It's rolling."

Later that night Loser Rred came into Beer Springs and sat down with Mordecai and Sal the Portagee at the far end of the bar, watching TV. Ethel turned down the sound after awhile when it looked like the announcers were only going to rehash the Watergate Hearings. "You see," Loser Rred said, jabbing a finger at the screen as the plan for domestic spying was displayed one more time, "all our conspiracy theories *were* true, man."

"Ahhhhhhhh," Sal the Portagee brayed, "*some* of them were, just some of them. But he's not going to get away with this one."

"Oh yeah? Did he get away with spying on the people? Sicking the IRS on people? Disrupting, man, political campaigns?" Loser Rred said. "And what about my bust, man."

"What? Your bust?" Mordecai said. "Were you on President Nixon's hit list too, Rred?"

"I was gonna organize the vets, man. I was gonna do it when the cops swooped down on me."

Sal the Portagee looked over at Loser Rred. Then he looked at Mordecai and winked. "Dirty tricks, eh Rred?"

"You're damn right," Loser Rred grumbled. "I was getting my act together when I got busted. They took my phone numbers, man, and they never gave them back. I had all the phone numbers for all the vets here and we were gonna march, man." Loser Rred looked down at the change in front of him and began to push the pennies around, in and out of the nickles and dimes and quarters. "This is how we were gonna *deploy* ourselves, see . . . ." He shoved the money around on the bar as Sal and Mordecai watched. After a minute of this Rred looked up, said "Oh!" as if he just remembered something, got off the bar stool and walked outside and turned right.

Ethel picked up Rred's beer and set it on the back counter. She carefully scooped up all of his change and put it alongside his beer. Then she went back to her stool beside the phone and picked up a copy of the TV guide.

Sal sipped his beer. "Looks like the gottas are getting em," Sal said.

"The gottas?" Mordecai said.

"Yeah, their gottas are getting them. I envy the guys your age," Sal said.

"What for?"

"Somehow you guys' gottas didn't get you all fucked up like our gottas did. See, those Watergate guys they're about my age. I had gottas, but those guys' gottas," he said, gesturing towards the silent TV screen, "*whew!*"

"What were your guys' gottas?"

"Oh you know. Gotta go serve your country, gotta get a house, gotta be a man, gotta act serious, gotta get a car, gotta vote this, gotta marry that, gotta get a TV, gotta go for broke, gotta drink, gotta have a blast, gotta hate commies. You know." Sal smiled. "Man, by the time I was seventeen, I had *more* gottas than I needed for the rest of my life. But those guys, those government guys, gotta re-elect the President, gotta get the Democrats, gotta do dirty tricks, eyes right, eyes left, whew! The next thing those guys know, they're up there during those Watergate Hearings trying to explain how their gottas turned into *havetas* . . . and hey! once they say them in front of everybody, why they sound totally nuts!"

Sal punched Mordecai in the arm. "And hey, you can see it in their eyes, they're saying their gottas outloud for the whole country to hear and suddenly, their gottas sound CRAZZZZ-EEE!"

"Well, we had our gottas too." Mordecai said. "Gotta go to college, gotta wear Kennedy hair cuts, gotta demonstrate, gotta sing "We Shall Overcome", gotta go to be-ins, gotta distrust anyone over 30, gotta smoke dope, you know. Just plain gotta do things different than any one older than us."

"Yeah, but those weren't *Official* Gottas, Mordecai."

"Still gottas."

"Yeah, but you talked up your gottas. Those gottas got talked up a whole lot. Our gottas, they was *silent* gottas."

Mordecai thought about that for a moment. "Well, Sal, maybe there comes a time when you *want* your silent gottas. Maybe when they're the only thing you have left."

Sal shook his head. "Nothing more deadly than a silent gotta."

— 26 —

That Sunday morning Mrs. Knauth stood by the front porch, holding a pot of purple hydrangeas. "Hello Mordecai," she said. "I was just taking these hydrangeas in. You see this?" she held up a purple blossom to him, about as large as a baby's bonnet. There were large flat flowers around the outside of the bloom. Inside the flowers were tight small bud shapes.

"Looks like they haven't bloomed yet in the middle."

"No," she said, "they've bloomed." Her hand went out and ran over the top of the plant, her papery fingers caressing the little flowers. "These are the fertile flowers, but the big ones here," she held one between two fingers, "they're sterile. The big ones are just for show."

"What's that called?"

"A lace cap hydrangea, it's a fairly rare plant," Mrs. Knauth said. "I thought I would give it a breath of fresh air today but it's too cold, I'm going to put it back on the porch. Francine gave it to me."

"Is Francine here?"

"No," Mrs. Knauth said. "I'm sorry to tell you she left, Mordecai."

"When?"

"This morning, about ten. Francine called the airport and booked a flight to San Francisco. She used a credit card. Only left this hydrangea." Mrs. Knauth smiled. "I don't know where she would buy it on a Sunday morning. Perhaps had it in her room already. I'm sorry she's gone, Mordecai. I enjoyed having another woman around. Those other two big galoots are so wearing on me." Mrs. Knauth walked up the stairs and Mordecai followed her.

"Did she say where she was going?"

"No, she thanked me for putting her up. Then she left after giving me the lace cap." Mrs. Knauth put the hydrangea down on the window sill. "I don't think these are in season. She must have got it at a nursery. So she must have had it in her room." Mrs. Knauth turned. "Go on up in her room, Mordecai, she might have left you a note."

Mordecai went up to the spare bedroom. The bed was made. The window was open, letting in a misty sea smell. Mordecai saw no note. He saw a saucer with a bit of dirt at the bottom of the knickknack shelf.

Mordecai went in the bathroom. Scrawled on the bathroom mirror in lipstick was:

Thanks for the melanoia
Say goodbye to the Three Blind Mice.

Mordecai took some tissue and cleaned it off, then he returned to the downstairs living room. Mrs. Knauth was wiping off the dinner table. "Was there a note?" she asked.

"Yes. She's gone back to take care of her gottas, I think." Mordecai said. "But now she's maybe got some help."

"Her what?" Mrs. Knauth said, her head coming up. "Her gottas?"

"Just a joke."

"I hope you don't feel bad, Mordecai. It was a pleasure having someone young around. You two weren't worrying about anything when you were together. I liked that. I liked the way she lived right here in the present. You too. That's hard to do. The past is all these others around here talk about. But, the past has a way of catching up with everything. Is that what you meant by her gottas? Anyway, I liked to walk into the room when Francine was there. It was sunny somehow. Sometimes she smelled like mown hay."

"I know," Mordecai said.

"But," Mrs. Knauth sighed, "there was something going on. There's always something going on, isn't there?"

Mordecai turned to leave. "And there's always something leaving. Only this time I think something of mine left—a little roll I was on."

—27—

The next morning Mordecai was tacking up a new poem by his shed door when he saw the landlord's car stop out on Alice Street. Mr. Zarri was a WWII vet who had bought the lot as an investment. He got out of his car and stared at the pile of split pine logs blocking the driveway. Then he picked his way through them and looked at the overgrown grass field leading to Buck's house. Mordecai stepped back into the shed and partially closed the door.

Mr. Zarri walked up to the steel frame picture window, now lying flat on the ground in front of the house. He looked down at it and viewed the matted tangled grass under it. Then he walked up to the door.

Inside the house Buck was taking a bath. Handel's *Water Music* was caroling out of the stereo speakers. Buck had drawn the curtain on the front door window to let in a little light. He was busy sudsing down his foot when Mr. Zarri looked in. Mr. Zarri did not knock. Instead he walked around to the Plywood Swamp. All the skins of the plywood were rippled and warped and waving in the breeze. Mr. Zarri looked at the corner of the house and saw the mossy water heater. Buck had moved it outside to make more room in the kitchen. He was going to build a shed around it sometime. Mr. Zarri looked in the kitchen window and saw the jagged sawed remains of the interior wall. Then he looked up.

The breeze was flapping the torn plastic around the skylight hole.

Mordecai stepped out of the shed. "Hello, do you want Buck?"

"No," Mr. Zarri said, "no, I don't believe I do."

"Was he going to do some work for you?" Mordecai said. He knew that Buck sometimes worked off the back rent with hauling for Mr. Zarri.

"No, I don't believe he's going to do any work for me." He turned and began to walk back to his car. Mordecai tagged along. He had to go get a pack of cigarettes anyway at Buster's Deli. "I don't know why he couldn't leave it the way it was," Mr. Zarri said, as if talking to himself. Then, to Mordecai. "There's not that much cheap housing left in Monterey. Hell, I wasn't going to get rid of the old shack. Now . . . ."

"Well some people can't help trying to improve their lot in life," Mordecai said. "Buck's that way."

"I wish your friend hadn't tried to improve *my* lot. Look, let me tell you something. I own a *bunch* of places like this and I've lost most of them in the past few years. These young people, hippies or whatever you call them, they don't pay PG&E. The company comes out and goes in and condemns them. That was the last hundred dollar a month place I owned. You ought to tell your friend in there that he's going to run out of room some day. There's only so much room to go around." He waved back at the house. "But what can I do?"

Buck received a short note about the back rent from Mr. Zarri a day later. Since Buck was broke, he lit it on fire and used it to start the pilot light on his oven. Mordecai noticed that his next note was a perfect haiku. It read:

The bulldozer will
be here to demolish the
house on next Friday.

Book Four
Monterey/Big Sur
Winter
1973-1974

MORDECAI ALWAYS thought that if humans were really funny bundles of light and water, then it was easy to understand why people move as other mammals, birds and fishes do in their peculiar migrations. The rays of light change, the angle and duration of the sun shifts, and the light inside their bodies responds, those pulsing sculptures called the heart, the liver and the kidneys—those light and water sculptures shift too, new destinations and dreams are secreted.

Mordecai felt this happening inside him. The angle of light off the Monterey pines gave him a clue. The light seemed to slide across the needles and slip into the ground in soft darts of energy. No energy seemed to remain above ground but dispersed in the earth in a solar hibernation. Inside him Mordecai began to feel his melanoia do a slow dissolve, drifting away.

He felt it drifting east, then going north. No more *pings* on his melanoia radar, no more days of following that elusive *someone*, no more gifts from total strangers.

Some Big Sur afternoons he was inclined to think this feeling was only a corollary of the winter's steady decline of light. And there were times when he thought this was merely a symptom of living in the canyon at the trout farm, where the sun barely pierced the fog until after twelve noon.

In short, Big Sur winter gloom set in. Their days at the Trout Farm were numbered, for one thing; Jasmine was due back from Hawaii. Buck and Mordecai checked around Monterey but rents were skyrocketing. One room shacks which used to be $100 were costing double. Unfortunately for the Blue Whale moving business, Sadie had continued her long distance sympathy sessions on Billy the Kid's credit. The Nose had descended on Billy's phone line and snuffed it, putting the Blue Whale calls into her nasal tape loops: *the number which you have dialed is not in service at this time. There is no new number.*

From the trout farm the national picture did not look much better. President Nixon was still busy pawing dirt on his associates, burrowing in and turning his ass to the public. The economic system seemed to be buckling and collapsing into a welter of random baby squeaks and tiny *gimmes*. There was a gas shortage; long lines of panicky tourists decorated Monterey's streets. Mordecai was sensible enough to know that not much of this Official Reality mattered. But it served as a grim backdrop for his feeling of lost melanoia. Somehow his fading melanoia and the tawdry lurch of the country's politics into public criminal banality seemed to be connected in some osmotic way.

After a few weeks of cabin fever with Buck and Mordecai, Sadie pronounced herself recovered enough to move into a commune down the coast, where she was going to help out with a alfalfa sprout farm. Before going she had expressed her condolences to Mordecai. "Living with Buck is not easy in the best of times, Mordecai. Good luck. And watch out for Buck's down country friend, Mr. Anarchy."

This was Sadie's mild way of registering her complaints about Buck's wake-up routine of blasting mummified loaves of Wonder Bread with the shotgun and then limbering up with a few rebel yells.

For any food besides fresh trout, Buck and Mordecai were reduced to making garbage runs to the Carmel Valley and Monterey Safeway stores, picking up castoff groceries. In Monterey, Steve Wire put a spare refrigerator on his front porch where they stored the Safeway milk products. Anyone who wanted some could stop by. Mordecai had also made friends with the weekend warehouseman at a local produce wholesaler. This kind soul kept cases of potential discards in the cooler for them. On Saturday morning they stopped by and he gave them cases of cabbages or avocados or cantaloups, bags of potatoes or onions and grapefruits. These they delivered to Jasper and a few of his pensioner friends, some poor families plus the Beer Springs regulars like Tom Soper, Steve Wire and Duane, who were all living off unemployment and facing a bleak winter. Their "customers" each gave Buck and Mordecai a dollar for gas and that kept the Grey Ghost running up and down the coast.

About this time Buck began having trouble keeping the baby trout alive. He was not the most regular feeder: Buck's morning trips to the hatching troughs were sometimes after 12 noon when the chill was off the long grass leading down the bluff to the trout pond grove. Then too, often the trouts' dinner was a moonlight affair. More and more of them began floating belly up in the water. Buck continued to find trout on the ground beside the troughs, as if they had been scooped out. "It's Old Sandpaper," Buck said. That was his name for the mountain lion that lived up the canyons. "Old Sandpaper's at it again."

Buck called the mountain lion "Old Sandpaper" because of his gritty purr. On one of his walks Buck had once come across the cat, lying up in a sunny tree half-asleep. Buck swore that the cat's breathing sounded like sandpaper on rough wood. Mordecai took his word for it. He certainly did not want to get close enough to Old Sandpaper to hear him breathe. But Buck's idea that the mountain lion was eating the baby trout did not seem right to Mordecai. Vainly he tried to argue with Buck. "No, he stands up on his hind legs and scoops them out," Buck insisted. "Saw the paw prints on the side of the trough myself. That's why those trout are missing. He's eating them. Cats eat fish, don't they?"

Mordecai thought it was racoons, if anything. Buck nailed down some chicken wire over some of the troughs but ran out of nails and ambition before the entire job was done. As the winter gloom set in, Buck got more and more fatalistic about the trout. "If the landlord comes by, he's going to shit little bricks when he sees how many trout are left," Buck grumbled. "Old Sandpaper's been at them again."

Buck put up a scarecrow but Old Sandpaper ignored that. The big cat made his usual nightly rounds, stopping to piss on the scarecrow's overcoat. Then Buck tied a string of tin cans on the troughs. That night there was a wild rattling down in the pond grove and then the rattling went up the southeast canyon and stopped. In the morning they could see the string of tin cans gleaming in the sun up the bushy cut of the canyon. Buck then strung some old barbed wire around the trough supports. The next morning the wire was delicately mashed down into a tangled pile around the base of the supports. Buck took an old Motorola portable stereo down to the pond. He ran an extension line from the freezer outlet on the shed and set the stereo up beside the troughs. That night he put a Gagaku record on automatic, hoping the high-pitched weird Japanese music would chase away the cat. Mordecai went to bed that night hearing *kwaaaangs* and *twa-wiiiings* and *eeeee-rrrows* coming from the grove. The next morning Buck found the stereo had been given a casual swipe of the big cat's paw and had landed upside down at the edge of the pond mud with the record missing.

"Boy, you're getting a *bad* case of cabin fever," Steve Wire told him when he visited the trout farm in November. "And I'd say you got a dab of shack simple thrown in, too." Buck was obsessed with the big cat's disdain for any of his ploys. "I'll think of something," Buck said, staring down the bluff at the trout pond grove. "I'll fix Old Sandpaper's wagon one of these days."

"Why don't you just shoot him, Buck?" Steve asked.

"Shoot Old Sandpaper?" Buck was offended. "I'd rather put the gun to my head than shoot a beautiful animal like that. What the hell are you thinking about anyway? There's got to be some way to chase him off." Buck stayed up late nights, scheming and brooding. Now and then he would go out at midnight with the shotgun and blast some more stale Wonder Bread loaves in the garden to warn off the cat. But more often than not, midnight found Buck snoozing beside the fire. In the morning Old Sandpaper's big paw prints would be all around the troughs.

In Monterey, Steve Wire scored an old fisherman's shack on Lottie Street. Built in the 1940s this palace displayed single-wall construction with a kitchen and a bedroom. A bathroom and shower were in a shed tacked on the side. From inside, the Southern Pacific markings on the shiplap wall boards were still visible; the house was about as long and narrow as a boxcar, too. Whenever Big Sur got to be too much for him, Mordecai would stay overnight there, camping on the floor in Steve's kitchen. It was here, in the midst of the winter gloom, that Mordecai had his last flickering after-image of melanoia.

Since Steve's shack was right around the corner from the Safeway store and the Forest Hills shopping center, in the morning Mordecai usually moseyed up to get the paper and check the bins at the same time. As he walked up Prescott Street toward the Safeway, Mordecai had a flash that someone was just ahead of him. When he got to the Safeway, he felt a tiny fading *ping* go off in his head. But instead of heading for the Safeway dumpster, Mordecai continued to the Rexall drug store. He bought a *San Francisco Chronicle* and then went around the back of the drugstore to their dumpster. On the bottom was one thing: a small square unmarked brown carton. Mordecai climbed in and picked it up.

When Buck stopped by that afternoon, he found Mordecai and Steve sitting at Steve's kitchen table with a case of razor blades open in front of them. Over a quart of Brown Derby beer they speculated on why razor blades would be thrown out.

"Hell, in these lean Republican times, one of the unemployed probably ate a blade in a suicide attempt and got botulism." Buck said. "And the concerned company pulled them off the market. But someone's got to try one. Mordecai? You still feeling melanoid? Why don't you shave and we'll watch."

Buck and Steve watched gravely as Mordecai shaved with the suspect blades. Mordecai did some figuring on shaves per razor and per year. He came up with the figure that the three of them now had enough razor blades to last the rest of their lives. While Buck went out for a second quart of Brown Derby, Steve waited for Mordecai to exhibit some symptoms. "How are you feeling, my son?" Steve said. "Sick to your stomach? Dizzy?"

Buck came back with the quart of beer and the evening Examiner. "Gawwdamn! Look at this," he said. He flashed the headlines at them. "That crook Nixon's given the court a tape with 18½ minutes erased off it!" Since Steve didn't own a TV set, they tuned in the radio and listened to the reports from the White House.

"This has *got* to sink that bastard," Buck said. "What are they going to have to do, drive a stake through his corrupt heart?"

They argued about how much longer the President could hold on. Then they got another quart of beer and began to discuss general corruption in the world. Steve entertained them with his stories of corruption on the Bay Area Rapid Transit tunnel under Market Street for the subway. "I had to quit, myself. Couldn't stomach it. Why, a carpenter told me one supervisor had the truckers delivering tiles and beams and lumber to his place up in the Oakland hills. Built almost his whole house with BART materials. Big place, too. This carpenter worked on the house. I heard this supervisor decided to sell the palace after it was built, but had to screen the buyers real careful. He didn't want anyone who would blow the whistle on him and point out that his forty acre bathroom had the same blue tiles as the North Berkeley BART station. Those were the days."

"Yeah, and me and Mordecai were making two hundred a day moving divorcees, getting a big check from the China Estate, living off the fat of the melanoia," Buck said. "Look at us now. All we got is enough razor blades so that we can even take a package into our coffins with us."

That night Steve and Mordecai announced in Beer Springs that they now had coffin security. Mordecai pointed out that this was better than 24 hour underarm protection. "The hair just keeps on growing, whether you're dead or not," Steve said. "But we got that licked. Now all we have to get is a throwaway case of deodorant sticks. One under each arm and one up our ass and we'll be set for eternity."

A day after this Mordecai went into several stores and noticed that the reason why the razor blades had been thrown out was because the packaging had changed. Buck immediately worked a deal at a little neighborhood store so they could return the razor blades for credit on wine and food. Each time they drove into Monterey, they stopped by the store and fobbed off a few more packages of razor blades. And this was how the product of Mordecai's last melanoia attack was frittered away. "Yeah I thought I was set up for death," Mordecai told the Beer Springs Chorus, "but it turned out to be only a close shave."

—2—

One December day a letter from the Armenian rug dealers somehow threaded its way through Buck's maze of forwarding addresses down to Big Sur. The letter said that they had sold as much of the China Estate as they could, and that Buck should drop by and pick up the remains and his last check for $47.63. Buck headed into Monterey, and borrowed some gas money from Ethel at Beer Springs, waited in line for an hour for the gas, and then drove to San Francisco.

When Buck came back to the trout farm, he had a load of groceries and a case of beer and a cardboard box full of China Estate rejects. "Wait'll you see what I got," Buck said to Mordecai. "Got something that is going to fry Mr. Sandpaper's whiskers off, let me tell you."

Mordecai looked into the back of the Grey Ghost but he only saw large black garbage bags piled in a big cardboard box.

"No peeking! Wait until dusk." Buck smiled and tapped his head. "Then I'll show you what I got. Let's eat."

After a heavy meal Buck sat in the kitchen and rocked in his easy chair and drank coffee and smiled down at the trout pond grove. "I'll show that cat who's in charge around here." To toast his new secret plan, Buck brought out a pint of brandy. He and Mordecai drank it, waiting for evening. As the light got dusky around five o'clock, Buck swung into action. "Come on, Mordecai, we're going to fix that baby trout eater once and for all."

Mordecai followed Buck out to the Grey Ghost. "Take two of these," Buck said, hoisting out a black garbage bag and handing it to Mordecai. "Don't look in them."

Mordecai hefted one of the bags. It was only about a third full but it was heavy. "Feels like dirt," Mordecai said. Then he caught the smell. "Jesus, what's in this?"

"Lion shit, Mordecai," Buck crowed. Buck handed Mordecai another bag, took one in each hand himself, and they started down the bluff for the trout pond grove. "African lion poop. Friend of mine from the old days in North Beach, artist type, works out at the San Francisco zoo. I went out there and got some genuine African male lion shit. Those big hairheads were spraying must and piss all over the place. Old Sandpaper is going to come down here tonight and get one nostril full of this, and he'll goddamn take off up into the hills and never come back."

Buck trotted ahead of Mordecai across the creek bridge and into the grove. "Old SP will be so goddamn freaked, he'll never be seen again," Buck muttered. "He'll think there's a *pride* of these big babies living there now. Heh-heh-heh. We'll show *him* who's the boss of this here canyon."

Buck and Mordecai got a shovel out from the feed shed and spread the lion shit up on top of the diversion dam first, then all along Old Sandpaper's trail down the feeder stream. They smeared it on the troughs and finished off by laying a circle on the meadow at the edge of the pond, then along the path back to the house.

"Old Sandpaper's going to have the olfactory shock of his life tonight," Buck muttered, tossing the lion shit around. "I'd love to be here when he comes down and gets his first whiff of this."

— 3 —

As the evening stars began to shine, Old Sandpaper padded along the narrow deer trail down the east side of the canyon wall, pausing now and then to sniff the chill night wind coming in from the ocean. When he reached a round rock hidden in the underbrush at the bend in the canyon, he stopped and listened. Then the cat stretched out and waited. From the narrow trail the cat was invisible behind the thick brush. When nothing came up the path, the cat slipped down and began to walk toward the trout pond. As the cat got to the bend in the feeder stream, he picked up his head and sniffed deeply. Up ahead, on the diversion dam, there were some dark mounds. The big cat smelled the wind, then let out a low snarl.

— 4 —

The next morning around nine o'clock, Mr. Chikes drove his maroon and red 1964 Chrysler Newport down the paved road into the canyon. When he got to the Y in the dirt road, he turned left toward the bluff and the grove beyond. Mr. Chikes was mildly disturbed when he had not been able to contact the trout farm. The phone seemed to be disconnected. He had not seen any rent now for two months and he thought it was time to find out what was going on. Then, there was the trout farm. He had been reassured by Jasmine that this fellow Buck was a country boy and knew how to tend stock of any kind. In Mr. Chike's memory some story about childhood catfish ponds in Alabama came back. Whatever the case, he had to restock the feed shed; in the trunk of his Chrysler were several sacks of feed.

As Mr. Chikes rounded the bend in the road, the first thing he saw was the vegetable garden. Among the stalks of dry corn and Brussel sprout plants was a blizzard of white fragments. For a moment Mr. Chikes thought they were sponge padding. Then he saw the red white and blue tatters of Wonder Bread wrappers fanning out down the hillside, blown by the ocean wind in a wider and wider pattern, until all the weeds down the canyon looked as if they were flying their own little gas station banners.

Mr. Chikes parked his Chrysler at the foot of the garden, next to the bridge leading across the creek to the trout pond. He eased his bulk out of the custom padded seats and stood up. Mr. Chikes was a portly man, a bit unsteady on his feet, and short of breath. He was puffing a bit from the exertion of getting out of his car when he saw a Wonder Bread wrapper at his feet. He grunted as he bent over to pick it up. The wrapper was full of shotgun pellet holes. He looked up toward the house. There was no sign of life, only a ratty gray Chevy truck and a Nash Metropolitan with a tarp over the top.

Mr. Chikes went to the back of his Chrysler and opened the trunk. He hoisted out one of the feed bags onto his shoulder and started along the muddy path to the trout grove, pausing at the creek to look at how high it was running. That was when he saw the school of fingerlings underneath the creek bridge. Mr. Chikes looked down at those fingerlings for some time. He didn't like the look of that.

Mr. Chikes continued along the path into the grove. As he reached the edge of the meadow sloping down into the pond, he stepped in something. He looked down at his foot, turning the shoe sideways. A rank smell assaulted his nose. "Son of a bitch," he said, scraping his shoe off on the grass, only to pick up more.

He dumped the sack down on a safe place and reached for a stick. As he knelt to scrape off his shoe, his knee sunk into another piece of shit. "Son of a *goddamn* bitch!" He checked the ground and knelt on the other knee, scraping the crap from his pants. Then he got his other shoe clean and threw away the stick. He bent over to hoist the sack again. From over the top of the sack he looked up at where the troughs used to be on the other side of the meadow. All he saw were their legs sticking up out of the grass. Some had big muddy paw prints on them. "What the hell," he said.

Just then a shotgun went off up on the bluff behind him and a wild rebel yell pealed out. This so startled Mr. Chikes he fell forward and knocked the sack of feed down. With Mr. Chikes on top, the sack began sliding on the slick wet meadow slope toward the pond. After about five feet it hit a rock and sent him bodysurfing down the dew and shit-slick slope toward the muddy water.

— 5 —

"So where is Mordecai staying now?" Ethel asked Tom Soper.

"He's sleeping around. He was at Katherine's, bunking down on the back porch, but then one of German Jock's motorcycle buddies came into town and he had to move out. He stayed a week with Morbid Tony but he said he had to leave there: too crazy. Then he babysat Loser Rred's apartment for a week while Rred was in jail in Salinas. I lost track of him after that."

"And Buck? They're not running together any more?"

"No, they're not. Buck was living in an old bread van parked alongside the road up by Steve Wire's house." Tom Soper laughed. "Yeah, it'll be hard for Buck to tear out the walls in that bread van. You heard about that, didn't you, Ethel? When the trout farm landlord came up to the house and saw all the interior walls leaning against the garage?"

"Uh-huh," Ethel said. "And the landlord had lion shit all over him too."

Tom laughed. "Wasn't that the *damnedest* thing you ever heard? That crazy goddamn Buck, you know, he was pissed off at *me*. He blamed me for the whole thing. See, I was suposed to get down there and put in a beam to hold up the damn roof, but Buck went ahead and took out the walls before I had a chance to do it. Why the hell the landlord would have been happy with lion shit all over him and a new beam in the house, I don't know. The first thing Buck does whenever he moves into a new place is tear out the walls. Needs the room, I suppose. Anyway, when Jasmine came back that week from Hawaii, she was about to strangle him."

"I wouldn't cross Jasmine in a million years," Ethel said. "Buck's gonna pay for that. I predict it."

"Oh sure, she'll get back at him," Tom agreed. "She had to put down five hundred bucks damage deposit and get me to put the walls back in the house before the landlord would let her move in again. Now Buck and his four thousand books are sitting in that bread van."

"Well, Mordecai's not starving, his mother sent him a Christmas check. I know. I cashed it for him," Ethel said. "She lives up in Washington. Mordecai was talking about going back up there. He seems awfully sad these days."

— 6 —

Mrs. Knauth put down her book. "I hated to have to turn Mordecai away like that," she said to Evan, "but we had to rent that room out. Might as well have a nice college student living here who's doing that cleanup work, too."

"Yes," Mr. Glimping said, "Mordecai took it well. He'll be stopping by."

"He hasn't been the same since Francine moved out, if you ask me," Mrs. Knauth said. "She took something out of him. That's what I think."

— 7 —

After her doctor's appointment, Sadie Strawberry stopped in for a club soda at Beer Springs before driving back down to Big Sur. "You seen Mordecai?" Ethel asked. Sadie said she had.

"You have!" Sal yelled from the pool table. "Beer Springs isn't

the same without Mordecai! Tell him to get his ass over here. General Sal wants him."

"He hasn't been around at all," Ethel said. "Everybody's worried that he's left town. Where'd you see him?"

"He was in the reading room at the Pacific Grove library."

"That's a good place to get warm," Jasper said. "Real quiet and pretty room, all that dark wood. I like it. Sat there myself many a time."

"Do you know where he's staying?" Ethel asked.

"No," Sadie said, "he didn't say."

"What was he doing?"

"Well, he was keeping out of the wind, that's what he was doing. And working on that Chinese writing. He was translating. I liked one of them so much, I got a copy. Let me see," Sadie began to rummage through her huge leather handbag. "Here it is." Sadie laid the piece of paper out on the bar. Ethel picked it up and read Mordecai's handwriting.

If you were a demon
Then I could not have caught you
So you must be human
Or how else could I know your face

Ah you were acting reckless
And now I am restless

"Now you see—a love poem," Sadie said. "And that is why I think Mordecai is pining away from a bad love affair."

"Mordecai? Love affair?" Ethel said. "I never even thought about that."

"Naw, Mordecai don't mess with women!" Sal brayed. "He's a beer drinker!"

"Did *you* ever see this girl?" Ethel said. Sadie shook her head. "Well, you see him again, tell him to stop by. His bar tab isn't *that* high." Ethel wiped at the bar. "It isn't the same around here without Mordecai."

— 8 —

Mordecai turned into Lottie Street from David Avenue and proceeded up to Steve's shack. Parked in the back of the shack was the big Wonder Bread van, the front end jacked up on wood blocks. On the other side of the shack was Buck's truck with the Nash Metropolitan behind it. Mordecai went up to the door and knocked on it. He opened the refrigerator next to the front door and looked in. Nothing but Safeway chocolate milk quarts and Christmas Egg Nog quarts. Buck opened the door. He was wearing a long T-shirt.

"Where's Steve?"

"You won't believe it, Mordecai. Last night in Salinas I put him on a train for Chicago." Buck walked back down the narrow hallway, his T-shirt hiking up with every other step, showing his bare ass. "I just got up," he added.

"I can see that," Mordecai said. "Why did Steve want to go to Chicago? It's goddamn January."

"Oh he got squirrelly as hell, getting up and drinking a quart a brandy every morning and wondering why and what and who, and the next thing I know, he got some kind of a check in the mail and he filled up one suitcase with his clothes and the other one with whiskey and had me drive him over to the train station."

Buck put on his jeans and got some coffee cups out of the sink. "Well, we've all been stoney ass broke. No goddamn phone, no jobs, no ads, no gasoline, no nothing. Safeway garbage and food stamps. I had to paint a Moving sign on the Grey Ghost, just to get my hopes up." Buck looked up at Mordecai. "What have you been up to? Got any new Chink translations? Your melanoia return yet? Any poetry in your soul?"

Mordecai shook his head. "Steve was going to drive me someplace this morning. I guess he forgot."

"Where you been bunking?"

"Rita's basement."

"Gawwwwwdamn! Boy, you must have been desperate."

"Naw, she's got herself this Ted Dune, you know him?"

"The dope dealer," Buck said. "Kinda wasted looking fellow, stands around with his chin in his hand, waiting for the phone to ring. Funny he looks that way, because he don't use the stuff himself. Waits for those calls from Mexico, flies down, flies back."

"That's him. He's a deal junky. Colder than hell in her basement. I boarded up one corner, keep the chill off me." Mordecai took out a pack of Bugler tobacco and rolled a cigarette. "I had to move out this morning, damn pipes busted. Almost soaked my footlocker. You do me a favor, Buck?"

Buck finished pouring the coffee. "Sure, you want to stay here? You can use the van. I'm not in it anymore. I got this dump for another month on Steve's last month's rent. If I can come up with one hundred and twenty-five, I can have it for two months. Gawwdamn, look at this place. I can't believe it costs that much. Rents are going crazy." He handed Mordecai a cup.

"Thanks, but I need a ride out to the Naval Institute. I thought I'd have a talk with that doctor who told me I had melanoia. See what he says."

"Now that you don't have it?" Buck was going to say something more but then he noticed how blue Mordecai looked. "Oh sure," he said, turning away. "No problem. Got to take the Grey Ghost, though. You know all that logging money I put into that new engine? Well, that thing wasn't worth a good spit. Up and turned into oily smoke one day. I don't know what the hell happened. I haven't had the nerve to look, tell you the truth, Mordecai."

— 9 —

At the information desk at the Naval Institute Hospital, Mordecai was referred to Dr. Sliccy, the Head Surgeon. Dr. Benouay, the shrink Mordecai had met in Chino's, had been transferred. Following her directions, Mordecai caught Dr. Sliccy just as he was leaving his office for the day. He was a white-haired man of about fifty with mild brown eyes and a bemused attitude. Mordecai walked with him to the parking lot. "Dr. Benouay is out of the service now," he told Mordecai. "In New Freedonia, I believe. Why did you wish to see him?"

Mordecai explained that Dr. Benouay had diagnosed his disease and that he wanted to follow up on his melanoia.

"Never heard of it," Dr. Sliccy said. They were walking toward Buck's truck and Dr. Sliccy looked at the newly painted sideboards. "Say, is that your truck there? I'm in a bit of a bind. I sold my house a month ago and all but my den and home office has been moved to my new apartment. These new people want to move in early. Why don't you come out to my place later on and give me a bid. Not much of a job, maybe two or three loads, but if you could do it, we'll have a deal."

On the ride to the mouth of the Carmel Valley, Buck was elated. He tried to convince Mordecai his melanoia was back. Mordecai disagreed. He said it was a dumb luck attack; he hadn't had a ping since they got the razor blades.

At Carmel Meadows Dr. Sliccy's long low white stucco was set in the side of the hill overlooking the river and delta. The garage was below the house. Behind it the Doctor had his den and office. Access was through some sliding glass doors, so the moving was a cinch. The only heavy things were a couple of map cabinets and his refrigerator. Mordecai left the bidding of the job to Buck and went up the stairs into the main house above the garage. He walked through the empty house to the patio and opened the door. Over the sand dunes he could see the ocean and beach. He saw a man walking towards the house with two animals on leashes. The animals didn't look like dogs and it wasn't until the man got closer that Mordecai saw that they were two pigs.

About then Buck and Dr. Sliccy came through the house. Dr. Sliccy saw the man approaching. "Ah, there they are," he said. "That's my orderly with my pigs."

"Your pigs?" Buck said.

"Yes, I kept them after I did surgery on them. Their skin is the closest to human skin and we try cosmetic surgery on them, you know, practice for war wounds, facelifts, that sort of thing."

"You did a facelift on a pig?"

"Oh yes, I even published the results of those two. They're actually famous. I don't know what I'm going to do with them. Now that I'm in this smaller apartment, I don't have room."

"You mean," Buck said, "you don't *want* those pigs?"

— 10 —

Before they left Dr. Sliccy's house, the new owner, Mr. Nord, arrived and hired them to move in his family, once they removed Dr. Sliccy's goods. On the drive back up the Carmel hill into Monterey, Buck explained to Mordecai how it was all going to work. "See, with the money from the first job, we can put in a phone and revive Blue Whale. And with the money from the second, I can put a down payment on Duane the Welder's truck. I need a bigger truck. That way I don't have to go out to the dump so much, see. Then I'll sell the Grey Ghost." Buck looked in the rear view mirror. The Grey Ghost was covering the caravan of cars behind them with a thick oily smoke screen. "Maybe throw a tuneup in it, raise the price a bit."

Mordecai nodded. "Right."

"Goddamn, Mordecai, you really have your dick in the dirt these days."

"Where do the pigs fit in, Buck?"

"Our pigs? Why I'm going to keep them out in back of the shack clearing ground for my herb garden. And I'll fatten them up on Safeway garbage."

"I hope they like chocolate milk."

"Christ, Mordecai, pigs *love* chocolate milk. We'll sell those pigs as Buck Bacon. Our ad campaign will be: *Breakfast and dessert in one serving.* Get all those diet conscious fatties in one stroke. Americans will flock to get their Buck Bacon."

"As your neighbors move away. You're not planning to breed them, are you?"

"Why not? Even people with cosmetic surgery are allowed to breed. That could be another angle: Buck Bacon for people who want that slim chin look. Remember folks, only Buck Bacon comes from pigs with facelifts."

"What's the pay for these two jobs?"

"Five hundred."

"I want half."

Buck looked over at Mordecai. "Of course, we've always gone fifty-fifty."

"Really, Buck. I want to go North for awhile." Mordecai paused. "I want a ticket and a cushion for the trip. Two fifty should make it."

"Sure, go back and see mom and the family, cheer you up. You're about as *down* as I ever seen you. Look, what do you think we should name our two pigs?"

"Name them?"

"Right, for the Buck Bacon ad. Two rosey-faced slim chin pigs with unbaggy eyes looking out from the billboard at the American public." Buck mused on this new problem. As they rounded the bend of the highway heading into Pacific Grove, Buck brightened up. "Ah! . . . I know. How about Zsa Zsa and Eva Gapork, in honor of their facelifts?"

— 11 —

The job of moving Sliccy out was set for Saturday that week, and the job of moving the Nord family in was set for Sunday. Mordecai would have preferred for them to do the jobs immediately. He knew what happened to Buck when he had the prospect of money: Buck became one loose caboose. It was in some ways worse than Buck *with* money. Five hundred dollars and the ownership of two medically famous pigs was enough to derail Buck. Mordecai knew that the chances were that in four days Buck wouldn't even be in town.

Mordecai was serious about returning to the Northwest. He was sure now that his melanoia had gone north. As much as he needed the money, he decided it was best not to move into Buck's van. He took up Tom Soper's offer of his garage. It had a false floor made of old pine packing crates laid over concrete, with a rug over those, and in the corner was a small potbellied wood stove for heat. Unfortunately that week it rained for three days straight. The garage was roofed with corrugated aluminum and by the second day Mordecai felt as if he were inside a Chinese water torture clinic. The wind blew in and out of the drafty old dump and he caught a bad cold. He curled up on the ratty damp couch next to the stove and fed bundles of old newspapers and butt ends of two by fours into the fire, trying to stay warm while listening to the ratta-tat-tat of the endless downpour on the roof.

Then, on the third day, something amazing happened to Mordecai. He was thinking about the Northwest—the weather reminding him of his days there—when he realized Francine had his melanoia. Even though he was rheumy-eyed and sick, he smiled. *It has got to be,* he thought. He laughed, he was so delighted. And about that time Tom Soper came in with some soup for him. Tom was nonplussed. "What are you laughing at?" he demanded. "You're snotted up and sick, what's going on?" But Mordecai couldn't tell him, he was so happy. All he would say was *she's got it.* Tom thought he was raving with a fever and later brought him a half-pint of brandy. Mordecai drank it slowly and went to sleep, dreaming happily of pale green waves washing over rocks on the Washington coast.

When Saturday came, the sky was clear but the day was windy. Mordecai had been up most of the night with his cough. He felt still rheumy and old but that didn't matter, he was happy. He put on his Army jacket and trudged up the hill to Buck's shack at eight that morning.

The Grey Ghost was gone. Mordecai stepped along the children's tombstones to the porch and knocked. The front door was open. Mordecai went in. He saw evidence that the three day rain had got to Buck, too. Camomile tea was on the table, along with honey and Vitamin C pills. There was a stiff breeze blowing through the kitchen. Mordecai looked over at the gas range and saw that the window above it was no longer there. Covering the hole where the window used to be was an old deerskin. Mordecai bent over the stove and lifted the deer skin. Lying in the tall weeds below the hole was the remains of the window frame and glass.

Mordecai heard the clatter and rattle of the Grey Ghost and then Buck came in. He had a pint bottle in a brown bag. He looked like death warmed over. "Arrrggggh," he said. "Holy mother of god." Mordecai sat down and Buck put a pan of water on the gas range and made them a stiff hot toddy before going out on the job.

The move from Dr. Sliccy's house to his new apartment took all of Saturday, three loads total. Buck and Mordecai viewed the work through the film of flu and brandy. Since there was no room on the third and final load, Dr. Sliccy asked Buck if they were going to come back for the pigs. "What?" Buck said. "Naw, they're okay on the patio, aren't they? We'll get them later."

"Sure," Dr. Sliccy said. "My orderly has taken their pens back to the base but they can't get out."

Just before they left, Buck went up to make sure that Dr. Sliccy was right abut the fence around the patio. "Hogs have a way of finding weak spots in any fence," Buck said to Mordecai. "We don't want to lose Zsa Zsa and Eva." Mordecai stayed downstairs, his nose running and his head aching. But that was okay. Mordecai was still happy. He was sure everything would work out for the best. He heard the loud click as Buck opened the sliding glass patio door. Buck called down, "Doc's right. Nothing but cement and cyclone fence." Mordecai heard the door slide back and Buck came down the stairs.

That night Buck went out shopping and returned with many remedies. They dosed themselves with chicken soup, Vitamin C and aspirin, followed by several brandy and lemon hot toddies. Sunday morning found them both as sick as ever. With a fresh pint of brandy in the glove compartment they drove out to Pebble Beach for the second half of the job. The guard there was reticent about letting them in, but Buck fixed his bloodshot, rheumy eyes on him and said, "Call the Nord family, jackoff, and be quick about it. We're working men." Buck turned to Mordecai. "And we're pissed off about it, aren't we, Mordecai?"

"That's right," Mordecai croaked. Then, to Buck. "I hope to hell this Nord family job is a snap."

"You didn't see that guy. Relax, Mr. Nord is real Wimpus Americanus, no trouble from him," Buck said. "It'll go just like yesterday, one, two, three."

— 12 —

In the hallway to their ranch house Mrs. Nord handed her son Julian the spraygun filled with ammonia. She handed a sponge to her daughter Cynthia. "And you'll wipe dry any of the wood parts Julian sprays. Be sure to get the legs on the tables and the couches and the dressers." She moved back down the hall and picked up the long nozzle of the vacuum cleaner. "First the moving men will stop here, turn the furniture upside down, and I will vacuum any of the dust off the bottom. Then they'll walk down the hall to Julian, you spray the legs, and Cindy you dry."

"Why can't I spray?" Cindy said.

"Because I'm older," Julian said.

"And stupider."

"Really Cindy, don't be so gross," Julian said, "I can't stand it when you're gross."

"Dear!" Mr. Nord said from the kitchen. "They're coming. The front gate guard just calllllled."

"Now I want you to all be in your places," Mrs. Nord said, ignoring him. "This has got to go smoothly. I'm holding you two responsible. Just remember, vacuum, spray and wipe."

"Deeeeear? Did you hear me?"

"Vacuum," Mrs. Nord said, "then spray, *then* wipe."

— 13 —

Mordecai heaved himself into the cab of the Grey Ghost. He popped open the glove compartment door, took out the pint of brandy, opened it, and drank a good slug. He heard someone coming up on the other side of the truck. He stashed the pint under his arm. Buck climbed into the cab. He put out his right hand without looking at Mordecai. Mordecai slapped the bottle into it. Buck twisted off the top, took a good long slash.

"What are they doing *now?*"

"They're all in the bedroom. Mr. Nord is still trying to take apart the bed frame. He's been at it ever since we got here."

"This is a nightmare," Mordecai said. "The flu gods have send us the Nord family, father. This has to be punishment for something *you* did."

"Yes, I know, my son." Buck drank more brandy and gave it back to Mordecai. "Never seen anything like these people. Pack of anal neurotics. *Vacuuming the bottoms of the furniture!* These people are goddamn insane."

The break came when the truck was half-loaded. Buck and Mordecai loaded a small old oak dresser and Buck climbed up in the back of the truck to shift the boxes around a bit. When he stepped on a box and then put his other foot on top of the dresser, the Nord boy let out a shriek.

"Oh my *god*," Julian screamed. "Look what he's doing to the dresser!"

Mordecai almost jumped a foot when the kid let out with his wail. He turned to look at the kid and the doorway was filled with Mr. Nord, Mrs. Nord and her daughter. All their mouths were open in horror. Julian was pointing at Buck in the back of the truck.

Buck was staring back at the Nords. "Whaaaa?" he said.

"Our dresser!" the boy hissed. "That's an antique! You can't *stand* on that!"

Buck looked down at the dresser under his right foot. Then he looked back at the Nord family in the doorway. All of them shook their heads, *no*. Buck looked down at his foot. He brought it off the top of the dresser and leaned back with his right arm using the opposite truck sideboard as a balance, and brought his right foot up so it was hovering in front of the dresser drawers in a karate kick position just as Mordecai lunged up into the truck and caught Buck's leg in his arms. "Careful, Buck, two hundred and fifty, Buck," Mordecai hissed.

"Well, that's *it!*" Mr. Nord said, hurrying out. "I guess we better load the truck ourselves."

Buck and Mordecai both turned to look at Mr. Nord incredulously. Buck smiled. "Okay, but *you're* responsible."

"Of course I am," Mr. Nord snapped.

"No," Buck said. "I mean, you're responsible for it staying on there. Not us."

"Of course," Mr. Nord said. He waited until Buck and Mordecai climbed out of the truck. Then he jumped up in the back and began to look at the top of the dresser. Buck picked up a moving pad and held it up to him. "You heard the man, Mordecai," he said, "we only bring the stuff out for them, they load it, they rope it down. I don't want you to tie a knot for them."

"We can tie knots," Julian Nord said. "Anyone can *do that.*"

— 14 —

In the morning sun on the Sliccy house patio, Zsa Zsa Gapork was rubbing her side contentedly on the ribbed aluminum frame of the glass door. The door was sliding back and forth with each rub of the pig.

— 15 —

In the city of Carmel, Sister Maria McQueeny was having herself
a walk, being in mind of an early morning stroll on the beach. She
was accompanied by Sister Rose Gioardo. They were both watching their step, for the sidewalk slanted down at a smart angle
toward the ocean. This being their annual vacation, they were
happy with the second good day of weather of the five they had
seen so far. They were a block away from the beach when Sister
Marie saw a cloud of oily smoke and then the overloaded pickup
truck turn the corner at the bottom of the hill and start up
towards them.

"Ahhh," she breathed, "now look at that." She pointed at the
truck and the upside-down chairs poking up and the tangled
crisscross of ropes looping around the chair legs, laundry baskets
and boxes of kitchen goods. "It looks like my ancestors descend-
ing on Sacramento," she said.

Sister Rose laughed. "Oh no," she said, "what a sight." They
both stepped back to face the truck as it chugged past. A blond
man in an Army jacket was just replacing the cap on a bottle as
the truck drew abreast of them.

"And I see the passenger has the same brand of gargle as my
grandfather did," Sister Maria added. "He said he never did get
the dust of the Great Salt Lake basin out of his throat."

They turned away and resumed their walk as the truck began
its assault on the hill. There was the sound of ropes straining, and
then a groan as the load shifted. Sister Maria put out an arm to
hold Sister Rose back from any danger. The station wagon behind the truck came to halt. The front door flew open and a man
stood up and yelled, "Look out! Sttttttttttttop!"

Just as he shouted, there was a loud *hunh*. The first box of
kitchen goods strained back against the ropes and then squirted
free. *Plop*, a bag of flour hit the cement, and then the ropes
sagged under the shifting weight and a whole box slipped out
and hit the street, sending a fan of broken cooking oil, glass, spice
cans and cooking utensils out behind the truck. Shrieks came
from the station wagon. Then the entire load vaulted out, taking
the ropes with it. It hit the street—kitchen chairs, card tables,
lawn furniture, boxes of food, books, a stereo set, pictures, the

whole load began to decorate the pavement.

Behind the truck all four people in the station wagon were now out on the street, screaming. The woman rushed forward and flung herself down on her knees in the street. "My casserole, my casserole!" she shrieked. "On the street! *The street!*"

Sister Maria turned to Sister Rose. "Why I believe we're about to get ourselves an Irish Opera this morning," she said. Then she leaned forward a bit and looked up the street at the truck. "You know, I just took a peek in the side mirrors there, and it appears those men in the truck are laughing."

— 16 —

In the driveway Mrs. Nord got out of their station wagon. She leaned back in. "No, you go back to the house, load up with as much as you can," she told her husband. "I'll wait for those men here. I can't believe the nerve of them going to lunch when we're two hours behind schedule. After they get done unloading here, I'll send them back. For god's sake, *don't* let them take anything breakable. And I hold you responsible for this."

"You're the one who tied the ropes down," Mr. Nord snapped.

"You were the one who couldn't," Julian said.

"Julian, puh-leeze," Cindy said.

"You were the one who hired them," Mrs. Nord snarled. "Cheap, you said. Yes, if you don't count the damage and *dirt!*"

She slammed the door and walked toward the Sliccy house. She mounted the circling flagstones to the front door. As she got to the top, she saw the station wagon turn out on the highway back to Pebble Beach. She looked at the front door and noted a scratch by the lock. Then she saw the dirty doormat. She bent down and picked up the green rubber Welcome mat and shook two burrs out of it into the garden and replaced it. Mrs. Nord searched in her purse for the key, found it, and opened the front door. She took a step inside and took the key out of the lock. She was just dropping the key back in her purse when she smelled something.

— 17 —

"I was coming up the Carmel hill yesterday," Ethel said on Monday morning, "and I saw some smoke and the traffic backed up. I thought it was a brush fire on the side of the road. As I got about halfway up the hill, I saw Buck's truck. The hood was up, and there was smoke, *oily smoke,* coming out of it. Looked dead to me. The traffic speeded up then, and as I came over the hill, I saw Buck and Mordecai walking along with two pigs. They were walking with their backs to the traffic and Buck had his left arm out and his thumb up, trying to hitch a ride."

"Only Buck would try to hitchhike with two pigs," Duane said.

"Well, as I said, the traffic was moving by then, so I had to get my blinker going before I could pull over. By that time I was a good two hundred feet past them. I thought they'd be happy to see me, but they just kept walking at the same pace. I got out of my station wagon and yelled back to them, *those pigs can ride, but you two will have to walk.*"

German Jock and Duane both laughed. "What'd they say?" Jasper said.

"Nothing, they were sober as Mormon judges. I put up my dog cage in back and Buck and Mordecai came up with the pigs, never said a word. I noticed that Buck's pig had a rope leash and Mordecai's pig had an extension cord for a leash. Mordecai put his pig in the wagon and walked around and got in the back seat. Never said a word. Then Buck put his pig in. All he said was, *careful, Zsa Zsa here is the naughty one, she burrows under carpets and shits.*"

Ethel looked from Duane to Jasper back to German Jock. "What do you suppose that meant?"

No one seemed to know. "So anyway, Buck got in to ride shotgun and I started off for Monterey. *Where to, Buck,* I said, *home?* Buck, he just nodded. Real quiet ride back, only ones talking were the pigs. Then, when we got to Lottie Street, Mordecai asks me if I could give him a lift out to the airport. I said sure. He gets out and Buck gets out, and Mordecai puts out his hand. Buck takes out his wallet, hands Mordecai a twenty, and says, *that's all I've got left. I put a down payment on Duane's truck last night.*"

"That's right," Duane said. "He came down here to cash that big check and I told him someone else was looking at the truck. He got all nervous that it was going to be sold out from under him and he gave me two hundred down. I only held it in my hand for as long as it took to give it to my landlord for the back rent."

"Your truck's not running, is it?" Jasper said.

Duane inspected his beer for bubbles. "Man's in a fever to buy something I'm not going to stop him."

"Well, who else was looking at your truck?"

"Junkyard man," Duane said, taking a sip. He seemed pleased with his beer. "I wasn't lying to Buck. Buck just didn't ask the right questions."

"Duane here never got over Buck selling him that Nash Metropolitan and then ripping the top off it," German Jock said.

"Well, anyway, Mordecai told me to forget about the airport and he walked off," Ethel said. "He looked about as blue as I've ever seen him, and you know Mordecai, he's not the type to get down. He sure looked depressed. But that's the story: pigs on a leash, a dead truck and no money."

Ethel looked around the bar. "Anyone know any more than that?"

"Two dead trucks," German Jock corrected her. "Looks like Buck now owns two dead trucks and two pigs."

"I guess we'll have to wait until Mordecai comes in and fills us in on the story," Ethel said.

— 18 —

But Mordecai did not come in. With his flu still raging Mordecai went back to Rita's and tried to fix the leaky basement plumbing himself. The room there was less windy than Tom Soper's garage. He lived in that damp place for another week, only occasionally leaving for the heat of the Pacific Grove library reading room. He wrote a letter to his mother and got a small money order in the mail, not enough for the airfare. The plumbing went out the next week. Rita swung a loan for the repairs and moved out to her new boyfriend Ted Dune's house in Carmel Valley for the duration of the remodeling invasion. Mordecai did more time in Tom Soper's aluminum garage but the rain and chill drove him out and he disappeared for days from the sight of the Beer Spring Chorus.

By this time they had pieced together the story of the Nord fiasco. On Wednesday of that week Buck got roaring drunk at Beer Springs and began muttering something about "not having possession of the pigs during the time of the infringement" and a few other legal terms. This indicated Buck had been boning up on the law. When the Sliccy check for two hundred and fifty bounced, Ethel called Dr. Sliccy up and got the whole story. Dr. Sliccy confirmed that both he and Buck were being sued for damages by the Nord family. Dr. Sliccy deemed it prudent to withhold payment until the matter of the pigs' rightful owner during the time of damages could be ascertained. Out two hundred and fifty dollars, Ethel had to inform Buck that he was no longer welcome at Beer Springs. The dumped load on the Carmel hill and the pigs burrowing under the living room carpet all entered into Buck and Mordecai's legend. The Beer Springs Chorus embroidered it with great care, feeling free to do so, since both actors in the drama were now absent and unlikely to interfere with the truth.

— 19 —

In the next few weeks the places Mordecai could stay seemed to vanish. Because of money problems Katherine's back porch had been remodeled and now she rented it to a college student. For the same reason, Tom Soper had to rent his garage to a mechanic. "I used to be able to work maybe 9 months a year," Tom Soper said, "and do unemployment for the winter. Now I can't make it that way. And there are no jobs." The usual sheds and attics and spare bedrooms seemed filled. The houses themselves were being priced off the market for any of Mordecai's friends. Mordecai moved into the back of a pickup truck camper in Pacific Grove. Mordecai had met the owner, Mr. Bruce, in the reading room of the library.

Mordecai still couldn't shake the flu. He assumed that things couldn't get any worse. Then he had what seemed to be the best offer of the winter from Rita. She said Ted Dune was looking for someone to babysit his house in Carmel Valley while he and Rita went to Mexico for a winter vacation. Rita drove him out to talk to Ted Dune. "Ted is particular," Rita said. "I've never seen him so picky about this. I've had three friends out now and he hasn't liked one of them."

— 20 —

Ted Dune was tall and skinny and his face had a perpetual five o'clock shadow. His most characteristic pose was leaning next to the water heater, his right hand on his chin and his left hand under his right elbow. Ted only came to life when the phone rang. Rumor had it that Ted was arranging planeloads of grass to fly north from Mexico. He had learned Spanish and made friends while living in Mexico City, playing at a beatnik lifestyle in the late 50s and finishing an electrical engineering degree on the GI bill.

Mordecai figured out that Ted held two attractions for Rita. First, she could speculate endlessly about Ted's state of mind. He said very little. And secondly, more than sex, she simply liked to have a man around. Ted didn't move all that much. Rita never had to call a bar to find out where Ted was. He kept liquor around but didn't drink. He never smoked pot. His only vice was the phone. A ringing phone made Ted's eyes light up.

Ted asked Mordecai a few "security" questions, then about his family—were they in the area? He seemed satisfied that Mordecai was a hermit at the moment, not seeing many friends. "Only bad habit I have is falling asleep in front of the TV," Mordecai joked.

So a deal was struck. Mordecai had the place for two weeks or more while Ted and Rita vacationed down in Mexico. The Dune house was a modest two bedroom ranch house with a sun deck. A golf course spread out behind the line of birch trees marking the property line. Ted had done some remodeling but then stopped at the guest bedroom, only building a deck out from it, and converting it to a temporary storeroom. Ted stocked the liquor cabinet with some wine and whiskey, put food in the refrigerator, and showed Mordecai the guest bedroom. "I moved the TV in here," Ted said. "Now you can sleep better."

After Ted and Rita left, Mordecai poured himself a drink, went out to the sun deck, and sat in the waning winter sun and viewed the bare birch trees and the green grass of the golf course. He still had the sniffles, so a box of Kleenex was beside him.

On the second night Mordecai decided to sleep out on the deck in a hammock. He took the down sleeping bag out under a partial sunroof over the hammock. Mordecai had taken a dislike to the house. It felt creepy to him. The outdoor smells pleased him, even though he still had some flu symptoms. The nights were mild enough. The Carmel Valley was having a warm streak. Mordecai enjoyed falling asleep looking at the stars.

The third night Mordecai went to sleep early at around eight. A good dinner and a few whiskies got him drowsy. He woke at midnight. He went inside the house but nothing good was on TV. He walked back to the deck. The night was warm. He felt awake and strangely restless. He decided to go for a walk on the golf course, follow it around, do some star-gazing and see what was up at the midnight hour in Carmel Valley.

— 21 —

The house where the party was going on had a bank of plate glass windows, leaning out at an angle over the patio. Around the edge of the patio potted shrubs made inky round blobs on the bright backdrop of the house. There was a piano in the middle of the room and behind it a white spiral staircase. Next to that was a rough pine wall with a huge black and red Navaho blanket hung above the fireplace. Most of the men were in tennis clothes, except for a few in suits and ties. The women were in evening dress. A Paul Simon record was playing on the stereo. On top of the piano were cocktail glasses on a tray. A man in a black suit with white gloves came through and swept the tray up, dimmed the lights via a dial by the wall, turned off the stereo and followed the crowd as it moved into another room behind the spiral staircase.

Mordecai was in the high grass under a cedar tree at the edge of the golf course. He turned and stepped in front of the tree, using it to shield himself from the light from the house, and examined the skies for his favorite star, Betelguese, which Mordecai had renamed *Bettlejuice,* in honor of the rootbeer and vodka drink he was drinking the first night he recognized its red brilliance. He had just located it in Orion's shoulder when he heard a door sliding open from the house and a familiar laugh.

Mordecai stepped back under the cedar and peered out from under the limbs toward the patio. A woman was standing there. She had a parka ski jacket thrown over her evening gown. She was humming *My Mother's Son-in-Law.* Mordecai walked from under the cedar limbs and started up the grass slope to the patio. The woman was staring up at the Big Dipper.

"Francine?" Mordecai said.

The woman turned, her face in shadow. Mordecai walked up to the edge of the patio, between two potted shrubs. "It's Mordecai."

—22—

Mordecai and Francine walked across the lawn away from the house. They sat in a golf cart parked in a small carport off the garage. "I'm sorry I had to take off like that," she said. "But I had to go."

Mordecai lit a cigarette. "Perhaps you should get back to the house. We could talk some other time."

"No. They're watching a movie. They won't even notice that I'm gone." Francine paused. "I'll start with when I was a lawyer's wife."

Mordecai tapped the ash off his cigarette and inspected the coal.

"My husband and I were separated before I came to Monterey. I grew up in Santa Cruz, met him at UCLA. When I left him, I knew that he would look for me either of those places, so I chose Monterey."

"He's here now?"

"Yes, in there," Francine said. "I thought I could get back to my beach days, go back and start my life over again. Wasn't that simple of me?"

"What made you split up?"

"My husband, he was connected to this Watergate business," Francine said. "He could have been called up to testify all spring and summer. He's been unlucky in his associates, . . . I'm so tired of saying that." She looked away. "Well, he could have got out— but at that time, three years ago, he didn't have much choice. It was his dream to be . . . I don't know, *influential*. He took what was offered him in hopes of something big. I knew things weren't right, but he kept saying it was okay. Phone calls at night and he would be gone for days. Actually I knew something was wrong, but it was exciting and I liked that feeling. I didn't know what he was up to until he left a folder by accident in his golf clubs with a bunch of clippings from underground presses. He must have been showing them to his golf buddies. I saw a name in there. It was our own private bogeyman, Mr. Pogson, we called him. We used to tell each other, you better be good or Mr. Pogson will get you. It was plain that he had been up to something."

"Which was?"

"One was an anti-war group. He apparently devised some way to drain the coffers after a funding rally in New York. He fabricated a security firm and the anti-war group hired them and they legally frittered the money away. That was just one of the things. The clippings said A. Pogson had disappeared with what was left of the funds. He thought it was all a big game. My husband sometimes thinks only in game terms. There were other things." Francine swirled the ice around her drink. "Later I decided that I wasn't angry at him, I was really angry at myself. Then I had to ask myself why? I decided that I liked living on the edge. But I realized I was living on his edge, not mine. So, I said to myself, go find your own edge."

Francine paused, then took a drink. "It looked like he was off scot free so I didn't worry about him. I knew his associates were worried about *me*, pressuring him to find me. They did not want another Martha Mitchell having midnight attacks of conscience and calling the press. So I came to Monterey where I was sure he wouldn't look. But then when Nixon fired the Watergate prosecutor I knew that everything could be opened up again with a new prosecutor. Peter couldn't go through that pressure a second time alone so I flew back."

"To where?"

"Salt Lake City."

Mordecai dropped his cigarette on the cement and stepped out of the golf cart to crush it. "I had the feeling you were across the mountains, then up North. Was I right?"

She nodded. "We visited an old friend of mine in Seattle and I worked for his firm. They want me to come back. But it was funny; I had your feeling that everything was going to turn out okay. I enjoyed it. It was more exciting than waiting for the roof to fall in and then coping. Well, it became clear that there would be no more investigations, no more hearings. The danger was over for my husband."

"If the danger's over, Francine, something else might be over too," Mordecai said.

Francine looked back at the house. "Yes, that might be true. Only I don't need it to feel alive. So I've got to decide." She nodded toward the house.

"I'm glad to hear you say that. Let me know when you do," Mordecai said. "I should go now." Mordecai stepped back from the cart. "You know, after you left the Three Blind Mice house I had a fantasy you were a radical bomber hiding underground. One of those Radcliffe Weatherman radicals." Mordecai smiled. "I was close, only opposite side. Look, I'm going to go up to the Northwest some time soon. Is there some place I can leave a message?"

"Here, this is the Wickerts house. It's in the phone book. They'll forward any mail to me. Nothing's settled." Francine put her glass down on the floor of the golf cart. "Mordecai, I thought I could live without that past. I made a mistake. I couldn't. It's mine. But now I have to decide in what way it's mine."

"If you've got my melanoia, you can keep it for as long as you want. I'm not attached to it, at least not enough to want to get it back from you."

"Well, maybe I do have it now."

"Besides, there's an old Spanish proverb that no one owns anything until one gives it away," Mordecai touched her hand. Then he turned and started to point down the golf course. "I'm staying down at the far end directly in front of the tee for the eighth hole," Mordecai said. Then he stopped. "Jesus."

Behind the line of trees far down the valley where Mordecai

was pointing there was a blaze. The trees were outlined in the red and yellow glow of the burning house.

— 23 —

Buck turned the Nash into the left fork of the canyon road. "You did good, coming to me. Who was that woman who dropped you off?"

"Someone who gave me a lift," Mordecai said.

"Boy, are you in trouble, Mordecai," Buck said. "You're legally a bum. No visible means of support. They'll hang you from your fingernails. They're saying arson in the paper. You can't go back to the house. Your footlocker was in the garage so they'll get your name off it. They know from the neighbors someone was staying there. They'll put two and two together and accuse you of setting the fire. Who knows how long it will take you to locate Ted. It's your word that he made you caretaker. And believe me, you don't know what Ted's going to say. I know Ted from Mexico. I'm sure he set you up. You burn up and he'd say he hired you as caretaker. You don't, you're some drunk who smokes. Son of a bitch. Luckily, no one knows where I'm taking you. Stay put, don't show your head outside until I check it out."

They drove past a line of junked cars along the canyon wall. Across the stream between the redwood trees was a narrow bridge. "That's his place up there," Buck said.

Mordecai couldn't see anything for all the redwood trunks and brush and rock. "Lester's homosexual," Buck went on, "but don't let that bother you. He loves company. I've known Lester for years."

— 24 —

Lester Towper was a short man with a slim, mild face. He wore a jade green short kimono and grey creased slacks and a white shirt, open at the neck. Lester had such a calm attitude that Mordecai often was not aware that Lester was in the room. His house was a long redwood shack, nestled into the hillside on a natural shelf of rock, almost completely invisible from the road below. It had taken Mordecai three walks before he located a turn in the road where a corner of the southwest window showed. Later in the week Lester told Mordecai about how he bought the house.

"I'm from Michigan, you never would have heard of the town. Both my grandmother and my mother were the town eccentrics. My mother couldn't hold a job and just painted. We were called artsy." Lester smiled faintly and poured another cup of tea. "And we were on welfare. When I turned eighteen, draft registration came up and I didn't want to have anything to do with the war. I tried to register as a pacifist. The draft board wouldn't let me. They didn't know that anyone could do that. My mother even pleaded with me not to do that. She knew what was liable to happen. The Principal of my high school told me that the school's *honor* was at stake. Our town had never had a pacifist. I said — what business is it of yours? or the school? It's between me and my conscience." Lester tilted his head to the side and looked up at the redwoods. "Everyone was dumbfounded by that. I thought our life there was all over. But things calmed down and after that I got interested in Indian tribes. I studied local Indian history, and one day I wore pink beaded moccasins to school to see what they felt like. The Principal saw this as his big chance, took me out of class, and had me declared legally insane. I spent the rest of my senior year in the State hospital. Actually I liked it better there, they had a bigger library. After I was released, I came to California. The first day I got here, I walked around San Francisco and I thought: *back home wearing moccasins got me declared insane. That won't happen here.*"

"Have you gone back?"

"Oh yes — for the funerals. Both my grandmother and mother died in one year. But I was a different person by then."

"When you were in California, did you talk about your past life?"

"Oh no. I let it be someone else's life until I was different enough not to let my old life bother me. Back home I actually ran into my Principal. He was convinced he was right. In fact he was so extraordinarily hostile that when I got back here, I thought it over. I couldn't get jobs at first because of my senior year in a

mental institution. I always believed in telling the truth back
then, so I never lied on job applications. I'm a bit of a pack rat so I
saved all of my job rejections. I wanted to get even so I hired a
shark lawyer with the money from my mother's tiny estate and I
sued the principal, the school district and the state and won. I
bought this house and have lived happily ever after."

— 25 —

Buck returned a few days later. Lester and Mordecai were sitting
on the polished wood deck, both nursing cups of tea and viewing
the light on the redwood boughs. "Ha! I knew you two would hit
it off," Buck said. "Look at ya, two old hermits nodding out over
the afternoon tea. Listen, I talked to the insurance guy. They got
ahold of Ted down in Mexico City. He said he stored the kero-
sene in the closet. So they're calling it an accidental electrical fire,
old wiring, which is how it started. You're off the hook."

"The outlet behind the TV set?" Mordecai said.

"Yeah. Why?" Mordecai shrugged. Buck paced around the
deck, lifted the top off the tea pot, sniffed it, and picked up a
handful of grapes instead. Buck leaned his head back and sniffed
the air. "Damn, it smells good down here. I sure miss the trout
farm. I'm positive our friend Ted set you up, Mordecai. No
family here, no one to go to bat for you, a drifter. As far as the
insurance claims go, he had a housesitter. Wouldn't be anything
for Ted to mess with the wiring. Think about it."

"I have," Mordecai said.

"Anyway, you came about *that* close to being fried, and if not
that, then *tried*, Mordecai. The guy at the insurance office said the
policy was upgraded over a year ago when Ted started that
remodeling stuff. He had mucho coverage, let me tell you. Never
finished remodeling. And I *know* that he got taken off in New
York just before that."

"Taken off? How do you mean?"

"He got robbed. Swung a dope deal and went to the Big Apple.
Happened to be with an old friend, happened to be waiting
outside the door while old friend went in on business, and happened to be escorted into the place by two of New York's finest

and his entire bankroll lifted out of his wallet. He was close to broke when he got back. Dope business was getting too serious, so Ted was getting out, but then he lost the money from what was supposed to be his last deal. That's why he stopped remodeling. Now he's got a big settlement coming." Buck craned his neck in at the kitchen clock. "I gotta run, Sadie's expecting me for tea. Be back in a few hours to take you back to Monterey." Buck went through the house and out the door. They heard him crossing the bridge across the creek.

"Lester, how'd you meet Buck anyway?" Mordecai asked.

"Oh, I picked him up," Lester said. "Not *that* way, hitchhiking. Buck wasn't quite so crazy in those days, I mean, not as raggedy crazy as he is now. Of course, who *isn't* raggedy these days. Anyway he was *young* crazy, you know what I mean. It was such a pleasure to talk to someone who was excited about art and books and wine. It took me a while to see that he was . . . well, so *unrelievedly* heterosexual, but by then we were friends. He steered me to the shrink that got me permanently out of the draft. So I was grateful to him. I was hesitant, in the closet sort of, about using a shrink to get out of the draft but Buck cured me of that. He used to say to me, *well shit Lester, you got to invent yourself. Don't let somebody else do it for you!*" Lester folded his arms across his chest and looked up at the slash of blue sky above the house. "So I did."

— 26 —

Mordecai moved back to Mr. Bruce's camper in Pacific Grove. The cramped quarters, the damp and the mold were not a welcome change after the clean high space of Lester's hillside house. The camper was on the back of a 1959 Ford parked in an alley between some blackberry vines and an old garage. From time to time Mr. Bruce would come out and invite Mordecai in the house to share a bottle of Thunderbird. The linoleum was yellow with age and the walls hadn't seen a cleaning in years. The house smelled of damp paper and bacon grease. Mr. Bruce liked to talk about naval battles of WWII. Mordecai missed his footlocker and its amusements. Buck went out to Ted Dune's garage to pick it up for him. But before he could do it, Buck got in a fight over Ted's suspected mis-use of Mordecai, blackened both Ted's eyes and returned without the footlocker. Rita dropped it off later that week. Mordecai holed up with his translations and reading. When Mordecai did go out, he spent most of his time walking out to the ocean. He avoided Monterey and Beer Springs. He became a hermit.

Book Five
Monterey
Spring
1974

A MONTH AFTER HIS mother passed away, German Jock went over to enlist Buck's help in cleaning out her house. Jock knew that Buck's Wonder Bread van was running. Buck had moved all of his books out of it into his shack in preparation for doing some hauling with the van. But, like all of Buck's maneuvers, he couldn't resist making further improvements. He tore out the driver's seat and installed a couch. The couch was not bolted to the floor. Buck had to hold onto the van door handle whenever he put on the brakes, so the couch didn't careen back into the load—or vice versa for that matter. This limited its utility as a work vehicle, something Buck ignored. He liked to talk about *how comfortable* the couch was.

On the drive out Buck got to talking to German Jock and Katherine how Mordecai thought his melanoia was gone. "I think it is too," Buck said.

"I hate to see Mordecai sad," German Jock said. "When he was living at Katherine's place, it was great to wake up feeling all rummy and burnt out and then see Mordecai out there on the back porch, real quiet and peaceful, working on his Chinese. I really usta dig where his head was at, you know? Does anyone know where he's staying?"

"Yeah, some old wino type's given him a camper in Pacific Grove," Buck said. "What Mordecai really needs is a little good luck to prime the pump."

"Yeah, you're right, Mordecai needs something to prime his pump," Katherine said.

The house was a little duplex out in Sand City. German Jock's mother had donated much of the furniture to her church, so there was only the odd chair and boxes of household goods left, except for Jock's old childhood bedroom, which was still filled with furniture and junk. Buck was manhandling a cheap pine dresser when the bottom drawer fell out, scattering papers and envelopes. Katherine helped clean it up. "Look at this. Jock's high school diploma." Katherine pretended to read the fine print. "Says here he majored in preliminary violence and airhead behavior."

"Johan Feuchter," Buck read. "Hey, that your real name?"

German Jock came out of the bathroom. "My name got me into more fights."

Buck held up a long white legal envelope. Three pieces of plastic slid out. "Hey, look at these credit cards."

"Whose are they?"

"Yours," Buck said. "Johan Feuchter."

"That ain't me," German Jock said. "I had my name changed legally to German Jock. When I was thinking of going back into wrestling."

"Are they still good?" Katherine said.

"Yeah," Buck said, checking the expiration dates. "All three."

"Those must have been renewed from the time I was working in the Harley shop and needed them for buying stuff. Mom must have put them in a drawer and forgot about them. Hey, you know what?" German Jock lifted the three cards out of Buck's hand. He smiled at Buck and Katherine. "I think Mordecai just got himself a primer here for his melanoia pump and a bitchin' good party to boot. Let's see how big a rip we can put in my friend Johan's credit. Whatta ya say?"

— 2 —

On the agreed day Jock and Buck met at Katherine's house. Jock gave Katherine one credit card for the food and redecorating her house. Jock reserved the second card for the airline tickets and Mordecai's new wardrobe. To Buck he gave the third card for the booze and the records and a new stereo to play them on, plus an extra drivers license with a bearded photograph of German Jock on it. "Tell them you shaved that mess off, Buck. Now, this has got to be all in one day, total burn, you understand." Jock checked his watch. "On your marks," he said. "Get set, go. Burn, baby, burn."

Buck drove off in his Nash toward Pacific Grove. Jock and Katherine watched the car drive away. "Hold some credit back on your card, Katherine," Jock said. "Buck will screw up somewhere along the line and we'll need extra booze." As Buck's Nash chugged over a rise in the road, Jock shook his head. "That Nash of Buck's sounds like a goddamn sewing machine and smokes like a one-car mobile smog alert. I thought he just put a new engine in that thing. Damn, there's gas lines all over the fucking city and here's Buck buying gas hogs right and left."

"He told me that was how Rockefeller got rich—buying in a crisis," Katherine said. "Somehow I don't think this is the right crisis."

— 3 —

Buck coaxed the smoking Nash up the Prescott Street hill to his house in a series of zigzag turns using side streets. He left the Nash in front of his Lottie Street shack and got into the Wonder Bread van. Parked on the east side of his place was the Grey Ghost facing out with its hood off and a brace over the empty engine compartment. On the west side of the shack was Duane's one ton truck, its backend jacked up and its driveline on the ground, lacking a back axle. Buck drove directly out to the Seaside junkyard. Buck had been feeling troubled that he could not lay the money for the Nord job in Mordecai's hand the night of the surprise party. He had a plan, though, for getting Blue

Whale back up on its flukes and making a little money. At the junkyard Buck purchased a used Chevy 230 six engine, an axle for Duane's one ton truck, and an exhaust manifold for the Nash. In Buck's mind the Grey Ghost would be for the small to medium hauling jobs, the one ton for the big jobs, and the Nash would function as the scout car for dashing around and making bids on the jobs. While he was at it, Buck bought a new head for the Wonder Bread van, which he decided would be a mobile warehouse housing castoff moving day goodies for any potential rummage sales. With a fleet of vehicles he would have no problem raising a measly two hundred and fifty. Buck drove back to his house with his load of car parts, the back end of the van scraping every bump in the road, and met the only mechanic in Monterey who would work on speculation for him: Loser Rred.

Actually Rred had forgotten that he had already done work on the Grey Ghost to pay off his debt to Mordecai for bailing him out of jail. He confused this debt with Buck's new mechanical problems. In part this confusion was due to the fact that Rred had also collared an old drug buddy, Morbid Tony, to help him. Always an opportunist, Buck caught them at a weak moment when he made his spiel. The two of them were squirrel-eyed on the first day of an amphetamine run. They were confident of success and pleasure since they also had Morbid Tony's backup supply of downers for the evening.

Buck helped them put the rear axle in place and turned them loose hoisting the used 230 engine into the Grey Ghost. He then drove off in the Nash to place three months worth of moving ads in the *Monterey Herald*, stopping by on the way to first subscribe to a phone answering service using Johan's credit card for both. He was chugging toward the Forest Hill liquor store for the party booze when a second try at the steep Prescott Street hill proved too much for the Nash—it expired beside the road in a flatulant bark of exhaust.

Buck walked out to Prescott Street and was hitchhiking up the last four steep blocks to his house, when a seventeen-year old Italian-American girl named Antonia picked him up. Antonia had just endured a raging fight with her family over her recent friendships with some surfers. All she wanted was to be treated like an adult. The day was warm and she was restless for some independent living.

Buck, warmed up from walking, took the opportunity to invite her for a swim in his private pool. As they drove past Lottie Street, Buck could see in a glance that the work on the vehicles was going well: both Morbid Tony and Rred were bent over the engine compartment of the Grey Ghost.

Antonia drove Buck out to the 8 Mile Drive motel court where Buck showed her his private swimming pool, which luckily the management had recently filled with water in anticipation of warm weather. And the day *was* hot by then. Buck appropriated Morbid Tony's one-bedroom apartment in the court by remembering what geranium pot the front door key was under. Antonia had her swim suit in the trunk of her car and she used Morbid Tony's apartment to change in. She noticed the art work pinned to the walls. She viewed Morbid Tony's intricate drawings of robots in geometric mazes. "You know artists, *too?*"

"Oh sure," Buck said. He pointed to a sketch of a robot drawn in pencil and pastels. The robot had the high-cheeked face of an Inca Indian and was followed through the convoluted and warped maze by a little robot on four legs with a tailpipe for a tail. "That's a variation on a classical theme—a boy and his dog."

"Really?" Antonia said, looking around at the disorder of the one-room dump. "I've never been in a real artist's studio before."

Buck waited out by the pool while she changed. He got so enthusiastic about the prospects for some more firsts for Antonia that Buck changed right there on the patio into the swim suit he kept in Morbid Tony's apartment. He was having an imaginary conversation with Antonia about art, books and life when he stripped off his jeans and threw them over the patio chair by the pool. Johan's credit card slid out of the back pocket, glanced off the pale green nylon back of the chair and nestled sideways into the azaleas lining the patio.

—4—

Later that afternoon German Jock drove up to Buck's shack to see how Buck's shopping spree went. He found Rred adjusting the carburetor on the new engine in Buck's Grey Ghost. Morbid Tony was sitting in a folding chair beside the Wonder Bread van. He had a thin paint brush and was putting the finishing touches on the van's grey primered front end. The painting was of a spider robot in the middle of the web with a face like an Aztec idol. German Jock got out and walked in the house, looked around, nothing there but the usual junk, sighed and went back to his bike. He drove away as Rred and Morbid Tony continued with their work.

— 5 —

"Right darling, the combo," Buck said before stepping out of the motor court apartment. "With anchovies. Gotta get that salt back." There was laughter from inside the apartment. Buck smiled and closed the door. In the dusky light coming through the trees and the fading smells of hot eucalyptus leaves Buck sauntered across the parking lot for the pay phone. "Ah spring," he said. He reached in the front pocket of his jeans and found a dime. He called Ace's Pizza. When asked how he was going to pay, he said, "Credit card" and he reached into his back pocket for the card because he couldn't remember what the number was.

— 6 —

The next morning Mordecai woke up in his camper to a banging on the door. The door opened and there was Sal the Portagee. "HEY! Mordecai! you wanna make a run with the General this morning? Got some missions for my army. I need support." He treated Mordecai to a breakfast at the Golden West Pancake house in Pacific Grove. Mordecai checked the General Delivery for any mail and found a money order for ten dollars from his mother. "My lucky day," he said to Sal as he got in the car. "You bet," Sal said. "Now first thing we gotta do is go a block and a half up the street and see this friend and then go to Salinas. Haven't seen you at Headquarters lately."

"Bar tab is too high. No mon, no fun," Mordecai said.

Sal drove two blocks up into downtown Pacific Grove and parked. They went up into the office building above the doughnut shop. Mordecai had never been there. He found this odd, as he had been in practically every semi-public building in Pacific Grove and Monterey in his wanderings. Sal went into a door marked with a notary public sign. Mordecai wandered around the halls, looking to see who rented these rather drab offices. As he came around the east side of the hallway, he saw a frosted glass door with these words on it:

NESTOR MARZIPAN
Imaginary Mysteries

Mordecai opened the door. The first thing he saw was a revolving wire rack of paperback books. A battered brown fedora slouched on the top of the book rack. To the side of that was a table with a large stack of papers and two big dictionaries, one Greek-English, the other Latin-English. A thin man with dark long hair wearing a hand-knitted sweater with alternating bands of blue and green and pink was seated behind a desk with his feet up. A dark brown muffler was around his neck. He was reading a book: *The Metamorphoses of Ajax*. He pushed up his glasses with one finger and looked at Mordecai. "Yes?" he said.

"Just curious, never been in this building before." Mordecai looked out the window behind the man and he saw the office door that Sal had gone into. "A friend went to get something notarized over there," he said. "I'm just killing time." Mordecai pointed at the dictionaries. "You use those?"

"Yes, from time to time," the man said.

Mordecai nodded. The man seemed to want to go on with his reading. "I had a rare disease once," Mordecai went on, "and no one was ever able to find it in any of their medical dictionaries. Perhaps you could tell me what the word means."

"Sure, what was it?"

"Melanoia."

"In Greek that would mean *black thought*," the man said.

"Gee," Mordecai said, "it didn't mean that when I had it."

— 7 —

Tom Soper and Jasmine watched Loser Rred and Morbid Tony drive away in the one ton from Buck's house on Lottie Street. Jasmine turned to Tom. "You sure you can have the work done by the time the party starts?" Jasmine said.

"Oh yeah, no sweat. That north wall of the crapper won't be any problem. Before I cut the studs, I'll rig the rope from that pine next to it," Tom said. "The whole shebang will be suspended from a pulley. All you'll have to do is cut it loose."

"Good. I'll give you the ounce of sensimilla when you finish," Jasmine said. She turned and walked back to her car. There was another woman sitting in it. Jasmine got in. "It's all set," she said. "The fish is in my trunk. We'll go down to my vet friend and pick up the bread. After three days with the cats that should be good and fragrant."

— 8 —

That night Katherine and Ethel arranged the food in the kitchen of Katherine's house. Out in the dining room German Jock was drawing off the suds of a newly opened keg of beer. "He won't know anything's up," Katherine said. "Sal's big mouth will make sure there's not a thought left in his head."

"Where did he take Mordecai?" Ethel asked.

"Salinas. Sal had another one of his pointless errands to run, I imagine."

German Jock came in with a pitcher of suds and set them on the drainboard. "Did you ever locate Buck?" Ethel said.

"Naw, the two squirrels are still up there, working on Buck's vehicles. I don't know where the hell Buck went. But there's no booze, no records, and no stereo at Buck's house, only two speed jockies riding their stash."

"Yeah, but wow," Katherine said, "you should see what Morbid Tony is drawing on Buck's one ton. That thing looks like an Inca Ice Cream Wagon. Morbid Tony got an airbrush from somewhere and is going to town. He started on Buck's van and then switched to the one ton. You know how Morbid Tony is, he'll paint anywhere but on canvas. He's got anxiety about canvas."

"And life. He's in a class by himself when it comes to needing tranks." German Jock walked back out to the dining room and stood in front of the window. "Jesus, here comes Buck. Wait, that's Rred and Morbid Tony. Look at how they painted that damn truck. Anybody looks in their rear view mirror and sees that face bearing down on them will have a heart attack. I wonder where Buck is?"

— 9 —

Mordecai felt numb from the ceaseless barrage of Sal's talk. Listening to him for a whole day was like taking brain novacaine. As Sal turned onto Hawthorne Street from Lighthouse Avenue, Mordecai's brain was barely registering perceptions, much less having thoughts. He did, however, look up a side street as they neared Katharine's house and see Duane's old one ton truck parked up the hill. A geometric spider web of black and red covered the front end, including half the windshield. In the center of the web was a spider with the head of an Inca god. Mordecai's brain didn't register much more than the words *"Morbid Tony"*. In the back end of Sal's Jeepster was a large crate of produce from the warehouse. (Sal had taken over the delivery of throwaway veggies when Buck's truck engine blew up.) They pulled up in front of Katherine's house. Mordecai got out and took a few avocados and a sack of potatoes and followed Sal up the steps into Katherine's house. Sal was babbling and Mordecai was only half-listening when Katherine opened the door. "Long time no see," she said to Mordecai and then stepped back. Mordecai walked in and looked to the right in the dining room and there was a big crowd of people jammed in there. "SURPRISE!" they all yelled. Mordecai was very surprised.

— 10 —

Mordecai's first gift was a new batch of clothes. German Jock took him in the bedroom and outfitted him in rust red corduroy pants and a brown wool sweater. Then he was led out to accept his other gifts. Sal gave him a lieutenants dress jacket and a pair of bars, making him the first member of Sal the Portagee's Army to go from NCO to Officer.

Loser Rred gave Mordecai his Swiss hiking boots. He sat down in front of Mordecai and took them off and handed them to him. Rred's eyes looked like revolving spirals of red veins.

"What are *you* going to wear on your feet?"

"What?" Rred barked. "What do you mean by *that*?" And he wandered off barefoot into the party.

Katharine presented Mordecai with the airline tickets for Seattle. Ethel gave him a scroll, cancelling his bar tab at Beer Springs.

Duane gave Mordecai a large brass key ring that he had welded himself. "In case you ever own anything that locks," he explained.

Jasper gave Mordecai a souvenir program of the 1944 World Series, the only series in history where the two St. Louis teams, the Browns and the Cards, played against each other. Mordecai was touched and thrilled by this. Jasper had remembered the year of Mordecai's birth.

Tom Soper's gift was a piece of old Chinese type which he had found between some walls in a remodeling job. Mordecai looked at it and was delighted. "You know what this is?" he asked Tom. "No," Tom said. "It's the ideogram for *jen*, or human-heartedness. It's a big idea for certain Chinese philosophers," Mordecai explained.

Sadie Strawberry gave Mordecai a gift certificate for her new business, a shiatsu massage. Morbid Tony handed Mordecai a bag of pills. "In case you get nervous on the flight back home," he explained. Jasmine also handed Mordecai a bag, but it was full of her primo mountain herbs. "In case you want to fly without tickets."

The last dramatic flourish was Buck, who presented Mordecai with a check for two hundred and fifty dollars. Mordecai looked at this closely. It was from a lawyer.

"The Nord family paid up," Buck explained, "I countersued

them in small claims court and even though their lawyer wanted to take me on, the Nord family decided to pay off out of court rather than admit for the public record that there had ever been pigshit under their carpets. That's what's known as *retroactive anal neuroticism*." Buck signed the check over to Mordecai with a flourish and Mordecai immediately gave it to Ethel to cash for him on Monday. "It's true," she told Mordecai, "I got my two hundred and fifty dollars back from Dr. Sliccy."

"And now," German Jock said, "let the party begin."

— 11 —

Five hours later Antonia was telling Mordecai about how the night before she had rescued the credit card from the azaleas by flashlight. "All I had to do," she said maturely, "was just go back and remember where Buck was each time he took off his pants. There were four times in all. So first we looked in the living room . . . ." Mordecai was listening to this ingenious explanation when he noticed that the party had entered what Mordecai called *"its half-life"*: there were now more dancers than room; the records had changed from The Persuasions and James Taylor to Marvin Gaye and Clifton Chenier; and people were coming in who either never should have been invited or he had never seen before; and the older folks, Ethel and Jasper and Sal had all left. "Then Buck and I went to the stores today," Antonia said. "He insisted I wear this beach outfit of mine—even in the tire store—and that's when I figured out that Buck was borrowing the card and he wanted me to act as a *distraction* . . . ."

About then Buck drifted over. "Ah, talking to my little Italian retriever," Buck said. "Yes, these people here would only be half as drunk as they are, had my Antonia here not turned sleuth and found the missing credit card." Buck put his arm around Antonia.

Mordecai looked up from this touching scene to see Jane James pushing her way through the dancers. "Buck," Mordecai said.

"My Italian Retriever of my lost youth," Buck continued, sliding into his W.C. Fields imitation, "such energy demands energy in return, the Third Law of Buckaramics . . . ."

"Ah, Buck," Mordecai squeaked.

Jane whacked Buck on the shoulder. *"There you are!"* Jane screeched.

"Hmmmm?" Buck said, turning. "Oh . . . my lord, *Jane!* Welcome to the . . . ."

"Don't give me any of that welcome to the party crap, Buck. Who's this *nasal bitch* who's been making those *nasty* calls to my parents about my brother Jesse's *phone* habits?"

"Who?" Buck said.

"And where's my books?"

"Your books," Buck said. "Ohhhh, your *books*. Well, Jane, I had them all packed up, wood packing crates, not any old cardboard, I know better than that. I went down to Chinatown and got the best, put them on my truck." Buck stepped back, letting his arm fall off Antonia's shoulders. "And then, after I had been all over the city looking for a shipper . . . ."

"I don't give a shit about the shipper," Jane hissed, "where did they go?"

"They were gone in the morning," Buck said, sliding behind Antonia. "Isn't that right, Mordecai?"

"That's right, they were gone all right."

Suddenly Jane smiled. "I don't give a damn about them. They were my first husband's books anyway. I never read them. Come on out and see what I got off my third husband. Cutest little Toyota you'll ever want to see."

"You got married in Missouri?" Buck said, "You were busy."

"Oh yeah," Jane said. She turned and regarded the heaving mass of dancers in the other room. "Some party," Jane said, "who's it for?"

— 12 —

"Who is that?" Loser Rred asked Mordecai. Mordecai told him.

"Jane's taking Buck out to look at her new car."

"She looks just like my first wife," Rred said. "She's a ringer for her."

"Maybe she is your first wife," Mordecai said. Rred nodded and slipped between the dancers, following Jane out the door.

— 13 —

In the backyard, under the two portable lights clipped to the back porch stairs, German Jock performed the last rites for John Feuchter's Life of Crime in credit. On a big old eucalyptus stump he pinned all three cards. People were leaning out of the back porch windows to catch the show. "The Master of Ceremonies, Mordecai," Jock called out.

"Yes," Mordecai answered. He stepped off the porch with Antonia. "Present and accounted for."

"Has it been determined that there is enough food and drink here for the duration of this party?"

"Yeah!" the crowd roared.

"Then Johan," German Jock said solemnly, taking the machine gun pistol out of his belt, "there comes a time of reckoning for us all." German Jock turned to face the crowd. "Johan Feuchter died in Vietnam so that German Jock could be reborn. When I went to Vietnam I was Johan Feuchter, and when I came back, I was who I am now." German Jock raised up his machine gun pistol into the beams of the lights. "And now Johan's credit must die." He turned and pointed the pistol at the stump. "So that our friend Mordecai's melanoia may be reborn."

Antonia pinched Mordecai's arm. "He's really nuts, isn't he?"

"He doesn't like to have that pointed out to him," Mordecai whispered back. Antonia giggled and hugged Mordecai's arm closer. "It's like some movie," she said.

"Mordecai, is your disease ready to be reborn?"

"Yes, it certainly is," Mordecai said. He took another drink of Budweiser from his Dixie cup. "Proceed."

"Johan," German Jock said to the credit cards, "been nice knowing your credit line."

He pointed the gun at the stump and let fire. That was the first time that night that the police were called.

— 14 —

At the same time out on Hawthorne Street Buck and Jane and Loser Rred were admiring the new Toyota. "Sure is a sweet little car," Buck said. "Did you see my one ton?" He pointed up the sidestreet.

"What's that on the front of it?" Jane said.

"One of Morbid Tony's Aztec spider webs."

"Did he have to paint the windshield?" Jane said.

"You know Morbid Tony, once he gets going . . . ."

"Yeah, well, anyway, like I said, I got this Toyota off my third husband." There was a blast of machinegun pistol fire behind Katherine's house. "He was a Vietnam vet," Jane said, listening to the gunfire. "Sane some of the time, bonkers most of the time." Jane stroked the fender of the car. "I got this without even going to bed with him. We got married and he flipped out in the bridal suite, got tucked away and I never saw him again, only his lawyers."

Loser Rred turned abruptly and walked away into the night as Jane continued. "I just don't seem to have much luck when it comes to husbands, only settlements."

Buck put his arm around Jane. "Well, that proves you're not working class then."

"No," Jane said, "but I can tawwlk it. I haven't had a chance to tawwlk that way for a while, Buck. My parents won't 'low it around home. You remember what I like to do when I tawwlk that tawwlk."

"Jane," Buck said, "I'd *like* to help you, but I'm kind of drunk and tired, to tell you the truth."

"That brown-eyed girl Antonia in there? She's so ditzy she doesn't even know you're gone. She's got Mordecai. Come *on*, Buck, honey," Jane said. "Don't want to get married no mo, just wanna *romp*."

"I really *am* kinda tired," Buck said.

"Well, you won't have to *do* anything, if that's what you're worried about."

— 15 —

Besides the machine-gunning of Johan's credit, there had been two fights, one public seduction and a broken marriage plus a visit from the police by the time Steve Wire got around to explaining to Mordecai why he had been hiding out in Seaside for the last month. "Chicago was so bad, man." Steve told Mordecai.

"*Real* bad. I only stayed there three days. Clark Street. Grunge City, man. So I came back on the Greyhound and stopped off in Reno to have a little fun gambling and I ran into this soccer team that needed a bus driver, so I drove them over Donner Pass. The bus broke down and the team sold it to me for my wages, and took a Greyhound themselves. I fixed the bus and sold it and then came down here where I got this job in Santa Cruz and the boss gave me his house in Seaside, so I been commuting to Santa Cruz and fixing up this house for the rent. I'm going straight from now on," Steve vowed. "Except I'm thinking of taking this job selling vacuum cleaners in Guam. I never been to Guam. You ever been to Guam?"

— 16 —

Morbid Tony and Loser Rred had locked themselves in Katherine's boy's bedroom and were occupied with a Leggo set. Morbid Tony liked the shape of the Leggo pieces. They reminded him of Inca Space Ships, the kind that landed in South America when the first space invaders put down on Earth. Rred was watching Morbid Tony build an Inca Space Ship facsimile, and talking about how he was sure that Jane was really his first wife, *in disguise*. "I knew she was really talking about me," Rred said. "She said Toyota but it was a morotcycle, my Triumph, man, that she got off me in the divorce. Not no Toyota. She's even lying about that."

— 17 —

At Lottie Street Jasmine stepped out of Buck's bathroom with several empty plastic garbage bags in her left hand. She took out an aerosol can of Glade Air Freshener and sprayed it around the house as she walked backwards to the front door. She put the spray can in her purse and took out a flashlight. Before stepping outside, she switched off the house lights. Then she went around to the side of the house, pausing to throw the plastic bags in the back end of the Grey Ghost. The bathroom jutted out from the

side of the house. It had been added on years ago. She inspected
the north wall of Buck's bathroom with the flashlight. Satisfied
that Tom Soper had done the job well, she located the master
switch for the electricity and turned it off. She walked around to
her car, parked half a block away, and got in to wait.

— 18 —

In Antonia's car in front of his shack, Buck handed the joint back
to Jane. "Holy mother of god, is that Jasmine's dope?" Buck
shook his head. "I'm tangled and twisted. Ooooo-weeeee!"

"That's nothing to what you're going to be," Jane said. "You
know what I'm going to give you, Buck?"

"No, whatcha gonna give me?"

"I'm going to give you a Dixie Hum Job. You remember that?"
She hummed Dixie. "Those high notes. You loved the high
notes."

"Ha!" Buck laughed. "Oh my . . . . *look away, look away.*"

"That's right, Buck-o," Jane said, "I knew you would
remember."

"*Hey, wish I was in the land of cotton,*" Buck sang. He shook his
head. "What was in that dope, anyway?" Buck rolled out of
Antonia's car and staggered to his feet. "That's *Rhino Polio* weed,
baby. Knock over a rhino with that weed! whew-weeee! Look at
those stars!" Buck fell back on the top of the car and stared up at
the sky. "Least I think they're stars!"

Jane got out of the car, walked around to Buck and took his
arm. She guided him toward the house. She whispered more
about what she had planned for him. Jane opened the door and
helped Buck in. As he came in the door Buck's hand automati-
cally went for the light switch. "What's that?" Buck said. "Must
have blew a fuse."

"We don't need any lights for what I've got planned," Jane
said. She stood Buck up against the wall and leaned in on him,
giving him kiss after kiss, unbuttoning his shirt first, then undo-
ing his belt.

"Ha!" Buck said, "Dixie! Oh the South is rising again!"

Buck stepped out of his pants and Jane danced him back,

naked and weaving, toward the bed. "Here we go," she said, stripping back the top sheets. "You ready for this?" She turned him around, so he was facing away from the bed. Then she started to kneel, her right hand sliding down Buck's belly. With a easy steady shove of her hand she sent Buck backwards into the bed.

Buck sat down in a waterbed covered with hundreds of cold smelt. "Gawwwwwwdamn!" Buck yelled, leaping up. He began flailing at his ass, trying to rub off the wet sticky smelt.

"What's wrong?" Jane said. She reached out for him, sending him sideways into the bed of slimy fish again.

"*Arrrggggh!*" Buck bellowed. He fought his way through the fish back to the edge of the bed and flopped off it, bringing many smelt with him. "Oh Jesus," he clawed at his skin, trying to get the small wet fish and slime off him.

"Here," Jane said, "oh my god, what is that? Fish?" She helped Buck up to his feet. "Here, get in the shower." She pushed Buck toward the bathroom door. Buck opened the door and stumbled into the bathroom. He pulled aside the shower stall curtain and was buried up to his knees in old Wonder Bread loaves soaked in cat piss.

Outside, in the moon-lit front yard, Jasmine listened to Buck's howl of rage. She gave a pull on the yellow rope that Tom Soper had rigged up. The north side of the bathroom fell away. Buck was standing there stark naked in front of the shower stall, up to his knees in Wonder Bread with smelt sticking to his back and legs.

He turned and looked at Jasmine. She had a camera with a flash pointed at him. "Smile, Buck," Jasmine said, tripping the flash.

— 19 —

Mordecai and Antonia were sitting on a front step across the street from the party. That's all there was in the lot, a front step; the house had been torn down. They were watching the party at Katherine's house. It was looking more and more like that's all that would be left of Katherine's house after the party: smoking ruins and a front step. The front door was open, the back door was open, and people were coming in and out of both. There seemed to be a separate party of Jock's biker buddies in the backyard now, as a bonfire was going there, ringed with motorcycles. "Buck will bring back your car," Mordecai told Antonia. "He probably went out for a beer run. It's about two."

"I hope he brings it back in one piece, that's all. He will, won't he?"

"Oh sure," Mordecai said, crossing his fingers in the dark.

"He left with that woman who came in."

"Oh, that was an old friend of his," Mordecai said. "They had a little argument to settle. He probably went off some place to make his peace with her."

"You mean, *get* a piece with her," Antonia said. She giggled. "I think I've had too much to drink. Maybe I'll just go home without my car. No one's home anyway. My parents went to San Diego." Antonia turned to the side. "Oh there's Buck now, getting in his truck."

Just then down at the party someone was thrown through a living room window. "I think it is time for us to go," Mordecai said. He stood up and saw that Buck's truck was rolling away from the curb. The truck started down the hill. "There goes Buck, he's going to pop the clutch to start it," Mordecai said. "Let's catch a ride with him before the cops get here again."

Mordecai began to wave at the truck as it coasted down the hill and turned onto Hawthorne Street. "Buuuuu . . . ." Mordecai began to shout.

The one ton truck took the turn and then swung wide and rammed into the back end of a Toyota parked at the curb, running the truck's front bumper up over the car's trunk and squashing the entire back end.

"Oh Jesus," Mordecai said, then he saw the dark figure leap out of the cab and run off toward Lighthouse Avenue. "That wasn't Buck," Antonia said. "He's taller than that."

"You're right," Mordecai said, "but that was our cue to leave." He took Antonia by the hand. "Let's split this scene." The party was emptying out of the house, some members helping whoever got thrown through the window back on his feet, and the others looking down the block at the wreck there. Mordecai and

Antonia turned left and started for Pacific Grove. As they passed over the slight rise in the street, Antonia wrapped her arm around Mordecai's. "Oh well," she said, "Buck'll show up when he does. And I haven't given you *my* present yet."

Mordecai kept walking. "And what was that going to be?"

"Hmmmmm," she said, "I haven't decided yet."

— 20 —

Mordecai woke up looking at a formal bonsai garden. Sometime while he had slept, the entire wall of the room had been tilted up like a garage door. The wall was made of clear white fiberglass backed with stained pine wood studs. Raised, it revealed a garden of dwarf pines and volcanic rock and white gravel. For a moment Mordecai imagined he had died and gone to heaven, especially when he looked behind him and saw that the room still had a pool table and a bar. The night before Mordecai hadn't known the garden was there. Now, he saw that he could play eight ball, drink whiskey and look at a Japanese rock garden. This was as close to heaven as Mordecai could imagine. Antonia was sleeping beside him curled up in a red blanket on a blue mat. Mordecai remembered how happy he was the night before just to get *inside* this house, one which he had passed many times in his rambles. He had been very curious about what it looked like inside.

The house was built on the steepest hillside in Pacific Grove. The building consisted of a modular series of columns with air shafts and inset gardens. Mordecai remembered taking a shower around four in the morning and marveling at the clear window which formed one wall of the shower stall. The window looked out on a small sand and ice plant garden at the bottom of one of the house's airshafts. When Antonia had taken him downstairs and showed him the pool room, he had felt that not only had his good luck returned, it was working overtime. But he hadn't known then that the whole wall tilted up to view a rock garden. He could not get over it. It was so wonderful he wanted to leave and let it remain a perfect memory, like the sound of the wind chime outside.

Mordecai located his clothes and put them on. He paused to

look at the tan brown skin of Antonia's arm and her smooth shining hair. Then he climbed up the stairs to make a cup of coffee in the kitchen. He took a tour of the house. It was constructed so that he was constantly surprised by the new spaces. It was a pleasant journey that Mordecai took, ending up on the rooftop patio, overlooking Monterey Bay. Mordecai drank the coffee there. It was good and strong. He was still slightly drunk from the whiskey he had drank the night before, and the coffee put the right edge on it. He went back down to the bottom level of the house. He wanted to take a walk around Lover's Point. Looking at the sleeping Antonia, he decided against leaving a note, so instead he wrote out one of his Chinese translations and pinned it to her blanket.

> Bright the white colt
> deep in the valley
> eating shoots in my garden
>
> Fresh food I need it too
> Talk to me don't be
> as rare as gold & jade in my life

Outside he saw that Buck had returned Antonia's car sometime in the night and that pleased him too. Mordecai started his stroll, first looking in his coat pocket at the airline ticket, to make sure that he was really leaving Monterey. That made the air seem even more magical and fleeting. He had the delicate excitement of living in the present while knowing it was already nostalgia. He felt as if he could *eat* the wind.

— 21 —

Two days later Mordecai was in the Pacific Grove Post Office with Buck. "I'm looking on this as an investment," Mordecai said. He took out the cash from the Beer Springs envelope and handed fifty to the Post Office clerk.

"Don't worry," Buck said, "you'll get your money back. And more. In fact, as soon as the insurance money comes for Duane's truck."

"Run that by me again," Mordecai said. "Who owns the truck anyway?"

"Well, *you* own a quarter share now with this fifty, and 10 percent of the profits," Buck pointed out, "I paid Duane two hundred down for it, but he agreed to deduct the cost of the new axle from the total price of the truck."

"So I own a quarter of your investment in the truck," Mordecai said. "I thought you got the new axle with Johan's credit card."

"Oh now, I want to be on the up and up about this. I never would have gotten to use Johan's credit card without you, so you have fifty percent of that."

"So I have fifty percent of the new axle and a quarter of the down purchase price," Mordecai said. He took the money order from the clerk and handed it to Buck.

"Well, see Duane doesn't know that the axle was credit financed, the cost is real to him."

"But he never signed the truck over to you."

"Right. And damn lucky he didn't. The truck still was insured through the iron worker's union plan, so technically it's his wreck and the insurance covers vandalism and theft."

"I get it. He owns the truck when it's a wreck and you own it when it runs. So who gets the money from the insurance claim on the truck?"

"I do," Buck said. "*I'm* the one who has to get the truck fixed."

Mordecai regarded Buck. "But then why can't you give him the insurance money for payment on the truck?"

"Oh, when *that* comes I'll use it for buying the pickup bed for the Toyota conversion."

"You're going to convert Jane's wrecked Toyota into a truck? So what's *my* fifty for?"

"That's to *buy* Jane's Toyota from her insurance company that Duane's truck totaled," Buck said, putting the money order in an envelope and sealing it. "Duane's already torched off the rear and I'm going to convert it into a truck and use it to go out on bids with it. That'll be the pilot ship for the new fleet. Save on gas."

"I'm glad we got *that* straight," Mordecai said.

Mordecai turned to the clerk. He was looking from Buck to Mordecai and back again with a mixture of pity and incredulity on his face.

"Got a stamped envelope?" Mordecai said. He put a quarter down on the counter. "The stolen painting is in the house next door," he added. The clerk pretended not to hear this last remark.

Mordecai took the envelope over to the phone booth and checked the phone directory for the address of the Wickerts. He wrote a short note, put it in the envelope, addressed the envelope to Francine, care of the Wickerts, and mailed it.

"Gawdamnit," Buck said, standing by the Wanted poster rack. He ripped a poster off and wadded it up. "It's one of those damn posters that Jasmine's been sticking up all over."

Mordecai uncrumpled the xerox copy. On it was a blown up Polaroid of Buck standing naked in his destroyed bathroom up to his knees in Wonder Bread with little fish stuck on his back. Above this photograph were the words: *Home Repairs Done Cheap.*

"She's plastered them all over the town," Buck grumped. "Every laundromat, bulletin board, and telephone pole in Pacific Grove."

Buck and Mordecai walked down the front steps of the Pacific Grove Post Office. "Well, what the hell, I should have known that Jasmine's no one to tangle with. Anyway, you see this way I'll have all the bases covered, Mordecai. Duane's one ton truck for big jobs, the Grey Ghost for medium jobs, the Toyota for small jobs and cheap long hauls, and the Nash for sporting events and scouting parties. The Wonder Bread van will be for my rummage sale runs to Santa Cruz to sell all the castoff goodies from the hauling jobs. Plus it has a forty-five gallon tank and I only have to gas it up once every two weeks and then siphon the gas into my other trucks. Avoid gas station lines that way during this crisis that goddam Nixon landed us in."

"Glad you have a plan, Buck," Mordecai said. "But what will your customers think when they see that huge Inca Indian head in the middle of a spider web on the front of your one ton?"

"Oh, I got that covered," Buck said. "See for yourself. Here's our new business card." He handed Mordecai a card. Above a phone number was:

INCA DINKA DO MOVERS
"Moving With an Olde
Tyme Smile"

— 22 —

On a hill of green spring grass in the Carmel Valley, Mordecai looked West and thought that what he liked about Monterey was that it seemed so easy to remember eternity there. The bay, the cypress trees, the ocean, the hills and the wet salt smell. They were as immortal as Buck was.

Mordecai looked down the hill at Buck. He was walking out of the ranch house with a chair in his hands. The Grey Ghost was parked in the driveway. The grey black asphalt and the bleached redwood fence and the new grass all around made a pleasing color combination. Mordecai checked his watch. Buck was running two hours late as usual. *It'll just take a minute, Mordecai,* Buck told him, *don't worry, we'll get you to the airport on time.*

Mordecai had Antonia acting as his backup ride to the airport in the event Buck was too optimistic about the time it would take to do this moving job. Mordecai went down to the house and made a phone call to Antonia. She said she'd be right out. Mordecai watched Buck carry the furniture out to the truck and load it. Buck had been adamant that Mordecai would do no work on his last day in Monterey. "You're in your new clothes, don't worry, I'll handle the job." He had already given Mordecai twenty-five percent of the advance on the job to show Mordecai how the money would flow north from his investment in Inca Dinka Do movers.

About the time that Buck had finished loading his truck, Antonia drove in. Mordecai's footlocker was in the front seat of the Grey Ghost and they transferred it to the trunk of Antonia's car. "Well, sorry I can't go out to the airport with you, Mordecai, but I got to get back to the old economic firing line."

"Sure, Buck. Well, see you again when I do."

"Right," Buck said. He gave Antonia a hug. "How you doing, honey? Haven't seen you in a while."

"Oh I'm fine, Buck," Antonia said. "We better run, Mordecai."

Buck and Mordecai shook hands. "Well, Mordecai, it's been real. Hope you find your melanoia again," Buck said. "Oh damn, I forgot the goddam patio table top. That thing weighs a ton. Will you give me a hand?"

"Sure," Mordecai said, "but first read this." He handed Buck a scroll of rice paper. Buck unrolled it and read aloud:

Rough water can't touch
the reeds if they're
bundled up
We're brothers
only you and I
whatever they say about me
don't you believe it

"Ah, Mordecai, I'm going to miss you and these poems. Having you around always kept a little poetry in my soul."

They walked through the gate onto the patio. A big round redwood table top was on its side, leaning against the fence. "Just need help getting it up in the truck," Buck said. He looked around for some place to put the scroll and stuck it into the center of the table top. Mordecai helped him roll it to the Grey Ghost and tip it up into the truck bed.

Mordecai and Antonia got in her car and then they drove down the hill to the highway with Buck following in the Grey Ghost. At the intersection Mordecai leaned out the window and waved goodbye. Buck turned right, heading into Carmel. Antonia waited for an oncoming car to pass and then she eased left onto the highway. Mordecai lit a cigarette and settled back in his seat. "Well, Buck seems to be pretty well set, three trucks, a van, and the Nash. That's how Rockefeller made his money, buying cheap during the Depression. Buck plans to buy more with the job money from today." Antonia slowed and downshifted. Then something caught Mordecai's eye in the rear view mirror.

Down the hill behind them the patio table top was rolling. It wiggled this way and that as it rushed down toward the back end of Antonia's car. "Uh," Mordecai said. Suddenly the table top veered right off the shoulder and plunged through the embankment weeds. Gathering speed, it hit the slat fence at full tilt. Mordecai glanced back and for a half a second he saw the slat fence disintegrate. Behind the fence was a swimming pool and a table. A man was sitting on the far side of the table, reading a newspaper. The man looked up just in time to see the table top destroy his fence and bounce up over the poolside and fly into the middle of the pool, sending a tidal wave over him.

"Buck will be okay," Antonia said, shifting into third.

Oncoming cars were honking wildly. Antonia looked back at them. "I wonder what that's all about?" she said.

— 23 —

Francine was sitting in a rented yellow Pinto in the parking lot of the Monterey Airport. She had on a white wide-brimmed hat, dark glasses, and a fetching pink frock. Around her right wrist was a carved jade bracelet. It jiggled up and down as she filled out some papers on the suitcase top.

She saw Mordecai get out of a car at the curb and a tanned young girl help him lift a footlocker out of the trunk. They set it on the curb and then they embraced. They held each other for a moment and talked, leaning back and looking at each other. The girl stepped back, they waved to each other, and then she got in her car. Mordecai turned and started to drag the footlocker toward the self-help carts. He dropped it and got the cart. The girl drove off. Mordecai put the footlocker on the cart and wheeled it into the airport terminal.

Francine went back to her divorce papers. When she finished signing all three copies, the jet had landed and was unloading passengers. Francine heard the call for boarding. She put the papers in a manila envelope. There was a printed address tag from a San Francisco law firm on the front. She got out of the Pinto and walked across to the terminal and put the envelope in a Post Office box. Then she walked back to the Pinto and opened the door.

— 24 —

Mordecai was sitting in the airplane's smoking section, looking out at the hills. He was remembering the first day he landed in Monterey, on his way to the language school to learn Chinese. He could also recall the day he landed there after his discharge and the first scent of the sunshine sea as he walked out of the terminal. He turned in his seat and looked back at the hills again. The scrub oak stood out like cardboard cutouts against the light yellow green new grass. Mordecai got the old feeling he always associated with California: *this is real/unreal.*

And as Mordecai remembered that sensation, how it was close to trying to figure out if something was shadows on light or light on shadows, he got a notion that there was someone ahead of him in the non-smoking section that he should see. He undid his seat belt and stood up.

"We'll be taking off momentarily, sir," a stewardess said.

"Yeah, yeah, yeah," Mordecai said. He started toward the front. A man stood up there and went forward into the first class section. Mordecai followed him. The man kept going into the cockpit. Mordecai thought for a moment they were about to get highjacked, when he realized that the man was part of the crew. Mordecai stepped into the first class section and saw a woman with a wide white hat unpinning it. Mordecai saw her hair and then he went forward and eased into the seat next to her.

"Hello, Francine, you still got my melanoia?" And as he said that he heard a tiny faroff *ping*.

Francine looked sideways at Mordecai and then she picked up the small leather drawstring pouch at her feet. She pulled it open. Inside a long silver handle was sticking up out of a pint cardboard carton packed between two blue ice packs. Francine took hold of the handle and levered it up. It was a spoon and on the end of it was a large scoop of french vanilla ice cream. "Open your mouth," she said.

PING

Other City Miner ⚒ Books

Fup (First edition)
by Jim Dodge. $25
ISBN 0-933944-04-7

Selected Poems: Six Sets, 1951-1983
by Howard Hart. $6.95 paper. $12.50 cloth.
IBSN 0-933944-06-3/0-933944-05-5

Bump City: Winners and Losers in Oakland
by John Krich. $3.95 paper.
ISBN 0-933944-01-2

Letters of Transit
by Frank Polite. $3.95 paper.
ISBN 0-933944-02-0

City Country Miners: Some Northern California Veins
edited by Michael Helm. $7.95 paper.
ISBN 0-933944-03-9

Passionate Journey: Poems and Drawings in the Erotic Mood
by Steve Kowit and Arthur Okamura. $7.95 paper. $12 cloth.
ISBN 0-933944-09-8/0-933944-08-X

Please add $1 for shipping. Send orders to: City Miner Books,
P.O. Box 176, Berkeley, CA 94701